A SURPRISE PROPOSAL IN THE ROSE GARDEN

MARGARET AMATT

LEANNAN
PRESS
INDEPENDENT PUBLISHER

LEANNAN PRESS

© **Margaret Amatt 2024**

The right of Margaret Amatt to be identified as the author of this work has been asserted in accordance with the Copyright, Designs and Patents Act 1988.

All rights reserved. No part of this publication may be reproduced, stored in a retrieval system or transmitted in any form or by any means, without the prior permission in writing of the publisher, nor to be otherwise circulated in any form of binding or cover other than that in which it is published without a similar condition, including this condition, being imposed on the subsequent purchaser.

All the characters in this book are fictitious, and any resemblance to actual persons, living or dead, is purely coincidental.

Glenbriar is a fictional town in Highland Perthshire, Scotland. Some of the historical sites and larger towns mentioned in this series are real. Homes, farms, features, and organisations are fictitious, and any resemblance to actual places or organisations is purely coincidental.

First Published by Leannan Press 2024

Book Cover designed by Margaret Amatt

eBook ISBN: 978-1-914575-56-3

Paperback ISBN: 978-1-914575-54-9

PROLOGUE

Genevieve

The world was spinning around Genevieve Harrington.

She rested the back of her hand on her forehead, unable to sit up or even move from the pillow. Her eyes didn't want to open either.

Hangovers were no strangers in her life, but it had been a while. And this one was bad.

Ugh, the prosecco! Always the prosecco.

The pain in her forehead almost buzzed out loud. No wait. It *was* buzzing. What was making that noise? It couldn't actually be her head. She let out a groan as a wave of nausea hit her. If she just breathed, it would pass. Wouldn't it?

The buzzing stopped – the external one anyway.

Where was she? Something on her left hand was rubbing against her face. It felt jaggy on her skin and not normal.

All she could remember was the prosecco. There had been a lot of that. And roses. Roses that smelt so beautiful. The thought took the edge off the nausea for a second. And what about the kisses? They'd been nice. A bit too nice. *He* had been nice too. Yes, *him*.

The buzzing started again. Gradually, Genevieve peeled her eyelids open. Was that her phone? Where was it? Morning light streamed into the room, casting a spotlight across the bedroom. *Ow!* It hurt her eyes. She squinted in the other direction, her neck stiff as it rolled on the soft pillow. *Oh no.*

He's here!

Someone banged on the door and her heart leapt, but her body was frozen and she couldn't shift it. She tried to shimmy her aching brain into remembering... remembering anything, from what she was doing here to how humans got out of bed every day.

'Genevieve? Are you awake?' a woman's voice said from the corridor.

She didn't reply. The man beside her stirred. Their eyes met. His irises were grey blue but surrounding them, the whites were slightly bloodshot. Were hers the same?

He stared at her, and she looked back, willing him to speak and explain what was going on. But his expression was as confused as hers.

Slowly, she slid her left hand off her face and held it out in front of them. Winking back from her long slender ring finger was a very unusual and extremely beautiful diamond ring.

'Oh my god,' she said. 'What did we do?'

CHAPTER ONE

Genevieve

The day before...

'*I'm thrilled to introduce you to my brand-new range of storage containers. Check out these beauties.*' Genevieve lifted a stack of elegant storage boxes with pretty patterns and held them to the camera. '*These boxes are not just any ordinary containers – they're your new kitchen best friends.*' With a flourish, she opened one of the boxes. '*Now, you know me and my love of all things sustainable...*'

'Oh my god.' Genevieve cringed and put her head into her hands. Beside her, her grandma chuckled and stopped the playback on her phone.

'I can't believe you follow me on social media.' Genevieve turned back to her grandma.

'Of course I do. I follow all my grandchildren. I know everything "The Vieve" gets up to.'

Heat stung Genevieve's cheeks. She bared her soul on social media as The Vieve – a single girl living her best life. Thousands of people were watching, commenting, liking, hating, judging, but her grandma?

'It's just a bit of a surprise.'

'Well, it shouldn't be.' Her grandma patted the cushion next to her on the sofa and Genevieve's French bulldog, Mitzi, jumped up beside her. 'Good girl.' Grandma tickled her chin as she cooed. Mitzi wriggled onto the old lady's knee.

'Are you sure she's ok there? She's quite heavy,' Genevieve said.

Her grandmother stroked little Mitzi's soft head. French bulldogs were cute, but Mitzi exceptionally so. Of course Genevieve was extremely biased. And after being on a waiting list for over two years to get her in the first place, she was going to cherish every moment with her.

'She's fine where she is,' her grandmother said. 'Lovely and warm, in fact, like a very cuddly hot water bottle.' The old lady rested her elbow on the sage green velour sofa arm. 'Does this online stuff make money?'

'Yes. I get sponsorships and freebies, sometimes partnership deals with businesses. The Vieve has a lot of followers.' She rested back on the sofa, crossing her slender ankles. Her grandma was in her late seventies and though some of her furniture was dated, it was always pristine. Gleaming photographs of her grandchildren shone from a wood and glass cabinet that took up a large part of the wall. Genevieve's face smiled back from the frames, ranging from the earliest days when she was a bald baby with bright rosy cheeks, through the school years with her long caramel-coloured hair in various plaits and styles – her teeth in several stages of gappiness – right up until now. Now, she was social-media perfect, of course; it went with the territory. The Vieve had a reputation to maintain. In most of the younger pictures, she was with her older siblings. Even then Cressida and Rafe looked more confident and able than her. She was the cute little sister who had adorable dimples when she smiled, but nothing much else to say for herself.

'I don't understand any of it,' Grandma said. 'Though I do enjoy watching you. You have a lovely way of talking online. Your cooking films are very good indeed and useful for me as a single woman.' Grandma winked and Genevieve giggled. Hopefully when she was that age, she'd have the same spirit.

'You know I can cook for you any time. I make so much food for the films, I always have stuff in the freezer,' she said.

'I would happily eat any of it and I really appreciate you dropping in. But aren't you going to your father's party this afternoon?'

'Yes, I am.' Genevieve got to her feet, walked to the window and looked out over the neat little garden and the similarly well-presented gardens of the other houses in the quiet cul-de-sac. Grandma had downsized to this bungalow six years ago, after Granddad had died. It was in a lofty location on the outskirts of Glenbriar. Beyond the house, across the road, was a view of the surrounding hills. The fields were a patchwork of summer green. Loch Briar was just visible too, glinting in the valley.

And Genevieve was procrastinating – big time.

'You don't sound too happy,' Grandma said. 'I thought you loved parties. I see lots of things on here about you and your parties.' She tapped her phone and Genevieve cringed again.

'I like parties, but this one isn't my thing. It's one of Dad's business parties.'

'Ah, but just think,' her grandma said with a mischievous glint in her eyes. 'Of all the young, single businessmen who might be there hoping to be "the one" for you.' She air-quoted like she was Genevieve's age, not almost eighty.

'Oh god,' Genevieve groaned.

Since she'd set herself up as a vlogger a couple of years ago, she'd marketed herself as a carefree single girl, showing women everywhere it was ok not to be in a long-term relationship. Her face was synonymous with independence and freedom. She was famous for her 'cooking for one' slots where she prepped and cooked meals for individuals or sometimes date nights. Well, every single girl needed a date every now and then. Plus, she did health, beauty and fashion reels. She posted that nothing could tempt her out of this blissful state except the truest, purest love. Whoever he was would have to be extra special, and she would have to know for sure that he was 'the one' before she committed to anything.

No one needed to know what a lie that social media face could be. Genevieve craved love as much as anyone but... Well, it was complicated.

'Why don't you fancy this party?' Grandma went on.

Genevieve slumped back into the seat. 'Because it won't be the first time Dad has done exactly what you said and tried to set me up with businesspeople he knows. One of the most embarrassing times was when he dragged me to Edinburgh at Christmas to meet some old friends. One of them turned out to be Gavin Sinclair, the CEO of Glenbriar Distilleries. Gavin brought his PA with him and she's the woman he ended up marrying. Dad was livid. I mean his daughter should be irresistible. Fancy Gavin bringing another woman. You know, to a date he knew nothing about.'

Grandma tickled Mitzi's ears, still smirking. 'Oh dear. Your father is an old romantic. When your mother was dating him, I wasn't quite sure if I liked him. I thought he was trying a bit too hard but actually he's just a natural charmer.'

'Yeah, and he's still trying too hard. I don't want to be set up with these people. I'm fine on my own.'

'Is that the real you talking or the social media you?'

Genevieve met her grandma's eyes and realised how shrewd the old lady was. Maybe the social media face didn't fool her. Could she see through the act?

'A bit of both,' Genevieve said.

'You seemed to get on well with the lad whose father owns Duchan Fayre. What happened there?'

'Oh... um...'

Her phone buzzed in that angry way it did when someone was calling her and she was glad of the interruption. It was the only time it made a noise at all. She got so many comments on her socials that she turned off notifications or she'd be ringing and pinging all day. She frowned at it.

'It's Elise. I better take it. She's going through a bad breakup and she's not herself.' She lifted the phone to her ear. 'Hi.'

'Oh, thank god, you're there.' Her best friend sounded a little breathless. 'I really need your help. I hate asking and I wasn't going to, but I've got myself in such a mess.'

'Oh no. What's up?'

'Finlay.'

That one word said it all. After Elise's short and not so sweet engagement to Finlay McBride had ended, she'd been withdrawn and quiet. Normally she was confident to the point of being pushy, but everything that could go wrong with her love life had gone wrong.

'What about him?' Genevieve almost didn't want to know. As if it wasn't hard enough sitting through months of her best friend being engaged... to *him*.

No one knew the secret about Finlay McBride she'd kept locked in her heart for so long. Except Mitzi.

Genevieve was the mistress of her emotions and she'd never let on to a soul how much she'd fancied Finlay for herself ever since she was a teenager. And she never would. It was too messy.

'He's selling his flat. He's got a new job in Dubai.' Elise sounded on the verge of tears.

'Dubai?' Genevieve's heart plummeted. He was leaving town – the country. Not that it mattered. She had no claim on him. But while they both lived in Glenbriar, there was always a chance of seeing him.

Christ, she had to stop this. It had gone on for way too long.

'It's all my fault,' Elise said. 'I don't think he'd have done anything like this if... Well, if we hadn't split. I'm not sure he even wants to go. He just wants to get away from the gossip. Oh god. I've ruined his life.'

'Hey, it's ok. He's an adult. He can make his own choices.'

Though Elise's words held some truth. She'd only started dating Finlay to get back at an ex – who happened to be Finlay's cousin. Dating her ex's cousin was a pretty shit idea in the first place, but it got so much worse. Elise had crossed the line Genevieve had always stopped herself at. Because Finlay was the brother of their other friend, Hayley. He was that cute big brother who'd always been around when they were kids. Hayley was one of the world's nicest people and hadn't objected outright to Elise dating her brother, but Genevieve could tell she'd felt uneasy. Now it was obvious why.

Breakups made everything awkward.

There was no escape for any of them now Finlay and Elise had split up. It put everyone in a tricky spot. Hayley was so loyal to everyone and didn't want to take sides. Genevieve, too, felt the repercussions. Since the split, Elise had relied on her so much more. She hated herself for the deep resentment that had brewed and festered inside her ever since Elise had got together with Finlay.

'But does it matter if he's moving away? In fact, isn't that going to be a relief? You were talking about moving away yourself,' Genevieve reminded her. Surely Elise didn't want to get back together with Finlay. Genevieve might be sick if that was the case.

'I suppose it'll be easier in some ways, but I hate myself for forcing him into something like this. He's not the kind of guy who does things like that on his own.'

'Maybe you've helped him get out of his comfort zone.' Genevieve wasn't sure why she was sticking up for Elise when part of her ached for Finlay. What a sad position for him. She understood what it was like to be rejected and feel the need to get away... far away. But that wasn't easy when it wasn't in your nature. She liked living here and couldn't imagine being anywhere else. This was her home. If Finlay was like that then the breakup with Elise must have been catastrophic.

'Maybe. I just wish... Oh, I don't know. Listen, the reason I phoned is that I have a lot of stuff in Finlay's flat. We were meant to be moving in together. He wants me to go around and take it all away. I don't want to face him alone.'

'Why not?'

'Because it makes me feel awful. I don't quite know what to say to him. I just wondered if there was any chance you could come with me?'

'What?' Genevieve coughed, taking in too much air too quickly. 'I mean, when?' She checked the time on her grandma's carriage clock on the oak mantelpiece.

'Well, now,' Elise said. 'I know I should have asked sooner but I thought I could do it.'

'Now? I'm not sure...' But how could she refuse? Elise was clearly upset and Genevieve had to keep up the pretence. No one could discover her guilty little secret. For a while, it had been a harmless crush. Ok, one that had lasted a long time. Then Elise had started dating him, and everything Genevieve had wrestled with for years had been turned on its head.

Why didn't I cross the line myself? Get in there first?

Her cheeks heated at the thought. How could she? He'd never taken her seriously. Not since... Well, she didn't need to think about that. She just had to act normal and not show how resentful she was feeling towards Elise or that she had any feelings at all for Finlay. 'I suppose I could, as long as it won't take too long.'

'No, it'll be really quick, I promise. Thank you so much. I'll meet you at yours in ten minutes, if that's ok?'

Ten minutes? Genevieve ended the call and let out a sigh. 'Sorry, Grandma, got to go. I'll come back next week and bring food and more Mitzi therapy.'

'Come any time,' her grandma said. 'You're always welcome and you're a good girl for coming at all.'

'I'd rather stay but Elise needs some support.'

'Young people and their dramas,' Grandma smiled. 'You don't need me to tell you, but when I was your age, I was already married with two young children.'

'You might have told me once or twice before.' Genevieve smiled as she lifted Mitzi from her grandma's knee, then leaned in and gave Grandma a kiss. Her grandma didn't need to know how much Genevieve would love to be married with two young children. Unfortunately, she suspected the partner she needed to bring that about wasn't going to be someone at one of her dad's business parties. Not if it turned out to be nothing but a business transaction like the last time she'd dated someone her parents set her up with.

Genevieve secured Mitzi in the back of her silver Audi and got into the driver's seat. She set up her phone on the hands-free to record as she drove down the street towards her own house.

'Just had a really interesting conversation with a wise old lady,' she said, not looking at the camera and watching the road. 'She might even see this, so I can't say too much, but it's made me think. Why am I not married? I'm twenty-seven and really, that's old enough to be settled down, don't you think? Except you all know how I'm married to my single life. And I've got Mitzi now. She's in the backseat being a good girl.' Genevieve checked in the rear-view mirror. 'I'd like to believe my soulmate is out there and

I just haven't met him yet. But there's no point in sitting around moping about that. I guess if he comes strolling into my life, I'll know. I'll feel the vibe, hear the buzz.' She laughed. 'Maybe as soon as I do, I'll let him put a ring on this single finger faster than you can say "hashtag, he's the one".' She waggled her finger. 'Or not. Anyway, I'll sign off for now. More later from the party. What party you ask? You see, no moping here. I'll let you know how I get on.' Without taking her eyes off the road, she stopped the recording. It may be superficial recording her life like this, but it made money and was kind of like free therapy. She could talk herself through her life choices and justify them completely – even if most of the time it was a blatant lie.

Chapter Two

Finlay

Finlay McBride flipped open the lid of the little black box and stared at the sparkling ring sitting on its moulded silk cushion.

Of all the stupid mistakes he'd made this year – and there had been some real clangers – this ring was one of the biggest. Not in terms of size obviously. In fact, it was small and delicate, hardly something likely to cause trouble. It wasn't even *the* ring, the one he'd had handed back to him, along with the confession that she'd never really loved him. This one was somehow more symbolic of his failure than anything else.

What to do with it now? He couldn't exactly use it for the purpose he'd had it refashioned for. And he couldn't have it changed back to how it was before. Nothing could do that and perhaps that was partly why it made his insides squirm. Would he never learn? When it came to women and relationships, he was a sad, sad case. Maybe he tried too hard. Well, not anymore. No more dating for a long time. He'd handed in his notice at the local High School and was going to teach in Dubai. Several friends he'd trained with had already done it and said it was a worthwhile experience besides paying well. Who couldn't do with a bit of extra cash? Especially after the amount he'd lavished on Elise.

He snapped the lid of the ring box shut and surveyed the sea of cardboard packing boxes surrounding him. This was one of those jobs that made everything worse before it got better. Most of the boxes were empty and he'd sat piles of books, pictures, old cables and electronics beside them, not sure exactly how to organise them. They were going into storage, so he wouldn't be unpacking them straight away. It would be nice to have them arranged in a way that made things easy to find. He also had clothes, bedding, towels, lamps, and kitchen goods to sort. There were even some trophies and medals from his bike runs and rugby matches. The little golden rugby ball one his junior team had won that year gleamed prominently among them. Just another thing he'd have to leave behind. That club would probably fold and die a death now that he was leaving. It was already just scraping by with barely enough funds to keep it going. Ah well, such was life. People moved on.

He'd never thought of himself as materialistic, but what a lot of stuff he'd amassed in his seven years in this flat. Seven years that had seen him engaged twice. Neither engagement had lasted more than a couple of months.

And what should I do with this ring?

If he hadn't acted so rashly and had it reset, he would give it to his cousin Aidan to give to his new girlfriend. But that wasn't likely to go down well for so many reasons. He shoved the box onto a side table away from the mess he'd piled up around the dining area. A couple were coming to look around later and he wanted to show off the place to the full, which meant temporarily shoving most of the stuff into the large storage cupboard in the hall. He also needed Elise to come and take her things away. How could one woman have so many clothes? He'd filled several bags, not to mention the ones full of the cushions she'd bought for 'when she moved in'. That day never came.

Elise drove a flashy little sports car and the bags probably wouldn't all fit.

'She can tie them to the roof,' Finlay muttered. He wasn't running after her anymore. She could come and get them herself. A lesser man would have chucked them out or burned them after what she did, but he wouldn't stoop to that level.

He tossed some books into a box, then started throwing some old cables into another. He probably should go through them all but that would have to be after the visitors had been. They'd asked to change the time from the evening to the afternoon and he'd agreed. It meant more rushing about now, but at least he could have a free evening. The sun was shining and his flat had a lovely balcony looking out over the River Briar. He'd like to sit out and chill with a beer, not think about anything and switch off to all the unnecessary drama in his life. He definitely didn't want anymore of that.

Speaking of the balcony, it was warm in here. He slid open the doors and let the air filter through the room. Voices from the path below drifted up as tourists walked along the river. Only a short stretch of lawn and rails separated the flats from the path and that was great for access when he wanted to go running or cycling, but in the summer, there was always a steady stream of people passing by, which lost it some privacy. This had been his life for so long. Time for a clean break. Maybe applying for the Dubai job had been rash, but it would be an experience, if nothing else.

Returning to his packing, he carried on sorting out the piles he'd made on the floor. His stomach burned as time passed, making him feel like he had indigestion, but it wasn't that. Eating something might not be a bad plan though; he'd barely touched a thing since breakfast. This needed done first however. Elise was coming soon and that was the reason hot acid was working its way around his stomach. She'd *said* she would come anyway. But he didn't trust a word that came out of her mouth these days. He'd rather not see her at all. Maybe he should push all the bags onto the landing and let her take them from there.

'Ah, screw it.' Why should he be bothered about seeing her? It wasn't like he'd done anything wrong. His only fault? He wasn't Aidan. That was who she'd wanted all along. Now she had neither of them. In the process, Aidan and Finlay had almost fallen out for life. Finlay winced at the thought. He and his cousin had always been friends. For a while, they'd been close. Then Aidan had lost his dad, upped sticks and gone off to Canada to do an endurance walk, leaving Elise behind with no word of when or if he was coming back. When Elise had turned to Finlay, he'd consoled her, not meaning for it to go any further. She was a friend of his sister and he'd known her in that capacity for a long time. She'd seemed so genuinely interested in him, which had surprised him as she never had before. As someone who already had one failed engagement under his belt, he wasn't going to rush into another one without being completely certain. And Elise had given him every signal that this was what she wanted.

Until Aidan came back.

Then everything fell apart.

And now he was here, packing up his life and trying to move on. Again. His eyes strayed to the clock over and over. Where was Elise? This was going to be cutting it neat for the couple who were looking around. It wouldn't give a good impression with several black bin bags piled in the corridor. And he really should change out of these clothes into something a bit less scruffy.

Finally, the front door buzzer rang and he chucked another pile of books into a box, dusted his hands together and checked the intercom. A very familiar face flickered on the screen: serenely beautiful with long dark hair and perfectly made-up eyes. Elise. And she wasn't alone. Finlay couldn't see who was with her. Maybe it was Hayley, his sister. That would make things a lot easier if it was. Hayley was good at smoothing things over, remaining neutral and somehow managing to stay friends with everyone, even when everything was messy... like now.

He buzzed her in and opened the door, waiting as the footsteps came up the stairs.

'Really nice apartments these,' the other woman said. Not Hayley. 'I fancied one but there weren't any for sale when I was buying.'

Her voice was familiar. She was another of Hayley's friends. The posh one whose dad owned a big renewables business in town.

Genevieve somebody-or-other. The one nicknamed The Vieve who did stuff on social media like she was a celebrity.

Like several of Hayley's friends, she was glamorous and well-turned out. She was also standoffish and a bit snooty. Finlay remembered, from when they were teenagers, offering to help her rollerblade at one of Hayley's birthday parties. She'd been struggling, arms flailing, looking like she might face-plant. He was just trying to be nice by holding out his hand and suggesting he walked alongside. But the look she'd given him was almost as cold and hard as a slap in the face. He got the message.

But it hadn't sunk in far enough... If it had, he would have steered clear of Hayley's friends altogether. For life.

Elise got to the top of the stairs first. She was slightly taller than Genevieve but together they looked like they'd stepped out of a fashion and beauty magazine. Neither of them had a hair out of place. Hayley would be proud; she was a hairdresser.

Finlay's eyes locked with Elise and where weeks ago he'd loved looking into those deep, dark orbs, he now saw nothing but cool serenity. She'd used him and it cut like a sharp dagger running across his cheek. He rubbed the spot above his closely cropped beard like she'd actually slashed him.

'Hi. Your stuff's in here,' he said, before looking away. His gaze met Genevieve's. She was as stunning as Elise. Long caramel-coloured hair glinted in the downlights and she held herself very straight, like she had an iron rod clamped to her spine. Her ice-blue eyes flickered over him before landing on something to his left, her usual expression of cool indifference maintained.

'You put it in bags.' Elise stared at the black bags in the corridor, biting her lip.

'I did.' He gritted his teeth.

Genevieve glanced at him and gave him a *don't be so insensitive* look. What he'd ever done to her to make her dislike him so much, he had no idea, but he got the vibes loud and clear. Elise's eyes were downcast as she stared at the bags.

'Feel free to take it out and check it's all there,' he said. 'But if you wouldn't mind doing it somewhere else.'

'It's not that. I just don't think there will be room in the car.'

'Well... Can you make two trips? Only I need it out today.'

'I haven't got time to make two trips.' She checked her phone. 'I'm going to work after this.'

Finlay clamped his mouth shut. Why hadn't she come earlier?

'Maybe it'll squash down,' Genevieve suggested. 'Let's try.'

'Ok.' Elise lifted a bag and handed it to Genevieve, then picked up another one.

Finlay lifted two and followed them out, hardly able to watch as they teetered down the stairs in their heels, looking ready to fall flat on their faces at any second. And they'd probably sue him for all he was worth if they did.

Having grown up with a mother and sister who took pride in their appearance and always had glamorous friends, Finlay was no stranger to beautiful people in his life. His first fiancée had also been stunning. But never again was he going to go for someone like that. As long as she had a good loving heart, he'd take the next woman in pyjamas, a just-out-of-bed updo and threadbare slippers. *I don't even care if she drives an old banger and eats biscuits for breakfast.* If he'd managed to attract two immaculate women in the past, he couldn't be wholly unattractive, so it stood to reason he could attract someone a bit less flashy but a lot more caring. And that meant looking far away from here. Away from his cousin's exes and his sister's friends.

Elise opened the tiny boot of her black sports car. After she and her friend shoved their bags in, there was no room for anything else.

'These will have to go on the passenger seat,' Finlay said.

'Then where will I go?' Genevieve asked.

'You go in first and I'll put them on your knee,' Finlay said.

'I don't think so,' she said, looking outraged. 'There are four more bags or something still up there. I'll be suffocated.'

Finlay gave a little shrug. It wasn't his problem anymore. 'Then get a taxi home. I don't know. I just need these bags gone now.'

He turned and walked into the house without looking back at either of them. They could figure this out for themselves.

Chapter Three

Genevieve

Elise shoved the bags into the passenger seat, then turned to look at Genevieve. Her eyes were glassy and she was sucking on her lip in a totally uncharacteristic way. Where had the self-assured woman gone? She might have been the one to instigate the breakup, but it had clearly hit her hard.

'I think you will actually have to get a taxi back.' Elise turned her focus to the bags again and put her hand to her lips. 'I didn't think I'd brought this much stuff.'

'What? Can't you come back for me?'

'I'm already running late,' Elise said. 'I left it until the last minute so I wouldn't have to stay long but I don't want to be late for work. I'm already in trouble there.'

'Why?' Genevieve rested a hand on Elise's upper arm.

'I've not been myself lately and I've made mistakes.'

Genevieve wasn't sure she should probe any deeper. Elise worked for a travel company... Had she maybe sent some holidaymakers to the wrong destination?

'Ok. I don't want you to be late for work,' Genevieve said. 'But I'm going to my dad's party this afternoon and at this rate, I'm going to be late too.'

'I'll call a taxi for you,' Elise said. 'I'll pay for it too. I'm so sorry.'

'On a Saturday afternoon? I'll probably have to wait an hour.'

'Let's ask Finlay. He'll give you a lift.'

Genevieve shook her head. No way could she let Finlay give her a lift. How could she be alone with him? Every time she was near him, she did something stupid, like that time years ago when he'd offered to help her rollerblade and she'd said 'no way' so quickly he'd gone off shaking his head like he thought her a rude bitch. Then she'd fallen and skinned her knees. So embarrassing.

'I don't think he'll want to,' she said. 'He looks busy.'

'Let me ask. He's a good guy really. I'm sure he won't mind.'

Genevieve's heart swooped in her chest. She couldn't go with him. 'Maybe I should walk.'

'Let me ask him before you try.' Elise eyed Genevieve's shoes.

Why had Elise been the one to cross the line? The one Genevieve had dreamed of crossing but never done out of respect for her friendship with Hayley. She smiled at Elise, though it was more of a rueful one at her own expense. Here she was telling herself she wished she'd thought to date Finlay before Elise, forgetting of course he would never have dated her. Not when she'd always been so cold towards him.

'Come on,' Elise said. 'Let's get those other bags and I'll ask him to drive you home.'

'I...er...' What could she say? If she protested, it would look strange and she was well-practised at being indifferent around Finlay.

She followed Elise up the stairs, trying to force a solution into her head. How could she get out of this? Elise went through the hall into the living area and Genevieve waited, not sure what to do with herself. This was so stupid. Finlay was nice. He was well-known for being nice... He'd tried to be nice to her.

At school, he'd always seemed popular, if a bit quieter than his fun-loving sister. Genevieve had watched him winning races at sports days and playing rugby, pretending all the while to be either tagging along with Hayley or cheering him on because they happened to be in the same house team. He'd always been athletically built and she'd imagined every plane of his body from when he was seventeen to now.

'Can you give Genevieve a lift home, please?' Elise's voice said from the living room and Genevieve listened from the landing through the open doors, her heart thumping a little too fast like she was still a teenager in Hayley's living room and he was somewhere else in the house talking to his mum in the kitchen.

'Are you kidding?'

Of course he didn't want to. Why would he? She could only imagine how he felt about her – not exactly a happy thought.

'No, not kidding,' Elise said. 'I'm sorry to ask. I didn't realise the stuff would take up so much room and now I have to go straight to work. I don't have time to detour by her house. I should be on my way already.'

Genevieve chewed on her tongue, half wishing she hadn't bothered coming, though if she'd been in this position, she'd have welcomed support too, so she couldn't blame Elise for asking.

'Yeah, fine,' Finlay said. 'Whatever.'

'Thanks so much.' Elise returned to the landing, playing with the cuff of her jacket. 'He's going to give you a lift. I'm so, so sorry.'

'It's ok. You get to work.' Genevieve fidgeted with the chain strap on her little bag.

'Ok. And thanks so much for coming.' Elise pulled her in for a hug and kissed her cheek. 'I appreciate it. I really do.' She picked up the other black bags and bolted down the stairs.

'Bye,' Genevieve said quietly, raising her hand.

'So,' Finlay's voice spoke from behind her. She turned around and her thumping heart almost leapt out of her ribcage. He was leaning his elbow high on the doorjamb, his fingers resting in his short dark hair. His broad shoulders stretched his tight khaki t-shirt, and his muscular arms were bigger than she remembered. In fact, he looked different somehow – even more attractive than usual, if that was possible.

'So what?' she said.

Why do I always sound so rude around him?

'You've been dumped.' He pulled a fake commiserative face. 'I know the feeling only too well.'

'Yeah.' She rubbed the skin above the neckline of her top and gave him a forced smile. 'Can you take me home then?'

'Yes. But you'll have to wait until these people have looked around. They're due in fifteen minutes and I've got to get cleaned up and changed before that.'

'Seriously?'

'Yes. Seriously.' He lowered his arm and opened a door off the hall. 'Feel free to wait inside.' He moved and held out his hand, inviting her to go in.

'But... Can't you take me first?'

'No. I might not get back in time for the viewers. If you can't wait, there's nothing to stop you walking.' He glanced down. 'Well, except your shoes, of course.'

With a deep breath, Genevieve moved past him, almost holding her nose. Not because he smelled bad, quite the opposite.

'The living room is through there,' he said. 'I'm going to get ready. See you in a min.' The door to what she assumed was his bedroom clicked shut and he disappeared from view. Genevieve stood in the hall looking towards the open airy space through the open door at the end, still barely breathing. Apparently, it was one of those days where everything could and would go wrong. Why had she said yes to Elise? Now she was alone in Finlay's home. Something was uncomfortably intimate about the whole setup. He wouldn't think so. In fact he was probably

extremely hacked off at her untimely appearance. But for her...
She mentally shook herself.

Get a grip. Act normal. Be calm. Be serene.

She could do that... or she could try for a taxi.

She headed down the corridor and into the living area, pulling out her phone. Bright sunlight shone in the French doors and the space looked dazzlingly clean. A sofa and a chair were set to look out at the river and a dining table served as a divider between the living area and the kitchen. Obviously Finlay had already packed away most of his stuff because there was nothing on the shelves below the wall-mounted TV or the bookcase in the corner, just a pile of telltale boxes neatly stacked behind the door. Genevieve stepped through the French doors onto the balcony where a white iron bistro table for two looked very inviting. She'd love to sit here looking out at the river and watch the people going by. She itched to make a quick film but she didn't, instead she googled local taxi companies. Filming Finlay's house without his permission wasn't right. She also didn't want to explain why she was here.

Her followers liked to think she was a confident person with all her ducks in a row. This afternoon had just proved the opposite. Not only was she running late but she was stuck in an apartment with her best friend's ex... One she happened to have secret feelings for.

She tried calling the only local taxi company she could find but there was nothing available for another hour.

With a sigh, she left the balcony and went back inside. How long would this take? Finlay was still in his room and wait... Was that the sound of running water? He was having a shower. Jesus. Every fantasy she'd ever had of what he might look like naked and dripping with water collided and fought for space in her brain. *Get out!* Mentally she shoved the images away.

What if the viewers showed up now? She didn't want to show them around – Finlay wouldn't want her doing that. Maybe she should wait outside. There was a bench on the riverside path. She could sit there. If she'd worn better shoes, she could have walked home. But Glenbriar was built on a hill and her house was a twenty-minute walk from here when she had on sensible shoes. Should she just go for it? She had to get back, get changed, collect Mitzi, then drive to her parents' country house. *Ugh.* Her body felt trapped in a tight band and there was no breaking out of it.

She slumped into the chair and checked her messages. She should send a message to her parents to say she might be late, even though they'd be busy getting ready and probably wouldn't look at their phones.

GENEVIEVE: sorry, running a bit late. I was with grandma, then something else came up. Will be there as soon as I can. xx

She hit send and as she did, the tension in her shoulders and chest relaxed a little. A strange loose feeling came over her and she allowed herself to imagine how nice it would be not to have to go to the party at all. No fake smiles and pretending to be interested.

No trying to hide from her dad's divorced business colleagues who fancied themselves as sugar daddies. No setups with guys who were happy with certain benefits.

The running water had stopped and cupboard doors banged shut in Finlay's room. Genevieve forced her brain forward, away from dangerous thoughts of what he might be like in the bedroom. She put her phone on her lap and drummed her fingers on a side table. A little black box sat on the tabletop. It looked like a ring box and it seemed bizarrely out of place in the empty flat. Unable to stop curiosity getting the better of her, she picked it up and flipped it open.

'Wow.' She goggled at the sparkling ring inside. It had an almost vintage shaped diamond in the centre but was clearly modern with three intricate bands studded with smaller diamonds, flaring from a central diamond, then meeting and forming one white gold band. She'd love to try it on but didn't dare. This wasn't the ring Finlay had given Elise. Elise had chosen one for herself a couple of weeks before breaking the engagement. Apparently Finlay had wanted to give her his grandmother's engagement ring but Elise hadn't liked it as it was an ugly yellow gold thing.

A cough made Genevieve spin around. Finlay was leaning on the doorjamb again, looking shower fresh in a crisp white shirt and black trousers. *Oh sweet Jesus.* How smoking hot was he? Her heart might have stopped. When they'd been teenagers, it was embarrassing to crush on a friend's older brother and she'd held back or been rude without meaning to. When he'd dated Elise, she couldn't bear to look at him. It made her sick to see him with her friend and she'd cold-shouldered him worse than ever. Now she couldn't drag her eyes from the slightly open shirt, broad chest and trim beard. *Do not notice. Stay aloof.* Bright eyes and firm jaw. *Not looking.* Neatly cropped hair and fresh eucalyptus scent so reminiscent of her favourite wax melts. *Don't care.* Her breath hitched in her throat. Who was she kidding? *He's gorgeous. He's always been gorgeous… but not for me. Repeat. Not. For. Me.*

He raked the hair above his ear and gave her a stern look.

He was a P.E. teacher and that was the *I don't take any crap* look if ever she saw it. She glanced down at her hand and swallowed. Oh shit. The ring. No wonder he didn't look impressed. *Caught snooping.*

Chapter Four

Finlay

'Still here, are you?' Finlay raised an eyebrow at Genevieve. He'd half hoped she'd have got bored with waiting and decided to walk home.

But hang on… What was she holding? Was that his ring? What a damn cheek.

'Um, yeah…'

'And give me that, please.' He marched across the room and held out his hand like he was about to confiscate something from a pupil in class. She flipped the box shut and handed it to him with one of her coolly indifferent expressions.

'Pardon me,' she said. 'I was just being nosey. That's a really beautiful ring.'

He raised an eyebrow. Why so polite? She was normally so snooty. 'Yeah. I think so.' He put it in his pocket and didn't elaborate. She didn't need to know its full history, and he wasn't about to tell her because she'd be straight back reporting to Elise. He never wanted Elise to find out the lengths he'd gone to before realising what an idiot he was. 'Now listen, the viewers will be here any minute. You need to…' He squinted down at her. 'Well, you can't just sit there. I want the flat to look as appealing as possible.'

'Oh charming.' She got to her feet. 'I'll go outside then if I'm spoiling the appeal.'

'That is not what I meant.' He held up his hands. 'I meant if you're here and they see you, they'll wonder who you are and what you're doing here. I want to give them a good impression, so just… I don't know… Look like you're my friend or something and that you think the flat is great.' *In other words don't sit and scowl at me or make snappy retorts.*

'How about I go into the kitchen and bake some bread? Or I could whip up a cake and serve it with a smile.' She pulled a perfectly angelic one, like she did on those films she made. Both Hayley and Elise had made him watch them at some point.

'No need for sarcasm,' he said.

'Too low for you? Your wit is of a much higher degree, is it?'

The buzzer rang before he could reply. With little hope she'd do anything other than pout or make snarky comments, he abandoned her to open the door.

'Hi,' he said, welcoming the couple into the hall.

'Hi.' They both replied at the same time and glanced around, starry-eyed. The man grinned at him and Finlay returned it but was surprised how hard his jaw was working to get it to show on his face. Seven years ago, he'd been that guy. He'd had a girlfriend and they'd looked at this flat together, holding hands and smiling. How excited about the future they'd been. But that had all changed now.

'So, we have the main hall here. The doors off lead to a bedroom and a cupboard on this side. Another bedroom and the main bathroom on this side.' He pointed with his hands like a flight attendant. 'And directly ahead, we have the living area. Oh, and the master bedroom on this side has an en-suite shower room.'

'Great,' the woman said. 'Maybe if we start with the living area.'

'Go on through.' He let them go ahead, crossing his fingers behind his back and putting up a silent plea. *Please let Genevieve be out of the way or at least looking happy.* She had such a constantly serene and unflappable expression it was impossible to know what she was thinking or what mood she was in. It made her perfect on screen but hard work in the flesh.

As the couple crossed the threshold of the living area, Genevieve spoke. 'Hi. Pleased to meet you. Such a gorgeous day for a viewing. The river looks so lovely from the balcony, don't you think?'

'Oh, wow, yes, what a great view,' the woman said.

'I don't think there's a flat anywhere in the town with a better view,' Genevieve went on. 'And with the windows all down this wall, it really brings the outside in.'

'Yes,' the man agreed.

Finlay frowned and strolled into the room after them. They made their way around the island cum table that split the kitchen area from the living room, eyes roaming all over it. Genevieve stepped forward like she was going to follow them, but Finlay gently took her arm and prevented her from moving past him.

'What are you doing?' she muttered, looking like she'd been grabbed by a mad axeman. God knew why she always looked at him like he might murder her.

'Same question right back at you,' he said through his teeth. 'Are you an estate agent or something?'

'No. But you told me to—'

'Does the flat have gas or oil heating?' the woman asked, looking over. Finlay still had his hand on Genevieve's arm. The viewers probably thought they were a couple. He internally rolled his eyes. Well, at least they didn't know him. The last thing he needed circulating was a rumour that he'd not only split with Elise but he'd already taken up with one of her friends just a few weeks later.

'It's oil.'

'Is that cost effective?'

How could he tell them it wasn't really, not with constantly fluctuating prices?

'If you're considering a more cost-effective and sustainable option, you could explore renewable sources,' Genevieve said. 'They can easily outstrip oil in a place like this.'

Both viewers turned their attention to her, and Finlay frowned.

'This area is perfect for green energy. Solar panels and heat pumps are really popular around here,' she continued.

'But do they really save money in the long run?' the man asked.

'Yes, they do. The initial installation cost might be an issue, but you can often get government grants. After that, you'll find they have lower running costs.'

Finlay's mouth opened like a goldfish. She seemed to know what she was talking about, or was this some learned-by-heart patter she spouted to her social media followers? Some of her films were hilarious, though they weren't meant to be. They reminded him of the games she and Hayley used to play as kids, where they'd make believe they were TV presenters. Now she'd taken that game to a whole new level and actually filmed herself cooking, cleaning, trying out beauty products and who knew what else. It all seemed totally frivolous to him. The kind of thing half his pupils wished they could do. Was it even a real job? He wasn't sure how it made money.

'If you go online and look up Harrington Energy Solutions,' she said, 'that's my dad's company. You'll get loads of information there.'

'Thanks. I'll save that info on my phone.'

The couple went back to looking around.

'Quite the boffin, aren't you?' Finlay murmured.

'When it comes to green energy, yes. My dad would kill me otherwise.'

The couple wandered into the dining area and smiled at Finlay and Genevieve. He suddenly remembered he was still holding her arm. It kind of felt necessary in case she decided to bound after them with another sales pitch. She beamed at them, then placed her hand over the top of his. Patting it and holding her fixed smile in place, she waited until they'd gone out the French doors before saying, 'You can let go of me now, unless your legs are about to give way.'

'Why would they?' He released her.

'Because you're so awed by me, of course. It's making you weak at the knees.' She batted her eyelashes and a smile he'd rarely seen on her before sneaked onto her face.

'Right.' He stepped away from her. 'Not just an estate agent wannabe and a green energy guru but an irresistible temptress too. I better watch myself or I'll be in trouble.'

'Who's being sarcastic now?' She folded her arms and eyed him over. Her lips quirked further and he had an odd sensation, kind of like something in that little movement said she didn't mind what she saw one single bit. Maybe he should be flattered but hell no!

No way was he falling into that trap again. Never would he ever so much as look sideways at one of his sister's friends again. No. No. No. It was because of another woman just like her he was leaving his job, his home, his family and the country.

Chapter Five

Genevieve

Genevieve drew closer to Finlay and watched the couple looking around his flat. She shouldn't be enjoying this. She really shouldn't. But how could she not? He wasn't scary, even if her heart was pounding like mad. He was actually a chilled guy and the aura surrounding him was steady and unthreatening. This was the kind of guy she wanted. In her teenage years, he'd been the actual guy she wanted... Maybe he kind of still was but she couldn't have him, so pretending was the way forward.

For the next few minutes anyway.

Her guard had dropped and it was ok. She wanted a flat like this and a man like Finlay. Someone steady and sensible. Playing house with him for this moment gave her a taste of what was missing from her life. Something she'd never successfully discovered: a real, deep and meaningful connection, not one that was nothing but a show or a business transaction.

Her followers knew her thoughts on 'the one' and how she was sure she'd know when he came along. But it wouldn't be Finlay.

Not now. It couldn't be. He was leaving and she couldn't cross that line she'd drawn for herself long ago.

She side-eyed him. He was looking back and her heart did that silly little flip-flop it always did in his company, but she was the mistress of it and knew nothing in her face would betray how she really felt.

'Can we see the bedrooms now?' the woman's voice said from outside the French door.

'Yes, of course,' Finlay said. 'Go on through. I... We'll wait here, if you have any questions.'

The couple crossed the room and went back into the hall.

'Aw,' Genevieve said, keeping her voice level. 'You said "we". How sweet.'

'Not sweet,' Finlay said. 'I just didn't want you following them in there. *We* are waiting here.'

'Why? I'm doing a great job selling your flat so far.'

'Yeah, but with your amazing capacity to adapt to any situation, I didn't want to risk you turning into a consultant in bedroom moves or anything like that.'

She glanced away, barely covering a laugh. 'You don't think my tantric instructions would be welcome?'

'I look forward to the video on your next vlog.' He wandered into the kitchen area.

'Oh ha ha.' But her pulse was racing. This was kind of like flirting, something she'd never let herself do with him.

'Funny, aren't I?' he muttered, lifting a packet of crackers from the cupboard. 'You want one?' He waved the packet in her direction.

'Er, no thanks. I better not. There'll be nibbles all afternoon at the party. And prosecco and champagne.'

'Nice.' He scoffed a cracker. 'I'm starving. I was so busy I didn't have any lunch.' Guzzling another cracker almost whole, he opened his fridge. 'I'll need to get some food for dinner too. I've got nothing left.'

'I'll bring you a doggy bag from the party. Honestly, the amount of waste will be awful and how my dad can justify it, I really don't know. Not when most of the time he's banging on about a greener planet.'

'What kind of party is this?'

Genevieve pulled a face. 'My dad has them every so often. He invites lots of businesspeople to the house and they spend the afternoon and evening pretending not to talk about business when, of course, they're all sizing each other up.' *Or trying to get me to date them.*

'Why do you have to go?'

'Well, who would turn down free drink and a free meal?' And she felt like it was a duty to do it. She didn't want to let anyone down.

'Good point.'

She was expected to turn up and represent the family along with her parents. Neither her brother nor sister were ever able to go these days. They didn't live as close or have the same 'needs' as Genevieve – 'needs' their parents had decided she had. Cressida was already married, so didn't require them to find her a partner. Rafe had married young and divorced a few years later. Since then, he always had a girlfriend, usually a very glamorous one, though they didn't seem to last long. It satisfied their parents however that he could find someone for himself. The fact he had his very own, and very successful, travel business also went in his favour – most of the time, though it sometimes annoyed their dad that he didn't want to take on the family business. Genevieve was a hopeless case in their eyes and if she stopped attending the parties, they'd worry she was even worse than they'd thought. A few years ago, it had died down when she'd agreed to date James Charlton, whose father owned Duchan Fayre, a country shopping centre and restaurant, full of designer brands, with a reputation for high quality and prestige. The kind of place both Genevieve and her mum loved going to for the day. James was in the same position as her with his parents always trying to set him up. Their relationship had worked for a while, but Genevieve had attached more to it than James. He saw it more like a friends-with-benefits arrangement. But the benefits didn't really work for her. If she'd even got a contract with Duchan Fayre to endorse their products she'd have been happy, but that hadn't been forthcoming.

Opportunity missed.

'The parties are usually quite smart,' Genevieve said, trying to convince herself as much as anything.

'Sounds very chic,' Finlay said, taking a bite from another cracker, just as the couple came back in. He hastily turned around and shoved the packet back into the cupboard, obviously chewing fast.

'Everything ok?' Genevieve asked, sparing him the need to turn around with his mouth full of biscuit.

'Yes. Great,' the woman said. 'I think we've seen everything we need.'

'That's good. Are you from the area or moving from somewhere else?'

'We're both from Perthshire originally, but we've just finished university in Glasgow and we're hoping to move back up here.'

'Well, good luck with your house hunting.'

'Thank you.'

'Yes,' Finlay added, brushing his lips as he moved closer. 'Thanks for coming. I'll show you out.'

Genevieve crossed to the French doors and looked at the river beyond. Funny how she'd been so eager to leave twenty minutes ago. Now she quite liked the idea of staying here. Maybe she and Finlay could crack open a bottle of vino and sit out. They'd had an enjoyable bit of banter. Probably more entertaining than anything she'd get in the next several hours at her dad's party. She sat down at the bistro table, resting her elbows on it and clasping her hands in front of her.

'So...' Finlay popped his head out the door. 'They're away. You ready to go?'

'I suppose.' She sighed.

He pulled out the other bistro chair and sat. 'You don't sound very enthusiastic. What's up?'

'Do you really care?'

He snorted. 'Ok. That's more like the you I'm used to.'

Genevieve huffed and shook her head, though he wasn't wrong.

'You know, Elise is some woman,' he said, and Genevieve winced. She didn't need to hear him telling her how wonderful Elise had been and how he missed her. 'It's the way she has people wrapped around her little finger that gets me. It used to be me. She does it to Hayley and you, it seems. I mean, why did you come with her when she dumped you straight away?'

'She was upset. I had to. We're friends and we help each other out.'

Finlay raised an eyebrow. 'Very noble. I'm surprised you want to come anywhere near me.'

'Why do you say that?'

'Well, you've never exactly been my number one fan, have you?'

If only he knew.

'I dread to think what Elise says about me,' he said. 'But it was her who broke up with me, you know?'

'I know.' Genevieve tapped the table with her nail. 'She never says horrible stuff about you. I think she's really sad about what she did. She was really cut up when she called me.'

'Oh yeah?'

'Really. I've known her for a long time and this has really affected her. I know she's made mistakes but she's not a bad person. After Aidan left, she just wanted everyone to know she was ok, she had everything together and was in a place to move on.'

'So she used me.'

'Maybe, but she also liked you.'

'Just not enough.' He tapped his linked hands on the table.

'At least she was honest. It would have been worse to have kept on living the lie, don't you think?'

'You think that if it makes you feel better. Now, are we going?'

'Hang on.' Genevieve put up her hand. 'Would you rather she pretended to have stronger feelings? What if you'd got married and then ended up being divorced years later, maybe after you'd had kids? Wouldn't that have been worse?' Was that not exactly what she'd hoped for with James? She'd hoped to squeeze something lasting from the relationship, knowing they didn't have particularly strong feelings for each other. Was that the very definition of desperate?

'Look, forget it. You're probably right, but I can't think about it like that yet. If she didn't have those feelings, why string me along in the first place? That's what I don't like.'

Genevieve let out a sigh. This was the mess they had to deal with. 'What does Hayley say about it?'

'Not much. You know what she's like. Always wanting to keep the peace, though I think she's withdrawn a bit from Elise.'

'Why do you say that?'

'Hayley at least knows where to draw a line. For example, Elise wouldn't even have asked her to do what you did this afternoon.'

Genevieve knew he was right. 'I just wanted to help.' She dropped her head into her hands before realising what she'd done. 'I should go.'

'Hey.' Finlay's hand grazed her arm and she looked up like an electric current had zapped her.

'You did help. You're a good friend to her.'

'Oh... Thanks... But, um...' she groaned. 'I need to get to this party now.'

'Fine, let's go. But you don't seem very happy about it.'

She brushed her skirt. 'I'm fine. Just fine.'

'Come on.' He cocked his head to the left. 'I've been around long enough to know when "fine" means anything but.'

She didn't answer. How could she? He was so right. Why had she let her façade slip in front of him, of all people? But he was so easy to talk to. He seemed genuinely concerned. Or was it just because she saw the resemblance to Hayley in him and she knew how kind she would be in this situation?

'If you don't want to go, then don't,' he said. 'You know there's this little word. It has two letters and starts with *N* and ends with *O*? Why not use it?'

She steepled her fingers at her chin and took in a deep breath. 'That's easy for you to say but it's not that simple. This is family. Me attending the party is important to them.'

'I know all about family loyalties. My parents are divorced, and both have had new partners. It's never easy doing the right thing, knowing who to visit, whose story to believe.'

'And the right thing for me is to go to the party.'

'I'm sure it won't be that bad once you get there. Sometimes thinking about things like that is worse than actually doing them.'

'All the guests think they know me because of my dad and social media, even if I don't know them. It makes conversation so awkward. Dad's usually told them a bunch of stuff he should have kept to himself. It puts me at an instant disadvantage.' She couldn't believe she was saying all this out loud or even admitting it. Normally she took it with grace and indifference but maybe the last straw had finally fallen.

'What kind of stuff does he tell them?' Finlay pulled a face like he wasn't sure he really wanted to know.

'My dating history mostly and how much I'd love to be happily married to whichever one of them can present me with the biggest cheque.'

Finlay chuckled. 'Ok, so I get that it's not actually funny, but when you put it like that.'

'Yup. Hilarious.'

'Come on, you're a party animal. I know for a fact you, Hayley, and Elise have been partying hard for years. And you've got the charm. Look at how you charmed those viewers. Why not just turn it on for a few hours? How hard can it be? You do it for the camera every day – fake it for a few hours.'

'That's what I have to do.' But she was tired of it. Really tired. Parties on her own terms were fine. She liked being surrounded by her crowd, dancing and knocking back the bubbly.

'Just drink as much as you can,' he suggested.

'Who knows what I might do then?'

'I dread to think.'

She rested her chin on her hand and gazed across the table at him. He looked so fit. She remembered Elise moaning about the amount of time he spent running, cycling and coaching sports clubs, but it had worked wonders on his physique. No doubt loads of the kids at his High School crushed on him. Sexy Mr McBride. She definitely would if she was still at school.

He put his elbow on the table and mirrored her pose with a very pronounced stare. 'Penny for them.'

No way! She couldn't let on what was going through her head at that moment – what had been going through her head for the last thirteen years. 'Do you fancy going to a party?' The words slipped out unbidden in the same way she'd let 'no way' slip out all those years ago when he'd offered to hold her hand as she tried the rollerblades. If she'd only said yes. How different things might have been and how much more would she have enjoyed rollerblading? She wouldn't have ended up with a sprained wrist and two grazed knees anyway and she might just have caught the boy of her dreams before he got too far out of reach and a hedge of tangled complications grew in the way.

'What?' He frowned.

'You know, come along to a party where you get to eat as much as you want, drink as much as you want and have a stunning and devoted date on your arm.' Her voice was a little hysterical, somewhere between manic laughter and ugly crying.

'Er…'

Why was she saying all this and digging herself a hole? Was she that determined to get egg splattered all over her face? But she couldn't stop now she'd started. 'Did I mention this date is the GOAT in the property market? A guru in green energy and an irresistible temptress with tantric expertise in the bedroom?'

Finlay snorted. 'You are having a laugh, aren't you?'

'Yes, just a mad idea that was never going to work.' She needed to leave and hopefully she'd never see him again after today. What must he think of her? If it had been bad before, it was downright hideous now.

'What kind of thing would I be letting myself in for with this tantric temptress?'

She huffed out a laugh and raised an eyebrow. 'Why not bring an overnight bag? You can find out.'

'Are you mad? What has got into you? I always thought you were so... Well, prim.'

She stood up and pushed her chair under the table. 'I am. It was just a silly moment. Forget it.' *Yes, forget.* She didn't need to persuade someone to date her out of pity or to save her from circumstances. That was James all over again. 'Now, would you please take me home?'

He got to his feet. He was so pleasantly tall; just the right height in fact, not so tall he was towering but enough that her eyes landed naturally on his face without having to crick her neck. His movement disturbed the air, and she was hit by his shower-fresh eucalyptus scent again.

'I didn't say no.'

'You didn't say yes either.' She arched an eyebrow, aware of the increase in her pulse tempo.

'Party or not to party, that's the question,' he said. His eyes met hers and he seemed to look at her for a very long time, perhaps trying to extract more information from her, but she pulled her serene face back on. She'd already given away too much in that convo. Hopefully he wouldn't go telling anyone. She didn't want a pity party or everyone dissecting her moment of weakness.

Was he seriously considering this? Part of her wanted that so much but the other part was ringing alarm bells.

'I'll grab my overnight bag and lock up then,' he said after a beat.

'You're coming?' She gaped at him. Jump for joy or cringe? What would she tell her parents?

'Yeah. What man could resist?'

Was he seriously thinking she'd been offering him—

'Free food and drink,' he said with a wink.

'Um... of course. And you're welcome to stay over. There are loads of bedrooms, but I wasn't really meaning we... You know.' Had her pulse rate just hit the red?

'I get the deal. I hang about and ward off the unwanted attention.'

'Exactly... While eating as much as you want from the buffet.'

'What are we waiting for?' He held out his arm for her to go inside, pulled the French doors shut and locked them.

Genevieve let out a breath. This day was getting stranger and stranger.

CHAPTER SIX

Finlay

Finlay tossed his overnight bag into the boot of his car and shut it with a thud. He rolled his eyes for what had to be the hundredth time in the last ten minutes. Only someone as gullible as him would have agreed to this. Clearly he hadn't learned his lesson. The one he'd been reminding himself about ever since the split with Elise. Hadn't he promised himself less than an hour ago he wasn't going to fall into anymore traps set by friends of his sister?

Yet here he was swanning off to a party with one of them. One who'd always disliked him too. Well, it was only a party. At least he wasn't leaping into an engagement with her. Her face when she was sitting at the table on the balcony – the look in her eyes was haunting. It was odd how a mask seemed to fall away and for a moment she was bare before him: the real Genevieve, not the ice woman he'd taken her for before. And he'd pitied her. How like him. That was how it had started with Elise. He was sorry for how Aidan had treated her and wanted to help her. *I never learn, do I?* He was a sucker for souls in peril. He always wanted to help the struggling kids at school, save the birds caught in the strawberry nets at his mum's house, and help lonely women who spun him a sob story.

Here we go again.

He jumped into the driver's seat and came face to face with a semi-smiling Genevieve. It wasn't wholly splitting her face but it was a lot softer than her usual look, warmer too. Almost like she was genuinely pleased to see him. Again, just like Elise. She'd turned on this act in the beginning too.

'This is only a party, right?' he said. 'Nothing else. Yeah?'

'Of course,' she said. 'What else would it be?'

'I'm just making sure.'

'Only a party. Let's just enjoy it,' she said. 'Live in the moment and all that.'

'You've brightened up pretty quickly.'

'Must be because I've caught myself a handsome date for the occasion.'

'Have you? And when's he arriving?' Finlay reversed out of the drive.

'Ha ha, very funny.' She gave him an obvious once over and it sent a weird tremor through him. He wished it didn't... But that wasn't the first time he'd caught her doing something like that this afternoon. Hopefully he was imagining things.

'What are we telling people at this party?' he asked. 'Am I a friend? A blind date you're never planning on seeing again?

A friend's ex-boyfriend you're dating for revenge because she dragged you out one afternoon and then dumped you?'

She gave him a stern look. 'None of the above, but you're right, we need to get a story.'

'What? Like *Jack and the Beanstalk* or something? Is it a bring-your-own-book party?'

She shook her head and looked like she might laugh. 'You know what I mean.'

'So, here's an idea. How about we say you came around unexpectedly and didn't want to go to the party alone, so you propositioned a guy you knew would otherwise be home alone in an empty house, and bribed him with the all-you-can-eat buffet?'

'Er, maybe not.'

'Well, do your parents know who I am? I mean, do they know about me and Elise? They must know Hayley.'

'My mum might put it all together, though she doesn't really like Elise. My dad never pays any attention to my friends and never remembers their names, but it's not like I want you to have a fake name or identity. You can still be you.'

'Well, that's a relief.'

'Sarcasm, Finlay.' Her voice was almost a purr, and it was kind of sexy when she said his name, though he shouldn't really be thinking stuff like that. 'Remember, it's beneath you.'

'Many things are, including a fake identity. So, what kind of story are you proposing?'

'Something about how we met, that kind of thing. We can say we haven't been seeing each other long, then if my mum twigs who you are, she won't think we were doing anything behind Elise's back.'

'Seeing each other? You want me to pretend I've been seeing you? What if someone there knows me other than your mum? They might think I was cheating on Elise and then I'll look worse than I do already.'

'Well, we can say we started seeing each other after that. I'm the rebound.'

'Can't I pretend to be your bodyguard and stand about eating food, stopping lechy blokes from bugging you, which is what I was originally engaged to do?'

'They have to believe we're together or they'll still try to creep their way in.'

'Are you enjoying this?'

'What?'

'Making up this little scene. I hope you're not planning on filming it and putting me all over the internet as some fake date experiment.'

A grin split her face and he almost put the car off the road. Why was he looking at her and not concentrating? That smile was... Well, it suited her more than the serene indifference. 'I wasn't planning a fake date experiment, but it's not a bad idea.'

'Don't bother. The school in Dubai I'm going to is very strict. If there's anything even slightly against me on social media, I'm in trouble. So no cameras. Got it?'

'Got it.'

He drove across town to her house, which was a pleasant, terraced townhouse on a new-build estate on the outskirts of Glenbriar.

'I need to get changed and grab my bag. Oh, and I also need to get Mitzi.'

'Who's that?'

'My dog.'

'You have a dog?'

'Yeah. She's a French bulldog. Come and meet her. She's so cute. She can play with Horace and Dax at my parent's. They all get on so well.'

'Who are Horace and Dax? I assume they're dogs too, or are they your little brothers?'

She flashed him that million-dollar smile again – so beautiful. 'They're black labs.'

He got out of the car and followed her to the door.

'I hope you're not allergic to dogs.'

'Oh, I am... I better go.'

'Seriously?'

'No.' He shook his head and laughed. 'I like dogs.'

'Phew. You had me going for a moment.'

'It's not difficult, is it?'

'Look who's talking, Mr Wellington Willoughby the third.'

'Eh?'

'That's your new name. For the fake identity.'

'Oh, very good.' He slow clapped as she opened the door.

'Knew you'd like it.'

'Nice house by the way.'

'Yeah, it's ok but I don't actually like it that much. The view of other houses is annoying. I'd love somewhere with a view like you have.'

'Feel free to buy my flat.'

'Actually, that's not a bad idea.' She stooped down in front of him and patted her knees.

He really shouldn't admire her backside from this position but he kind of couldn't help it.

A scuffling and snuffling noise came from her feet and she cooed. 'Hello, beautiful. Yes, mummy's home and look who's with me.'

'Daddy?' he suggested.

She straightened up and goggled at him. 'That's a bit pre-sumptuous, isn't it?'

The dog scampered out the door and sniffed around Finlay, wagging her bottom and her little stumpy tail. 'Maybe not.' He bent over and tickled her. She dropped onto her back, displaying her tummy and he rubbed it. 'Definitely not.'

'Yeah, well, we're not sharing custody. Now, in you come, both of you. Come on.'

'What did you say her name was?' he asked as he entered the hallway. He blinked before taking a second look. This was like a show home. Social media perfect.

'Mitzi. How about you wait with her in there and I'll get ready as fast as I can?'

Fast for Genevieve was snail-pace compared to everyone else. After half an hour of playing with Mitzi, Finlay lay his head back on the sofa and sighed. Mitzi jumped up beside him and crawled onto his lap. 'You're a funny little thing, aren't you?' He tickled her and she turned to mush, sticking her legs in the air so he could rub her belly. 'Not as odd as your owner though. What's her deal?' One minute so serene, then suddenly the guise slipped. Now she was bubbly and as happy as anyone going to a party. 'Must be my natural charm,' he muttered.

Eventually, he heard footsteps on the stairs, and a few seconds later, the door opened. He was used to seeing beautiful women, immaculately dressed – his mum, his sister, Elise. But it didn't stop the jolt of electricity that walloped him when his eyes latched onto her.

'Wow,' he said. How could he help it?

'Is that you being sarky again?'

'Not at all. You look stunning.'

'Thanks.' Her cheeks bloomed and she smoothed non-existent creases from the front of her figure-hugging dark pink dress. The sweetheart neckline dipped at her rosy cleavage and the off-shoulder sleeves were like cuffs on her upper arm. Her long caramel hair tumbled around in wide, elegant waves. Yup – stunning was accurate. Utterly stunning, gorgeous, beautiful.

Take care, he warned himself. But it was nothing. He was just getting into the part. Gently lifting Mitzi off his knee, he got to his feet and approached Genevieve.

'What are you doing?' she said, her face slipping, her eyes suddenly filled with a different look – worry perhaps, or was it the old serenity returning?

'Just looking.'

'Ok, good. I thought you were going to do a practice kiss before we got there.'

'Excuse me?'

She giggled and looked away. 'Joke! Got you again, Mr Willoughby.'

'Oh very funny.' He moved closer. 'But perhaps you might permit me...' He raised an eyebrow.

'To what? I've just done my lipstick, and...'

'I wouldn't presume. But how about...' He took her hand. 'This?'

'You want to kiss my hand?'

'May I?'

'Um... Well, ok... I guess. You go ahead, Mr Willoughby.'

With a smile, he held her gaze and raised her hand. 'Mr Willoughby sounds like a bad guy.'

She nodded and looked like she was holding her breath. 'Yes, but they're always... hot,' she said, her voice slightly hoarse.

'Hot, huh? Well, isn't that something?' He pressed his lips to her soft skin, still keeping his eyes on hers. What had actually got into him? This was fun but crazy mad. Just as well he was leaving the country in a few weeks.

Maybe there wasn't any harm in a final farewell before he went.

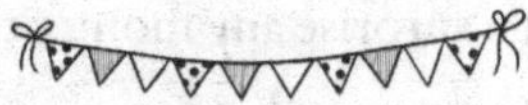

The drive to Genevieve's parents' house didn't take long. Finlay knew the road well. He often cycled in these purple hills and found new tracks down steep slopes, across streams and through rocky terrain. When they arrived at the house, he realised he'd seen it before many times from one of his favourite rides. And really it was unmissable: a custom-built eco-house in large grounds. Its design was such a bizarre mix of space-age and rustic that Finlay couldn't remember seeing anything quite like it. It was the kind of thing that featured on *Grand Designs* with its own solar field and wind turbines. The living roof made it seem like the house was curling out of the ground. He drove down a steep curving drive around the back to a parking area, too awed to speak.

'Everything ok?' Genevieve asked.

'This house,' Finlay said. 'It's... Well, wild.'

'I told you I'm a renewables guru. This is why. My dad is the king of green. Even the house is called Greenacres. It's kind of a theme.'

'Wow.' Finlay got out of the car, glancing around. A lot of other cars were parked in the car park but no other people were about. 'Are we very late?'

'Yes.' Genevieve checked her phone. 'But don't worry. It goes on all day. My mum has replied to the message I sent earlier. She hopes everything's ok.'

'She's going to get a surprise any moment. When you turn up with Herr Van McHoover or whatever my name is now.'

Genevieve grinned and strolled around the car to meet him. 'I'm starting to regret this. You better behave.'

'No chance.'

'Not even for all the salmon blinis you can eat and prosecco on tap?'

He moved his head from side to side, weighing the idea. 'That might work.'

'Let me get Mitzi out. We can leave her with the boys before we go in.'

'Are they somewhere else?'

'They have a kennel and a run for when my parents are out or busy. They'll get back in later when it has calmed down a bit.'

Kennels and a run conjured an image of a shed and an area fenced around with chicken wire... But this. Finlay goggled at the large space with a building more like a garden office than a doghouse. 'Pampered pooches these, aren't they?'

'Of course.' Genevieve smiled, and Mitzi tugged on her lead, desperate to get to her friends. Two black labs appeared at the fence wagging their tails wildly and panting with big slobbery smiles. 'Hey, boys,' Genevieve said, and their tail-wagging approached somewhere around a hundred miles per hour. Mitzi zoomed forward and started jumping up at the other side, her paws scrabbling on the mesh.

'Someone's happy,' Finlay said.

Genevieve moved to the door and unbolted it. The two labs bounded up and by the time she'd fully opened the door, their noses were in position, ready to sniff all over Mitzi. Giggling, Genevieve unclipped Mitzi and gave all three dogs a pat before closing the doors.

'I guess I'm not going to be missed.' She hung up Mitzi's lead on the outside of the door and they walked back the way they'd come, passing the fenced off area on the way. The three dogs were outside, chasing each other around the run.

'They look like they're having the time of their lives,' Finlay said. 'If only the same could be said for us.'

'And here was me thinking you were.' Genevieve looked up at him. 'Please don't wreck my illusion.'

'Your illusion? This coming from a woman who's always hated me.'

'I didn't *hate* you.'

'You did a very good impression of it. And in return, I'm sure I can do a great impression of enjoying myself.' He looked around. 'I mean, I can't imagine anywhere I'd rather be.' He gave her a Sean Connery wink and she laughed into the back of her hand.

'Should we hold hands or something? You know, make this look authentic, like we're really into each other.'

'Aren't you anyway?' She tossed him a sassy look, as if daring him to say otherwise.

'Sure. How could I not be?'

'And you're the least sarcastic person I've ever met.'

'Why thank you,' he said, holding out his hand. 'Shall we?'

She looked at his hand, then at his face, and raised both her eyebrows. 'I think you're insane.'

'Me? Says the woman who asked me here in the first place, even though she's barely spoken two words to me in ten-plus years.'

'Yeah.' She ran her fingertips down her decolletage, still looking at his outstretched hand, then reached out and took it. Her palm was warm and her grip was firmer than he expected. He returned her hold with equal pressure and she glanced up, looking almost uncertain. He knew why. They were about to enter an eco-house with turbines and solar panels... But neither of those methods could generate as much energy as the connection from their combined hands. Finlay's body felt stronger, like he was a superhero changing from his human form into something gigantic and powerful. Whatever the next few hours threw at him, he could handle it. And more than that, he was going to enjoy it.

The path wound ahead, bending around the house that, from the side and the top, seemed to blend in with the hill. The bright green lawn continued perfectly across the roof. Finlay's jaw dropped as they walked towards the front. What a masterpiece of weathered timber and glass: symmetrical with two-storey wings on either side of a giant roundhouse in the centre. The doors were wide open on the ground floor and people milled in and out seamlessly.

'Wow.' He gaped at the tear-drop shaped lawn built effortlessly into the swirling paths around the garden. Large white trellises were dripping with roses.

'You like it?'

'Stunning. I've never seen anywhere quite like this – except on TV.' He glanced up and saw that all along the upper floors were rooms with balconies and French doors. It reminded him of his apartment building but this was one house. Every well-placed eco brick sang money. It must have cost a fortune to build.

'There's my dad,' Genevieve said, leading Finlay into the throng. 'Let's get this meeting out of the way, then we can introduce you to the buffet.'

Finlay let out a snort laugh. 'You really are my kind of girl.'

'I'm sure my dad will be delighted to hear that.'

'But we still haven't sorted out our story.'

She twisted her lips into a pout. 'You up for winging it?'

'Oh sure. I love living dangerously.'

With a smirk, she led him over to a grey-haired man in a blue shirt. He looked around sixty and was good looking with a trim figure. There was something of the silver fox about him. Finlay could imagine his mum eyeing him up.

'Hey, Dad.' Genevieve tapped him on the arm and he dropped out of the conversation he was having with a group of people.

'Ah, you made it,' he said with a broad grin. His gaze almost instantly fell on Finlay, taking in their joined hands. His expression was pleasantly curious.

'I did. Sorry I'm late.' She leaned up and kissed his cheek, still not letting go of Finlay. 'I got held up.'

'No problem. And who do we have here?'

'This is Finlay, my, er...'

'Boyfriend,' Finlay supplied. 'Though I'm possibly too old for that term.'

'Oh I don't think so,' her father said. 'You look like a young lad to me. And I'm very pleased to meet you.' He pushed out his hand. 'I'm Geoff.'

'Pleased to meet you too.' Finlay shook his hand.

'I had no idea you were seeing anyone,' he said to Genevieve.

'It's all quite new.'

'Wonderful,' Geoff said. 'Let me find Hilary. She'll be delighted.'

'Listen, Dad, while you're looking for Mum, we'll get some food. Finlay's been... er, renovating a flat and he hasn't eaten much today.'

'Well, you better get to the buffet then, hadn't you?' Geoff ushered them forward. 'Are you in the property business, Finlay?'

'No. I'm a P.E. teacher.'

'Fantastic. What sports do you like?'

'Everything. Cycling is probably my favourite and I enjoy rugby. I play, coach and watch it.'

'Good, good. I like the rugby too. Not a bad show this year at the Five Nations either.'

'Yeah. Pretty good, all things considered.'

Inside, the large glass circular room was laid out with a huge buffet table and Genevieve gave Finlay a little smirk. A server passed by with a tray of drinks. Genevieve lifted two glasses, handing one to him. How warm his hand had got in hers; the cool glass chilled his skin.

Geoff disappeared to look for his wife and Finlay took a large gulp of prosecco. Elise loved this drink but he'd never fully appreciated it.

'Chin-chin,' Genevieve said, clinking her glass on his. 'Here's to a—'

'Long and wonderful relationship with my new girlfriend?'

She giggled. 'Sure, I'll drink to that.' With a wink, she took a sip. He glugged back some more.

'Not much in these really, is there?'

'You're supposed to sip it, but there's enough here to satisfy the five thousand. Here...' She waved to a passing server, laid her half full glass on the buffet table and took two more glasses. 'This is what you're here for, after all.'

'Indeed.' Finlay knocked back the remains of his first glass. 'Not forgetting the tantric experience later.'

'Yeah. Well, you *can* forget that. Now, behave. Here's my mum coming.'

'Noted.'

A smart woman was marching towards them with Geoff. She was an older version of Genevieve – very pretty and well turned out in a bright green cocktail dress. A huge smile cracked across her face as she got closer.

'Hello, hello.' She opened her arms and embraced Genevieve, then pulled back and looked up at Finlay. 'You must be Finlay. How wonderful to meet you.' She pulled him in for a hug too. 'I think I've seen you somewhere before.'

'Very possibly.'

'Well, I'm so pleased you're here with Genevieve. We always hope to introduce her to some nice young men but she's found someone delightful herself. It's so exciting.' She almost did a happy dance on the spot.

'I'm right here, Mum.' Genevieve finished her first glass of prosecco and lifted the second one.

'I know. And you are such a wonderful girl.' She clapped her cheeks affectionately and beamed like Genevieve was a cute little toddler. 'Here. Your drink's almost finished.' She flagged down a passing server and handed Finlay another drink.

Vaguely aware he probably shouldn't drink too much on an empty stomach, he wafted the thought away and took another sip. The buffet was calling but Mrs Harrington wanted to chat and it was easier to let her.

'Call me Hilary,' she said. 'We don't stand on ceremony here.'

'Of course,' Finlay said.

'Geoff tells me you're a sports teacher. Do you like golf?'

'Yes. I haven't played for a while but I enjoy it when I do.'

'I enjoy golfing with some of my lady friends,' Hilary said. 'We play on Thursday afternoons. I find it very relaxing, though I must say I'm a fair-weather player. Can't be doing with it in the rain and having to dig out all the waterproofs.'

'It's definitely more fun in the sun,' Finlay said, wondering if he was really required to reply. Hilary was rattling on like a long-distance truck and she was still going.

'Oh yes. We've played on the Algarve and we even had a round at Kiawah Island one holiday. That was amazing.'

Finlay gulped almost all of his drink in one. How well-off were they? Just as well he wasn't dating Genevieve for real. No way would his teacher's salary stretch to this kind of lifestyle.

He glanced at her and found her looking back with a grin, like she was struggling to hold back a laugh. Hilary became distracted by some other guests and she and Geoff slipped into another conversation.

Genevieve leaned towards Finlay and, like she was a magnet pulling him, he moved closer. Their bodies touched and a frisson of awareness drifted over him, interspersed with a raw urge to kiss her pretty lips. *That's the alcohol talking.*

'They absolutely love you,' she said, her words soft and warm in her breath.

'What can I say?'

'They've never been so enamoured by any of my real boyfriends.'

He put his finger to his lips. 'What are you suggesting? That I'm not a real man?'

She smirked and raised her finger to his cheek. 'You've got something there...' With her fingertip, she brushed his cheek above his beard line. He clasped his hand over hers, holding it to his face.

Their gazes were locked and Finlay's brain jammed. Words seemed to want to come out, so did feelings... so did raw lust.

'Finlay,' Genevieve whispered. 'We—'

'Aw, look at you two,' Hilary Harrington said.

Finlay released Genevieve, smiled at Hilary, and took another drink from a passing server. He almost downed it in one. What was happening here? His mind and emotions were all over the place. Maybe he just needed food. Yes. Food would do the trick.

CHAPTER SEVEN

Genevieve

Genevieve's father took hold of Finlay's elbow. 'Come and meet my friends. They're all golfers and could do with some tips,' he said. 'I told them I know just the man.'

Genevieve's heart was pounding in her ears. Everything that had happened since she'd invited Finlay to the party was insane. He'd kissed her hand, walked hand in hand with her and been so present. Their talk was like flirting, and she wasn't backing off because the enjoyment was powerful. He was fun to be with. She couldn't remember being this at ease with a man in a long time.

'He is wonderful.' Her mother sipped on her drink, watching Finlay with a dreamy smile. 'Well done on finding him. How did that come about?'

'Oh... He's a friend's brother.' Maybe she shouldn't have said that. Too close to home?

'Ah.' Hilary nodded with a slight frown, quite obviously trying to place him. The good thing was that her parents never paid much attention to her friends. Even when they'd been at school, Hilary hadn't really befriended the other mums. 'Which friend?'

Uh-oh.

Genevieve didn't want to say. Her mum had thought his face was familiar and she might remember that a few weeks ago Hayley's brother was engaged to Elise. Did Mum pay that close attention to what her friends were doing? She couldn't risk it. Instead, she glanced around, feigning that she hadn't heard and hoping to see someone she recognised or could comment on. Why was there no one? She lifted another drink from a passing server, aware her mum was watching her.

'Pardon? Oh, by the way, I saw grandma earlier,' she said before her mum could ask again. 'She was looking well.'

'That was kind. She'll have appreciated it.'

'I'm going to cook some meals and take them over. Something she can easily heat up.'

'That sounds perfect. She'll like that. She always says she sees you cooking on the internet. Is that what you're focusing on these days?'

Genevieve didn't bother replying. She just nodded and took another sip of prosecco. Her mum didn't really understand what she did, so what was the point in explaining?

An older man approached and Genevieve took a large sip of her drink. He wasn't quite her father's age but Genevieve put him around fifty. Her stomach twisted. *Here we go.* This was exactly the kind of man she was used to having advance on her at parties like this. Men who were attractive enough and usually pleasant... but far too old. When they talked about having kids who were in their late teens or twenties, Genevieve wanted to curl up and hide. Her ideal partner needed to want kids now and not be 'well past the baby stage' or 'ready for the next adventure'. While she was sure these guys would be fun to be around and could probably afford to let her live the highlife on endless holidays and cruises, she wasn't there with them. Being a trophy wife was not her scene.

'Hi,' the man said and his voice was smooth and mellow. 'Nice to see you again, Hilary.'

'Alan.' She took his hand in hers. 'Delighted to see you here. How are the boys?'

'They're doing just fine.'

Genevieve edged towards Finlay, who was laughing with her father and his friends. Yes, she'd promised him endless food and drink, but he had a job to do and right now he wasn't doing it and she needed him.

Alan turned his attention to her. 'Is this your daughter?' he asked her mum, though still keeping his eyes on her.

'My youngest daughter, Genevieve. Cressida is my other daughter; she lives in Edinburgh with her partner. And Rafe is my son. Do you know him?'

'I've heard of him, but we've never met.' He smiled at Genevieve. 'And are you enjoying the party, Genevieve?'

'Sure.' She tried to return his smile, but in moments like this, a squashing sensation overcame her. She tapped her toe to dispel it. She wasn't twelve years old, wearing braces, with awkward limbs which either dangled uselessly at her side or knocked together underneath her. A beautiful and confident fifteen-year-old Cressida and handsome and very sure of himself eighteen-year-old Rafe weren't hanging around to deflect the interest. She'd have to fend for herself, but did she have any more to say for herself than she did back then? When her camera was running and she was alone, she was like someone else. A confident person, talking to an army of unknown followers, but in situations like this, she was just a small fish who had to constantly explain herself. Her siblings had gone on to fulfil their potential, but she was still here. Still standing before her father's business friends, hoping she wouldn't have to explain what an influencer was... yet again. The only reason this man was interested was because she had an adult body he might find pleasure with. If she did end up with a man like him, he wasn't exactly going to love her for her mind or the things they had in common.

'We could maybe grab a dance later,' he said with a smile.

'I...um... Well, I...'

Finlay turned and spotted Alan. 'Hi.' He moved in beside Genevieve and put his arm firmly around her waist. She tried not to faint at the touch. This was what she'd wanted forever, and it was actually happening. Finlay was hers; he was protecting her and she could enjoy it. For a few hours anyway.

'Ah, I'm sorry,' Alan said. 'I didn't realise you were with someone. Put the dance on hold for now.' He gave Finlay a brief once over then shifted his focus. 'Hello, Geoff.'

'Alan.' Geoff wrung his hand.

Genevieve couldn't hold in the sigh that burst from her chest. She sagged into Finlay and he didn't let go. Warmth seeped from his palm, through her dress and into her soul.

Is it wrong to be enjoying this so much?

How she'd cry come morning, but no one would ever know except Mitzi. And Mitzi really was her best friend – the best listener and completely nonjudgmental.

'Are you ok?' Still holding her close, Finlay put his other hand on her upper arm, moving her slightly so she was facing him.

'I am now.' The words came out on a shaky breath.

He kept his eyes on her and she tried to talk to him without actually speaking. If she kept looking, she could will the message over and let him know how much she appreciated him being here. And more than that. She liked his company. She liked *him*. He thought she hated him but she'd never done that. Distancing herself and putting up a front was self-preservation.

But she wasn't supposed to like him. Not really. She couldn't. And this was just pretending. She was good at that. Really good. She'd convinced thousands of online followers she was a happy single girl living the dream. But it wasn't true.

Finlay dropped his head even closer and for a heart-stopping second, Genevieve thought he was going to kiss her. Her heart trembled. 'Can I eat something now?' he whispered.

She managed a little laugh and the movement brought her head close to his lips. 'Of course.'

'Thank you.' He swept his hand gently around her face, curving it up to look at him again. Such a swoony moment. She almost obliged by fainting on the spot. She held her breath. 'You're the best girlfriend I could ever wish for.' Releasing her, he turned to the buffet table and picked up a plate.

Genevieve shook her head, taking slow, deep breaths, and trying not to appear weird or look like she was having a seizure. *Just act normally.* Her mum was standing not far off, still chatting to Alan, her dad, and some other friends, but her eyes were moving back and forward between her own conversation and watching Genevieve and Finlay. Mum smiled a very satisfied smile and took a sip of prosecco. Finlay made his way along the buffet table and Genevieve edged closer to her mum.

'He is adorable,' her mum said, stepping away from Alan and her husband.

'Who?' Genevieve glanced at Alan.

'Finlay, of course. I absolutely love him. He just said you were the best girlfriend he could ever wish for. He's a keeper, all right. I already feel like he's perfect for you – so steady and sensible.' She looked him up and down as he stretched over the buffet table and spooned olives onto his plate. 'Not to mention very handsome and fit.' She gave Genevieve a little nudge. 'And I see he has a healthy appetite.'

'Mum!'

Her mum chuckled. 'Just hang onto him.'

'I'll try but it's too early, you know? To be sure about any-thing.'

'I've got such a good feeling about it.'

Genevieve's insides plummeted. How would the conversation go in a couple of days when she had to tell her parents she and Finlay split up or confess this hadn't been real? She picked up a plate from the buffet and chose some food.

'I should mingle,' her mother said. 'I see James Charlton over there. Your dad said James wanted to talk to you. Apparently, he's got some contract thing to discuss. It's nice to see the two of you are still friends, even though things didn't work out.'

'What?' James was here. With a contract? Could this be the moment she'd been waiting for? Should she abandon Finlay and find out?

Her mother moved off to chat with James, and Genevieve tapped her toe. Should she go now?

'This is so good,' Finlay said, polishing off a salmon blini, and coming to her side again.

'Have you tried these?' A woman close by pointed to a plate of spring rolls.

'Oh, not yet.' Finlay wandered over to get one. 'Two secs.'

'I'll just—'

'Genevieve!' The woman who'd spoken to Finlay turned to her and beamed. 'So wonderful to see you.' Genevieve recognised her as a well-off local woman named Flora MacDonald. The fact she shared a name with the Jacobite heroine of old wasn't lost on anyone – especially her. She played on it and was well-known for being a little eccentric. Her dress was somewhat hippyish with a long burgundy skirt, draped shawls and bright beads. Geoff Harrington invited her to everything, claiming she was a close friend of the family, but Genevieve knew his real motive. Flora was famous for throwing her cash into all sorts of projects and Geoff was always on the lookout for investors.

'Is he the young man your father's been telling me about?' she whispered, indicating Finlay with a nod.

'Um... Yes.' Genevieve looked between her, Finlay, then back to James... Where had James gone?

'Good, because I have got exactly the thing for you,' Flora said, placing a heavily ringed finger on Genevieve's arm. Genevieve examined her face, trying to work out her age. Maybe fifties? It was hard to tell. She looked in some ways older and in other ways younger. She had no children and, as far as Genevieve knew, no partner.

'For me?'

'This will be right up your street.'

'Indeed?' A lucrative sponsorship wouldn't go amiss. Could this be her lucky day? She might get a deal with both James and Flora?

Flora leaned in conspiratorially. 'I'm opening the castle for a couples' only retreat this summer.'

'Oh?'

This was another strange thing about this woman. She lived in a castle, though Geoff scoffed at it a little in private. Only a small part of the original keep remained and the rest of it was a relatively modern house – and not even particularly pleasant architecture, according to him.

'Yes. Ever since I bought Storminch I've thought it was the perfect place for it,' Flora went on. 'I've had a wing completely overhauled, installed an enormous four-poster bed and a giant wet room. There's a balcony with a hot tub, loch views and access to a private garden. Meals will be provided. How does it sound?'

'Absolutely amazing.'

'I knew you'd love it now that I hear you have a boyfriend.'

'Um, yeah. I'm sure I would.' She knocked back some more champagne. No point in telling Flora she wouldn't actually be using it anytime soon because her boyfriend was fake.

'This food is great,' Finlay said, rejoining them.

'It really is,' Flora said. 'So, you're the boyfriend Hilary was telling me about. And what is it you do, young man?'

'I'm a P.E. teacher.'

'Oh dear. That was my least favourite subject at school.'

Finlay smiled. 'Yeah, it gets a bad rap, but I try to make it fun.'

'I'm not a big sports fan.' Flora nibbled on a sausage roll. 'Though I do like rugby.'

'Me too,' Finlay said. 'I coach the junior team, though I'm not sure it'll keep going after the summer.'

'Oh, why not?'

Genevieve cast him a warning look. He really couldn't mention he was off to Dubai and blow their cover.

'Lack of funding. We've scraped by the last few years but it mounts up and it's not fair to charge too high because that makes it elitist, which is something we're trying to eliminate from sport.'

'Ah... Of course. That is a pity.'

'Flora,' Hilary said, distracting her and Genevieve frowned. Where had James gone? 'Did Geoff tell you about Cressida's latest venture?'

'No...' Flora smiled at Hilary, before turning back to Genevieve and Finlay. 'Lovely to chat to you both.'

Hilary winked at Finlay and Genevieve shook her head. What on earth were her parents doing? The way they were telling everyone about Finlay seemed like *they* were the ones putting on an act. Not that they were ever rude or mean to people she'd dated in the past, but there was always that awkward first meeting when conversation was a bit slow. None of that this afternoon though. They were acting like Finlay was already their son-in-law and they'd known him forever.

'Have you taken one of everything?' she said, checking out his plate.

'Pretty much, and two or three in some cases. Sausage?' He held up a mini cocktail sausage.

'No thanks. I'm not keen on them.

'Do you like cheese?'

'Who doesn't?'

'There you go then. I'll sacrifice a cube for my favourite girl.' He lifted one from his plate and popped it into her mouth.

Genevieve covered her lips and chewed it quickly. 'Listen, you better lower your voice or tone down the mushy stuff.'

'Why?' He bit into the cocktail sausage.

'Because my mum thinks you're so amazing I should be marrying you. I can see her being disappointed if we're not engaged by tomorrow morning.'

Finlay laughed. 'I'm sure she'll get over me. More cheese?'

'Go on then.' She held out her hand.

'There you go, darling.'

She threw him a look but her heart flip-flopped. Why couldn't he be real? Her mum was right; he was adorable.

'Oh, come on. Don't kid me on that you don't like it. Not even a little bit?' He grinned.

'Listen, there's a man here… He, um, might have an offer for me.'

'What? Like his hand in marriage or something? Am I redundant?'

'No, but…' The crowd at the door moved outside and a man and a woman came in. She was very pretty with long blonde hair and a sleek black dress. He was handsome and smartly dressed. Genevieve held her breath.

'Oh no,' she muttered.

'What?' Finlay moved in beside her. 'Is there another sugar daddy on the radar?'

'No. It's Gavin Sinclair, the CEO of Glenbriar Distilleries.'

'And? Oh… Is he the man with the offer?'

'No. Dad once tried to set me up with him and I had a totally cringy meeting with him a couple of Christmases ago.'

'Is that him there with the blonde woman?'

'Yes. She was with him when Dad dragged me along to meet him. They're engaged now. It's just so embarrassing.'

'Why?'

Genevieve didn't even know for sure. Perhaps it was something to do with the fact his fiancée was so similar to her in age and even looks. She'd managed to capture the eligible CEO while Genevieve hadn't snared anyone. It must be over a year since she'd even had a second date with someone.

'Oh no. They're coming over.'

'Well, don't worry,' Finlay said. 'It's not like he's going to come onto you now. If he does, he's a total bastard.'

'He won't do that. It's just—' They were too close to continue and Genevieve smiled at them. 'Hi,' she said brightly, like they were old friends.

'Hi,' Gavin said. 'Nice to see you again.' He glanced across at her parents. 'And in better circumstances this time.'

'Oh definitely. That was a bit of a nightmare the last time, wasn't it?'

He smiled. 'It was somewhat unexpected.'

'And I hear the two of you are engaged.'

'Yes. Not long until the wedding.'

'Aw, that's lovely to hear.'

'I'm not sure you properly met Felicity the last time, when—'

'My parents tried to set us up?'

'Yes. Felicity was my PA back then and we weren't together, but it was awkward.'

'Just a bit.' Genevieve smiled at her. 'Nice to meet you properly. And, so you know, I never had any interest in Gavin. It was all my parents.'

Felicity laughed. 'It's ok. The whole thing was pretty mortifying, especially in my reindeer jumper.'

'Oh gosh, I'd forgotten about that.' Genevieve covered her mouth. 'Oops.'

Felicity glanced at Finlay.

'Sorry,' Genevieve said. 'This is Finlay. My—'

'Boyfriend.' He shook hands with Felicity, then Gavin. 'Nice to meet you.'

'And you,' Gavin said. 'Are you also in the energy business?'

'No. I'm a P.E. teacher.'

'Oh gosh,' Gavin said. 'Respect to you. Anyone who braves school pupils deserves a medal.'

'Yeah, it has its moments.'

Gavin had his hand on Felicity's back and though it was possibly territorial, it looked natural. In fact, together they appeared perfect, relaxed and in love. Genevieve frowned. Love radiated from them. What did they see when they looked at her and Finlay? Two individuals making a poor mockery of what they had for real?

Finlay moved closer and put his arm around Genevieve's shoulder. She melted a little. Had he somehow picked up on how lonely she felt? Felicity's head tilted a little and it looked like she went to say 'aw' but smiled instead.

'Have you had food yet?' Finlay asked, holding his laden plate aloft with his free hand. 'Honestly, this stuff is so delicious.'

'That's why we came in,' Gavin said.

'Well, we'll leave you to it,' Genevieve said. 'Hopefully see you again later.' She headed towards the wide-open glass doors leading to the garden, swiping another glass of prosecco as she passed a server. She'd lost track of how many glasses she'd had but she didn't feel too bad. Sometimes prosecco went straight to her head but she seemed to be ok this time. As they reached the door, she glanced back at Gavin and Felicity. They were talking and pointing at the food, then Gavin dipped in and planted a kiss on her lips. It seemed to go on for an indecent length of time but Genevieve couldn't look away.

'Do you fancy him?' Finlay asked.

'No.'

'But you did, didn't you? That's why it embarrasses you thinking about him.'

'No.' She let out a sigh. 'I don't think I ever really fancied him. He's a nice guy but... Well, maybe I fancied the idea of him.'

'You mean because he's the CEO of a big company?'

'Yes. I wanted to impress him and I was sure I could, but he wasn't interested.'

Finlay let out a snort. 'More fool him, but is that what you normally look for in a man? How many employees they have?'

'It's definitely what my parents look for when they're scoping potential dates.'

She wasn't sure what she was looking for anymore… or if she was really looking at all. The Vieve certainly wasn't and mostly it was easiest to maintain that persona. She still quite fancied the idea of Gavin Sinclar but it was nothing to do with his career and everything to do with the way he was with Felicity. That was the kind of man she wanted. Someone who loved her just because – not because she was Geoff Harrington's daughter or someone who would look good on their arm, but because she was a person in her own right, and that was important to them.

'Why do you let your parents scope dates for you?'

'It's not like I have much choice and, as dates go, Gavin wasn't too bad. He's actually quite attractive.'

'Oh yeah? You just said you didn't fancy him.'

'I don't, but he does have some very attractive qualities. Like the way he… Well, the way he looks at Felicity, like she's his whole world. They also work together. They're equals. I know what I mean in my head but I don't think I'm expressing it very well. I must have had too much prosecco.'

'I know what you mean.'

If he did, he was a great interpreter because she'd waffled. 'I just love the way he kissed her, like no one was watching.'

Finlay let out a little chuckle. 'If I'd done that to Elise, she'd have pushed me off and been annoyed.'

Genevieve pulled a face. 'I'm sorry to burst your bubble, Finlay. But that's because Elise never really got over Aidan.'

'Oh, believe me, I know that now. No need to drive that nail in any further.' He shook his head. 'Her loss, huh?'

Genevieve nodded. And she meant it because letting go of a man like Finlay seemed pretty stupid from where she was standing. 'Definitely her loss.'

'Thanks… and if I had a girlfriend who wanted to be kissed like no one was watching, then I'd do it.'

Her eyes locked with his again, as they'd done all afternoon. That's where they wanted to look, and it was a sight that set a fire burning inside. 'You do.'

'I do what?'

'You do have a girlfriend who wants to be kissed like that. She's right here.' Her heart started banging a tattoo in her chest. This could be one of the stupidest things she'd ever said or done, but it was true. The prosecco had nudged out words she'd never normally have said. But she wanted to kiss Finlay more than anything right now and she wanted him to kiss her back. So long she'd thought about it. How would it feel for real? Or at least kind of real.

He drew back slightly and looked her over with a frown. 'Are you serious?'

'It's all part of the game, isn't it?' she said. A game she'd tried to play with James but it had never really worked. She vaguely remembered she'd been looking for him but that didn't seem to matter now.

'Isn't it just?' He moved closer and gently slipped his arm about her, holding his plate of food at her back. 'Shall we?'

Her hand slid around his face, his stubbly beard grazing her palm, and she drew him close, her heart racing to the finish line before almost stopping completely. As his lips made contact with hers, her eyes closed simultaneously. The gentle chitchat and clink of glasses seemed to die away as she relaxed into the kiss. Her stomach flipped over and desire burned deep inside. He didn't push or rush, just considerately moved his mouth with hers, lingering slowly on her bottom lip. His hand at her back anchored her to him while the other cupped her head firmly. She let out a sigh as molten heat filled her from the top down.

This. This. This.

This was the moment she'd waited for forever and it had finally arrived.

CHAPTER EIGHT

Finlay

Finlay drew back, furrowing his brow slightly as he looked at Genevieve. She still had her eyes closed, like she'd be quite happy if he dipped in and kissed her again. And honestly, he'd do it in a heartbeat. Why were the words of 'The Shoop Shoop Song' ringing around his head? His brain had adapted the lyrics to suit him and the woman in front of him. *It's in her kiss.* If love hinged on one kiss, that was a pretty good one to start with. But hang on… Love? What the hell? Why was he thinking such nonsense? This was what he'd done with Elise – shut his eyes and leapt in without thinking and look where it had got him.

Genevieve's eyes were open now. Her hand gently slipped off his beard and she blinked like she was coming out of a trance. 'We're good at this, aren't we?' she said with a slight twist of her neck.

He smiled; her deflection was excellent. 'At what exactly? Pretending to be lovers? Or kissing?'

She lifted an eyebrow and did a quick sideways glance. 'Both.'

'You're not wrong. Now let's get some air.' He put his hand on her back as they moved into the garden. He half expected her to recoil or move away from him, like Elise did. She always shrugged him off or got touchy about him 'helping her' to walk when she could move perfectly well on her own, which wasn't what he was doing at all – or he certainly never meant it in that way. Genevieve, however, didn't seem bothered. She glanced around, smiled at him, then pinched some tortilla chips from his plate. 'You should have got your own plate,' he muttered.

'It's not like you can't go back for more. There's enough there to feed several hundred people and, believe me, there will be leftovers. There always are. Mum hires caterers but they box up the spare food and leave it at the end.'

'They can send it my way. I won't complain.'

They walked along the very clean path towards the trellis fences he'd spotted when they arrived. Red roses tumbled around them. 'It's like a fairy tale garden this,' he said, nibbling a prawn sandwich. 'I've never seen so many roses.'

'My mum loves them. Come through the gate and see this.'

He followed her through an archway in the trellis.

'Oh wow.' The garden opened up into what looked like a maze of more trellises and hedges. As they walked, it became obvious that the route was planned to relax and not tease like a real maze. Although there seemed a natural way to follow, it was wide enough to not feel boxed in and there were plenty of openings and lower fences, so there was no chance of getting lost.

Set into alcoves were pretty little white wrought iron benches and loveseats. In some there were statues. One had a fountain. 'What is this place?'

'The rose garden,' Genevieve said. 'Mum had someone design it. It's supposed to be a blend of a maze and a stately garden. I think it's a bit strange. You can't really get lost but it still makes me a bit dizzy.'

'That's the prosecco.' Finlay's gaze roamed around. 'I think there's something magical about this place. I like it.'

'It is pretty, and it smells so beautiful. There's a pond in the middle. I think it would have been better if there was a hot tub.'

Finlay shook his head with a grin. 'Don't they cost an arm and a leg to run? Probably doesn't sit well with your dad's eco business.'

'He would have it running on solar panels. It's one of his bestselling lines among his friends.'

'Solar panels for hot tubs.'

'Yup. I'm not joking.'

'I don't even see how that's possible.'

'Well, you need a big garden because it's a minimum of four panels, plus you need to be south or west facing.'

'Not one for my balcony then?'

'No.'

Finlay plonked himself on one of the wrought iron benches. 'Let me finish this. I'm so hungry.' He wolfed down the rest of the food. Genevieve sat beside him, stealing a few things and bouncing her toe; her shiny heeled pumps glinted in the early evening sun. 'Have you got restless leg syndrome or something?'

'I'm bursting for the loo. It's the prosecco.'

'Well, go then. We don't want an accident.'

'Very funny. I was being polite and waiting for you to finish.'

'That's me done. I'll get me some seconds while you're at the loo.'

They headed out of the rose garden into the main area where people milled around the lawn. A few stopped to speak to Genevieve. Finlay stuck close by, keeping his hand on her back and liking the way she drew closer to him whenever a likely lad approached.

'I love their reactions when they see you,' she said as they got to the main door.

'I said I should be your bodyguard. That's what I feel like.'

They were in almost exactly the spot where the kiss had happened earlier. 'Are you ok to go to the loo by yourself? I don't have to accompany you in there, do I?'

'No, but wait for me at the buffet table, so I know where to find you quickly.'

'Ok.'

She hastened away and Finlay strolled to the buffet table and added seconds to his plate. Servers were still dotting around with drinks. He nabbed another glass. Maybe he should go to the loo too. He'd knocked back a fair bit of this stuff already.

'Hey, Finlay. I didn't expect to see you here,' a man's voice said.

Finlay spun around, almost spilling the contents of his glass. Who did he know here? 'Logan, hi.' He relaxed a little. Logan was a friend from the cycling club, laid back and fun. Not someone to gossip, though he was sure to know all about the Elise debacle. Who didn't?

What would he make of Genevieve and how quickly Finlay had apparently moved on? His eyes darted towards the doors, checking for ways out. Maybe he could shake off Logan before Genevieve returned, but he didn't want to be rude. 'What brings you here?'

'Geoff Harrington is a big supporter of my camping business, Heather Glen. We won a grant from him a few years back and we've kept up the working relationship.'

'That's great.' Finlay looked at the young woman who moved in beside Logan. She pushed her blonde hair behind her ears and smiled a little shyly.

'I don't think you've met my wife,' Logan said. 'This is Eleanor. Eleanor, this is Finlay McBride. He's in the cycling club and the tug-of-war team.'

'Hi.' Finlay shook her hand. As he did, he noticed her other hand curling around her tummy, cradling an obvious baby bump. Making sure nothing untoward showed on his face, his insides slumped. Not because he wasn't happy for these two. He just wished one day it might be him standing next to someone carrying his baby. He was ready. But he hadn't found a partner who was on the same page.

'And what about you?' Logan asked. 'Why are you here?'

'Oh... Um... I'm with my girlfriend.'

Logan's brow furrowed slightly but he kept smiling. 'Sorry. I must have got the wrong story. I thought you'd split up.'

'This is' – he cleared his throat – 'someone different.'

'Oh.' Logan looked happily surprised. 'Well, that's great.'

'Yeah. I know it seems fast. But—'

'When you know, you know.' Logan smiled at Eleanor. 'We pretty much fell for each other the second we saw each other. It happens.'

'Ha. Doesn't it just.' Finlay knocked back almost the whole glass of prosecco. So far, it really hadn't worked out that way for him.

'Hi.' Genevieve appeared at his side and took his arm. 'Oh...' She looked at Logan and screwed up her face like she was concentrating hard. 'I recognise you.'

'I'm Logan Ramsay. I own Heather Glen Campsite and Water Sports Centre.'

'Ah, yes. I met you a while back. Gosh, ages ago actually. I came around with Dad. He was with his friends, the Langfords.' She pulled a face and Logan nodded.

'How could I forget? They were... interesting, shall we say.'

'You don't need to sugarcoat it for me. I think they're as mad as a box of frogs.'

He laughed. 'What do they do these days? Have they succeeded in their dream of moving up here?'

'I honestly don't know. Dad hasn't mentioned them for a while.'

Logan gave a little shrug. 'So…' He looked between Finlay and Genevieve. 'Is this your girlfriend?'

'Indeed.' Finlay slung his arm around her and pulled her close.

'Do you two know each other?' Genevieve said.

'Uh-huh,' Finlay said. 'Logan and I are in the cycling club and tug-of-war team together. And this is Logan's wife, Eleanor.'

'I think I've met you before too,' Genevieve said.

'I was there the day the Langfords were looking around Heather Glen. It was before we were married.'

'Ah, yes. Now I remember…' Genevieve glanced at Finlay, her somewhat manic grin not totally hiding the panic in her eyes. 'Well, we, um…'

Logan and Eleanor looked like they were waiting for her to finish or perhaps chat more about how Finlay and Genevieve had met – especially as Logan clearly knew about Elise and the breakup.

Finlay took a deep breath. Nothing much they could do about it. The cat was out of the bag now. *Oh well.* In a month, Finlay would be in Dubai. He wouldn't see Logan or anyone from here for a long time. They could gossip about him all they wanted.

'It's like Logan said when you were at the loo,' Finlay said.

'What did he say?' Genevieve glanced from Finlay to Logan and back.

'If you know, you know.' Finlay gave her a squeeze. 'And we pretty much knew right from the minute we clapped eyes on each other how perfect we were, didn't we?'

Genevieve's mouth fell slightly open. 'Um... Yes. We did.'

Logan chuckled. 'You two are really cute.' He gave Finlay a little wink and picked up a plate from the buffet.

'Um, yes.' Genevieve gaped at him.

'Nice chatting to you,' Eleanor said.

Genevieve lifted Finlay's plate and beckoned him to follow her. She opened a door off the large circular room that led into a corridor. 'What are you doing?'

'Playing along.'

She slapped her hand to her forehead. 'You're mad.' Her voice was a little raised but she looked ready to burst out laughing – perhaps hysterically.

'Is that the loo?' Finlay asked.

'Yes.'

'My turn. Grab us another drink, will you? We can go back out to the rose garden and eat. It's quieter there, so it'll keep us out of trouble.' He nipped into the somewhat space-age toilet with blueish lighting and all the fittings built in with curved lines. Presumably this was a private bathroom and not the one the other guests were using. He washed his hands in the gleaming basin and headed out to find Genevieve.

'Finlay,' she called to him from behind and he looked back down the corridor.

'What are you doing?'

'Help me.' She was beside an open door and looked like she was trying to lift something. 'I've found a stash of real champagne. Let's take a bottle or two.'

'What if your parents are saving that for something?'

'Ah, so what? They can buy some more. Honestly, they won't even notice. If they do, they'll think some old charmer like Alan found his way in and nobbled them.'

'And here was me thinking you were a perfect angel.' He took the two bottles she handed him and cradled them in his arm.

'I am an angel, of course.' She handed him his plate and batted her lashes. 'You may add it to my résumé.'

'Along with tantric temptress and all that other stuff.'

'Precisement.'

'Since when did you become French?'

'A la now.'

He rolled his eyes. 'Are you drunk?'

'Probablement.'

'I'd say certainement.'

'Mais oui, Monsieur. Definit-ement.'

He laughed and shook his head. 'Let's get out of here.' As they crossed the circular room, Finlay kept his eyes forward. He didn't want to bump into Geoff Harrington while he was making off with his expensive champagne. He could always tell him it was so Genevieve and he could celebrate their forthcoming marriage.

If his earlier reaction to their being together was anything to go by, he'd be ecstatic.

Genevieve swiped two glasses from a passing server and they headed back to the rose garden.

'If you go that way, it leads to the middle. We can sit by the pond,' she said, pointing a glass towards a wide opening.

'And pretend it's a hot tub?'

'Whatever tickles your fancy.'

'Is that part of the tantric experience?'

'Oh, ha ha. Aren't you funny?'

'You know... I think I'm drunk too. I feel a bit—'

'Please don't say nauseous. I hate sick.' She screwed up her face.

'I was going to say giddy.'

'As long as it doesn't lead to you throwing up.'

Finlay laughed and stopped to wait for her. 'You know what?'

'What?' She gave him a pained look, possibly still fearing he might vomit all over her.

'I think I do fancy you.'

'What?' She gaped. 'Are you serious?'

'Yeah.' He laughed too. 'Why not? You're fun to be around.'

'Wow. That's like... Well, a really nice compliment. And...' She turned a little pink and her smile suddenly looked a little less certain. 'I always fancied you.'

'Yeah right. We're definitely drunk,' he said. 'But I'm not drunk enough to believe that. At least we're happy drunks. Ah, look. This must be the pond.' He peered around a trellis into a small, paved area with a sunken pond covered in water lilies; a fountain rose in the centre and water cascaded down the sides. One of the pretty wrought iron benches was at the opposite edge. He made for it, resting his plate on a low wall and putting the bottles on the ground.

Genevieve sat and he moved in beside her. She handed him a glass and they clinked them wordlessly then simultaneously took a sip. With an almost huffy exhale, Genevieve bent over and put her glass on the ground. 'You know what?'

'Tell me.'

'I was telling the truth. I *have* always fancied you.'

He frowned, not sure whether to believe her or not. His head was so light he wanted to believe it but this felt like such an Elise-style game that he just couldn't. 'Ok, even though you've always been like the ice queen around me?'

'I was embarrassed.'

'Really? So... do you, um, want to do something about it?'

She eyed him over, then slowly nodded. 'I'd quite like to sit here and kiss you.'

'You would?'

'Yup.'

'You know how insane that is? Because we're just messing about for the duration of this party, right?'

'Fully aware.'

'And you still want to...?'

'I do.'

'Well, how can I resist?' He never bloody could. Dumping his glass beside his plate, he turned to face her. She seemed to move at exactly the same time, taking his face in her hands as he slipped his arms around her and their lips met.

A fairly drunk kiss ensued. Her lips were warm and tender, but they were both smiling, so the kiss was definitely lacking in finesse. It wasn't screen perfect and wouldn't win any prizes, but it was pleasurable. Genevieve let out a little moan and tilted her head, allowing the kiss to deepen. Suddenly it became hot. A bit too hot, maybe... or maybe not. His brain was addled by alcohol and happy hormones.

Whatever.

He relaxed into it even more and Genevieve let out a little sigh. The sound sent bolts of lust bursting through Finlay.

'Genevieve.' The word came out like a breathy growl sent from somewhere deep in his subconscious.

'Yes?'

'I think we've officially taken this too far. I mean... Well, no one's even here. We don't have to pretend.'

'I wasn't.'

Their eyes locked, and he wanted to kiss her again, but he didn't. He turned and retrieved his glass. 'This is madness. I'm not on the market, you know that?'

'Who said I was? This is just fun, isn't it?'

'Well, yes. But we shouldn't really...'

'Because you're on the rebound.'

'Not exactly. But I'm done with dating and complications. I'm leaving the country to get away from, well, everything.' He gulped back his prosecco. 'Let's open that champagne.' He lifted a bottle and started prising off the foil cork cover with the wire.

'You're leaving the country?' She furrowed her brow. 'I think Elise told me that. Is it Dubai?'

'Sure is. I've had enough of being messed about.'

'By Elise?'

'She was the last straw.'

'Oh dear.'

'Do you want to know why I proposed to her?'

'Because you loved her?'

'I wish that was the reason, but it's not really. I liked her, and we ticked along together.' He shrugged and ripped off the cork cover. Slowly he manipulated the cork with his fingers.

'Haven't you got one of those knives with the corkscrews?' she asked.

'No, but do you have a key?' He fished in his pockets. Had they come in his car? He couldn't even remember. 'Here I've got mine.' He pulled his keys from his pocket and as he did, he felt something else. A box. *What is that?* His mind slowly waded through memories. The ring. Christ, he'd shoved it in there earlier when Genevieve had picked it up. He had to remember it was there. That ring was too valuable to lose, especially when he was already guilty of defiling it.

He wound his house key into the cork.

'So, why did you really want to marry Elise?' Genevieve asked.

'Call me sad if you like, but I just wanted to be normal. A guy with a wife and a couple of kids. I want to raise a family, take the kids to sports club and the park. I'm ready for it but... Well... You see what happened.'

He tugged on the key and with a soft pop, the cork shot out.

'It didn't work out.'

'Yup. Story of my life.'

Chapter Nine

Genevieve

Genevieve poured her remaining prosecco into a nearby bush and held out her empty glass. Finlay sloshed some champagne into it, then did the same in his own glass. Some of it spilled down the sides. And he looked a little uncoordinated. Unsurprising, as they'd packed away quite a lot already. Maybe champagne on top wasn't a great idea, but hey, life was short and this was a party.

'Here's to us.' She held her glass high.

'Who's like us?' He took a mouthful. 'Damn few and they're aw deid.' He added in a much broader accent than usual.

'What are you talking about?' Genevieve chuckled.

'It's a toast my dad always makes. It starts with "here's to us". I couldn't help saying it.'

'I've never heard that before. It sounds a bit morbid.'

'Yeah. Let's not be morbid and spoil the evening.'

'You know what?' Genevieve took another sip, then let out a long sigh. 'I'm really sorry for what Elise did to you. All her friends, including me and your sister, thought it was very strange when she started dating you. We all wanted to believe she was doing it for the right motives.'

'Yup. Me too. Shows how easily duped I am. Honestly, my friends, colleagues, even some of my students, look at me with pitying faces. They think I'm a gullible idiot.'

'But you're not, are you? You're a really sweet and sensitive guy.' She traced a finger over his adorable, closely trimmed beard.

'Thanks.' He shook his head at his glass.

'I told you I always fancied you.' Of course he didn't believe her, so why the hell was she telling him? The prosecco had loosened her tongue to level dangerous. 'Elise was stupid. If she'd stuck it out, she'd have had herself a great guy.'

'Hey, you told me to quit with the mushy stuff. What's got into you? Where's the serene vlogging The Vieve face gone?'

She slugged back more champagne. 'She's not really me. I'm just a normal person really. I want the same things as you. Two point four kids, a house with a garden and all that jazz. But my public image has made that so hard to find. People see me as this cool single girl who has everything under control. I go on dates and friends like to set me up with people, but whenever I meet guys, it never plays out right.'

'Why?'

'I've made such a big deal out of finding "the one", but I have no idea how I'll know. Will there be a lightning bolt moment or something? Because I have to be bloody sure he's the right one or I'll look like a right idiot.' When she was a teen, she'd wanted

Finlay to be the one, but she'd stuck to the friend code and stayed well away. It wasn't like he'd ever have looked at her anyway; no doubt she was too young and silly in his eyes. And she always got so tongue tied around him. Then he'd got a girlfriend and life got in the way, but she'd never forgotten how it had felt the first time she'd noticed him.

He stared at her. 'You've set yourself up to fail. That's waiting for some kind of perfection that's never going to happen.'

'How do you know? Lots of people meet "the one" and just know. It's a well-documented fact. That Logan bloke was just talking about it in there. Usually the people who don't believe it are the people who've never experienced it.'

'I'm not denying things like that happen. Sometimes you make an instant connection with people and other times it takes work. I work with students every day. Every time we get a new class, it's the same. Some of them I have an instant rapport with, others not so much. The same is true for colleagues and people I meet at clubs. So, of course, I believe it can happen for love as well. But if you're waiting for it and obsessing over it, then it's unrealistic.'

'Why? Like you say, in your class, there's a few students you have an instant rapport with. Doesn't it stand to reason if I go on enough dates, then at least a small percentage have the chance of being right?'

'I'd say a small percentage stands a chance of you liking them and being more comfortable around them – maybe even fancying them more than the others. But you're talking about finding one person to top all the others. I mean, I'm not sure how that's even possible.' He shook his head like he was contemplating climbing a sheer-faced mountain, then frowned and put his hand on his forehead as if settling a dizzy spell.

'You do realise sometimes people who really like other people act the opposite way?' she said.

'How do you mean?'

'Sometimes when you really like someone but know you can't have them, it's easier to act as if you don't like them.' She slumped back on the seat.

'I can see how that might happen.'

'It's impossible to meet the right person at the right time, isn't it?' She'd tried with James. He was a good enough guy, just not her guy. Playing at love wasn't the same as being in love.

Finlay shuffled up beside her. 'Don't ask me. I've tried twice and failed.'

'Did you really believe they were "the one" both times?'

'I don't really know. I'm not sure I've ever looked at it like that. They were people I liked and enjoyed being around. But my head and my heart feel so bruised by it all, I can't remember clearly what I thought. It's such a mess.'

She leaned on his shoulder and it was so warm. He lifted the champagne bottle from the seat beside him and refilled their glasses. They sipped them in silence for a few minutes.

'I was that girl, Finlay.'

'What girl?'

'The one who pretended to hate the guy she fancied.'

'Do you mean me?'

'Yup. I keep telling you. I didn't want to do anything when I was a teenager. I was too young anyway. If anything had gone wrong, I didn't want to fall out with Hayley or put her in a difficult position; she was always such a good friend. When Elise started dating you, I couldn't bear it.'

Was it her imagination or had her words become over dramatic? Oh god. Was she slurring? But she couldn't stop.

'How could Elise do that?' she said. 'She broke the rule I'd stuck by and took the guy I wanted. The one who never looked at me. The one I got so bloody embarrassed around.'

'Genevieve, where is this all coming from? Why are you saying this stuff?'

'Because it's true. And I hate what she did to you. You're a good guy. This afternoon has been amazing. I haven't felt this free around a guy for... Well, I don't know when. It's what I always dreamed of.'

'I enjoyed it too,' he said, putting his arm around her shoulder and squeezing it. 'And I'm sure I never meant to upset you when we were younger. You were so much younger at that point it would have been weird. But you know what? I wish it had been you and not Elise. You're much more my kind of girl. Elise was always a lot more tense. You've been more open with me in one afternoon than she ever was.'

They fell silent and Genevieve stared into the water dripping from the fountain into the pond until her eyes glazed over. She wanted to cry. A pain rose in her chest. Why hadn't she been the one he'd found? Why did it have to be Elise? The tinkling of the fountain and the gentle breeze in the roses were the only sounds. The early evening fragrance from the flowers was heady and enough to induce drowsiness.

'You know what I think?' Finlay said a little hoarsely, and Genevieve blinked. Had she fallen asleep?

'No.'

'This is fate.'

'What is?'

'You and me. This is it. This is the lightning bolt moment. I am "the one".'

She turned slowly to face him, her eyes widening. 'I know. That's what I've been telling you. It was always you.'

'Then, let's do it.'

'Do what?'

'Get married.'

'Just like that? Vegas style?'

'Yeah. That's what we both want. You said so just now. We've both been waiting for the right moment and it's finally arrived.'

She blinked, and something on the edge of her brain signalled a warning, but she couldn't be bothered examining it. 'So, what are you going to do?'

'I propose that I propose.'

'Oh my god.' He couldn't be serious, could he?

'I mean, I am the expert at proposals, after all. Look at the experience I have.'

'Then hang on. Let's do it properly. Here.' She pulled out her phone from her little clutch bag and propped it on the wall beside the seat. It took her uncoordinated fingers several attempts to get it in the right place. 'I want to make sure I don't forget this momentous momentum... moment... thingy.' She hit the red button and smiled. 'Can you believe this?' she said to the camera. 'I've found "the one". He's here.' She clenched her fists and squeed.

'Does that red light mean this is live?' Finlay muttered.

'Just recording.' She turned back and smiled at him.

'Well...' He adjusted the collar on his shirt. 'Let's make this third time lucky.' He dropped to one knee in front of the seat and took her hand in his.

Genevieve held her breath at the sight. It was too sexy and adorable for words. He really was the most handsome man; the one she'd always wanted.

'Genevieve,' he said. 'I can't believe I found you when I'd almost given up hope, but here you are. I think you're wonderful... and beautiful. And... I love you.'

She bit her lip, holding on to a laugh that could easily become tears. 'I love you too,' she blurted. 'You're the sweetest, funniest guy ever.'

'Would you make me the happiest man alive and do me the great honour of marrying me?'

She unleashed a smile and gripped his hands. 'Yes, yes, yes.'

'Oh... And I almost forgot.' He let go of one of her hands and fished around in his pocket. He pulled out a small black box. 'For you.'

'Oh my god. You have a ring?'

'It's a very special ring for a very special woman.'

She took the box from him and flipped it open to reveal the gorgeous ring she'd seen earlier. Somewhere in a deep chasm in the back of her mind, the warning voice asked, 'why did he have this ring in the first place?' But she was drunk and too caught up in the moment to pay it any attention. Still on one knee, he prised the ring from its resting place on a silk cushion. Genevieve waggled the fingers on her left hand and Finlay slipped it on. How did it fit so perfectly? And look so beautiful? Like it had been made for her. She stared at it.

Finlay got up off the ground and sat beside her. 'It looks gorgeous. Just like you.' He dipped in and kissed her. She returned it, moaning as his tongue touched hers along with the taste of champagne.

Suddenly she remembered she was recording and broke away with a smile. She held the ring up to her phone. 'Check this out. I'm engaged at last.' She hit the stop button and tossed her phone in the bag. She could edit it all another time. Right now, she was too sky-high to think. Finlay poured more champagne and toasted her.

'To my fiancée.'

She drank and raised her glass again. 'To my fiancé.'

They both downed the rest of their champagne and Finlay drained the dregs from the bottle, then kissed her once more.

'I need the loo again,' Genevieve said, stifling a yawn with her left hand, then noticing the ring again and smiling.

'Maybe we should call it a day.'

'You mean go to bed and consummate our engagement?' She winked.

'That kind of thing.' He put his arm around her and they tottered out of the clearing with the pond. Trellises and hedges seemed to be in the way when they hadn't been before and it took a long time to find the arch into the garden. They couldn't stop laughing as they knocked into flower beds or sank into hedges as they stole kisses. The main garden was still full of people. Genevieve had no idea what time it was.

'This way.' She led Finlay to the back entrance. 'Let's grab our bags from the car and I'll get us in the back way.' Singing 'Stars' by Simply Red, she made her way to the car parking area. Finlay laughed and joined in by humming the background music like he was an electric guitar.

With a lot of staggering, they had the bags and made their way into the house via the backdoor. The wooden stairs were too high. Genevieve pulled off her heels and Finlay half dragged her up. At the top, they went along the gallery corridor and Genevieve opened her bedroom door.

She was so bursting for the loo she didn't even close the door on the en suite bathroom. Did it matter? Finlay was her husband-to-be.

Clothes fell off all around the room and Genevieve hit the pillow, smiling. Finlay's warm body moved in beside her and she nuzzled into his chest.

'I think I'm too tired to do anything,' he said.

'Me too.'

'Let's just cuddle.'

'Cuddle. Yes. That's good.' Genevieve closed her eyes and let out a dreamy sigh. Finlay's hot palms rested on her naked back, keeping her safe from anything and everything. She'd found her happy place and nothing could spoil it.

Chapter Ten

Finlay

Who was banging like that? What did they want? Finlay couldn't open his eyes. If he did, his head might split open. The agony would make him throw up... It would happen any minute now. He couldn't stop it.

Move!

But he couldn't move. Why...?

A woman's voice spoke from somewhere far away. 'Genevieve? Are you awake?'

Genevieve? With an immense effort, he opened his eyes and shifted his head on the pillow. A woman lay facing him with her hand resting on her forehead. His eyes met a pair of beautiful blue irises; they looked slightly glazed. He squinted at her, frowning. Why was she here? In fact, where was here?

Slowly, she slid her left hand off her face and held it out in front of them. Hang on... That ring! How?

'Oh my god,' she said. 'What did we do?'

Finlay tried to sit up but the movement made him want to vomit. 'Genevieve,' he said, and his voice was hoarse. 'Why are you wearing that?'

She swallowed. 'I think I'm going to be sick.' She threw back the covers and bolted.

Finlay closed his eyes, but it couldn't blot out the sound of her retching. *She doesn't like being sick.* The thought drifted into his head. How did he know that? Breathing very purposefully, he got out of bed. He was naked. *Christ...* What else had they done? The en suite door was open, and Genevieve stood by the toilet, also naked and shaking.

'Hey.' Finlay approached her. Just in time, he moved her hair out of the way as she threw up again. The sight was almost enough to make him do the same, but somehow he mastered it.

'Sorry,' she said, crossing her arms over her bare breasts. 'This is gross. I hate being sick.'

He flushed the toilet. 'Here, have a drink.' Moving to the sink, he filled a glass with water. 'As much water as you can.'

Still shivering, she took the glass.

'I think I might be sick myself. Don't look. It'll make you worse.'

She hastened out and Finlay only just made it to the toilet. This was awful. Even as a teenager, he didn't remember having a hangover this bad. Once his stomach was purged, his muscles ached, and he filled himself a glass of water. The thought of putting anything else in his stomach made him wince, and his hand shook slightly, but he downed the water, then filled it up again.

Genevieve was still standing in the bedroom, shivering. 'Hey, it's ok.' He crossed to the bed, pulled off the top sheet and wrapped it around her. She leaned into him and went weightless, like she couldn't stand without him holding her. He closed his arms around her.

'How much did we drink yesterday?' she said.

'Far too much, by the looks of things.'

She pushed her hand out from under the sheet and held it out again. 'Do you remember this?'

He groaned and closed his eyes. His brain didn't really want to do anything as complicated as thinking and it fought hard, like it was willing him not to go back to yesterday evening. The kisses, the rose garden, him down on one knee... 'Oh my god,' he muttered. 'I did it again.'

'Did what?'

'Proposed.' He groaned and wanted to collapse into the bed and stay there for a very long time. 'But it was all just drunken nonsense, right? We had way too much prosecco. You can take off that ring and pretend it never happened.'

She pulled out of his embrace, set the glass down on the bedside cabinet and took hold of the ring, ready to slip it off. 'We should do that, shouldn't we? It's not like anyone else knows. And... We don't really want to be engaged, do we?'

'No. We were just messing about. We don't like each other like that... Not for real.' A buzzing started somewhere on the floor. 'Is that your phone?'

'Must be.' She massaged her forehead. 'But I don't know where it is.'

He raked through the clothes on the floor. Spying his boxer briefs, he snatched them and pulled them on. It seemed a bit more civilised than wandering around naked. 'Neither of us are dressed... Did we...?' He glanced up at her.

She sucked on her lower lip and looked at the rumpled bed-sheets. 'I don't think so. We would have remembered, wouldn't we?'

'Would we? This little engagement isn't going to end in an accidental pregnancy, is it?'

'I doubt it. I've got the implant.'

Finlay half closed his eyes, trying to keep his breathing steady. 'I'm really sorry. I've never done anything this irresponsible in my life. What the hell was I thinking?'

Genevieve shuddered and clung to the sheet. 'I think we just fell asleep. I'm sure we didn't do anything.'

'Except get engaged.'

'Yeah, but like you said, I can just take this ring off and—'

The buzzing started again and Finlay spotted Genevieve's bag under her discarded dress. 'I think it's in here. Someone is desperate to talk to you. You better take it.' He handed her the bag and sat back on the bed, leaning on the headboard and closing his eyes. Maybe when he opened them this would be nothing but a bad dream. If he had more energy he'd pinch himself and check but he couldn't bear to.

'What does *she* want?' Genevieve muttered.

'Who?' he said, keeping his eyes shut.

'A friend I haven't seen for ages. And why do I have so many missed calls? What is going on?'

'Answer it and find out.'

'Hello.'

'Congratulations!' The voice on the phone shrieked so loudly Finlay heard it like she was in the room with them. Could he shut his ears too?

'What?' Genevieve said.

'On your engagement. I saw it live last night.'

Finlay's eyes pinged open when he realised what the woman had said.

'Live?' Genevieve turned and looked at him, her expression pale and shocked.

'It was so romantic with the roses and the fountain. But who's the man? When did you meet? He actually got down on one knee... And he had a ring. Aw! Tell me everything. I thought for a moment it was Finlay McBride, but the camera angle wasn't too clear.'

'It was,' Genevieve murmured.

'It was? What? It *is* actually Finlay McBride you're engaged to? Bloody hell, you're a fast mover. What does Elise make of it?'

'I... um... Listen, I can't talk now. I'll call you back later. There's stuff I have to do.'

'Ha ha, yes, sure there is. Like bedding your new fiancé. You get to it then.'

Genevieve ended the call and stared at Finlay. 'Did you hear that?'

'How could I not? She might as well have been on the other side of the door.' But his mind had jammed. 'Hang on though. Rewind a second. You filmed it live?'

She shook her head. 'I don't think so. Did I? Oh god, I must have or how else would she know?' She fumbled with her phone, opening screens and scrolling. 'I'm so used to recording live... I must have pressed the wrong thing. Why did I film it anyway?'

'That's not the question. The question is, why did we do it at all?'

'Holy shit.' She gaped at her phone and turned up the volume. Finlay cringed at the sound of his own voice. She rotated the phone, and he scrambled closer so he could see. Should he be proud or horrified? Considering how drunk he must have been, it was actually a decent proposal, but what the actual fuck was he thinking?

'Does that say 7k?'

'Yes.'

'Seven thousand people have watched that already?'

'Yes.' She half raised her eyes to him, almost like she expected him to lash out. The sheet hung loosely over her shoulders.

He blew out a breath and looked away. Her barely concealed, beautifully formed breasts were very distracting – and not in the way he needed right now. 'Ok. So, it's not like we can just pretend that it never happened. I don't suppose you can take that down.'

'I can and I will, but so many people have already seen it. Look at all the comments. Oh no.'

'What?'

'Some of them know it's you. And my friends are messaging me about it.' She scrolled through them. 'They think you've done it for revenge on Elise.'

'What? For fuck's sake.' He put his head in his hands.

'And Chloe says I've broken the girl-code and what was I thinking?'

'Who?'

'She's a friend of mine and she wants to know if Elise has done something to upset me and can't understand why else I'd have "pulled a stunt like this". Just bloody great. Do they really think I'd do that?'

'Is this all public?'

'No. It's on messenger.'

'Listen, please take that video down. I know people will have seen it already, but if my new employers see that, who knows what they'll make of it? I hope to god they never find out about it. They're super conservative and if I turn up in Dubai without a fiancée four weeks after I proposed to her online, they are going to ask a lot of tough questions.'

'People split up. That's life.' She clutched the sheet across her body.

'You're telling me? You're talking to the man who's already had two failed engagements and is about to add another shitshow to his list of life flunks.'

'I'm taking it down, ok?'

He leaned back, rubbing vigorously at his face, and groaned. 'What time is it?'

'Quarter to ten.'

'Bloody hell. We must have been comatosed to sleep that long.'

'Right. I've taken it down, but that doesn't mean there aren't other ways of people seeing it. Anyone could have saved it.'

'Oh man.' He covered his face.

'Hey.' Genevieve put her hand on his and gently moved his fingers to look him in the eye. 'I'm so sorry.'

'Don't be.' He took hold of her left hand and ran the pad of his thumb over the ring. 'It's nobody's fault or if it is, it's both of us.'

'Yeah. We were very silly.'

He huffed out a laugh but it hurt his head. He focused back on the ring. 'It does actually suit you though,' he said with a wry smirk.

'How can it suit me more than anyone else? It's just a ring on a finger.'

'I know. But when you look at it, you smile, and your smile is... Well, it makes me smile too.'

He looked deep into her eyes, letting his brain wander into an imaginary world. What if they'd woken up like this and it was real? How would that make him feel? But no. That was insane. He couldn't be engaged to someone he didn't really know and who'd always disliked him... Or had she? Hadn't she said last night that she fancied him? Or had he dreamt it? Dreamt it probably and just as well, because she needed to find her real 'one' and he had a new life starting in another country.

'What we need is some way of ending this without making you look like you were heartbroken by "the one" just hours after he proposed and without making me look like a prick and a serial fiancé who goes about engaging himself to any woman, then splitting with her a few days later,' he said.

'How? I mean, I could post that it was a prank and just tell the truth. We were drunk.'

'Yes.' He nodded. 'That'll work. Do that.'

A knock on the door made them both jump.

'Genevieve? Are you awake?' Another knock. 'Are you ok? Are you even in there?'

'It's my mum,' she whispered.

Finlay tapped an imaginary wristwatch. 'She probably wants to know why you're not up yet. I think she was knocking earlier. I heard something, but I wasn't awake enough to figure out what.'

Holding the sheet firmly around her, Genevieve went to the door and opened it a crack. 'I'm fine,' she said.

'Oh darling.' Her mum pushed the door open and Genevieve staggered back. Finlay grabbed the duvet and pulled it over himself, though there was no hiding the clothes strewn about the room.

Shit.

'Mum! What are you doing?'

Hilary Harrington had thrown her arms around Genevieve. 'I am over the moon. We all are.'

'About what?' She side-eyed Finlay. He kept the duvet at his chin, not sure where to look. This was a first. He'd never been caught like this by a fiancée's mother before.

'Grandma called earlier to say she'd seen you getting engaged on your internet thing.' Hilary glanced over at the bed where Finlay was trying to sink into the background. 'Oh, Finlay, I'm so sorry to butt in here like this. You must think me a mad woman with no manners at all. Please forgive me. I am just so thrilled for you both. When you didn't get up, I was panicking. No one saw you last night and until your grandma's message... Oh look, never mind. Here's me rattling on. I'll leave you in peace. Come down when you're ready. Your father's ecstatic. He wants to get you both an engagement present and throw you a party. I have some ideas, but you put your thinking cap on, and we'll see what we can come up with.' She gave Genevieve another hug and Finlay a brief wave before leaving the room.

'Jesus Christ,' Finlay said, lowering the duvet. 'Are we likely to get anymore visitors? Maybe we should sell tickets.'

Genevieve slumped onto the end of the bed. 'Who's going to break the news to them that this is simply drunk nonsense? You or me?'

Finlay shook his head and groaned. 'If we're going to do it, we should do it straight away. God, they're going to hate me, aren't they?' He buried his face in his hands.

'At least you won't have to live with it. I'll have their disappointment to deal with every day for the rest of my life.'

'I hope Hayley doesn't know.' He peered at her. 'I don't want to message her in case she doesn't, then she'll wonder what I'm talking about.'

'She'll find out soon enough. Most of my friends know. Even if she didn't see the film, they're bound to tell her.'

'I just hope she doesn't tell my mum.' He sighed and threw back his head. 'This is such a mess.'

'Where's your phone? See if they've messaged you.'

'I'm not sure I want to know. It's in my overnight bag, though the battery might be dead by now.'

'I have a charger.' Genevieve crossed the room and pulled his bag off the chair. She plonked it on the bed beside him. 'Is it an iPhone?'

'No, but it's ok, it still has twenty per cent,' he said, pulling it out. 'Oh god.' Even from the amount of notifications, it was obvious everyone knew already. He flipped up the screen, and it opened to his face. 'Yup, my mum knows, so does Hayley... Oh, and my dad. Just great. And Aidan. Fantastic. Seriously?'

'What?'

'My friend, Oliver; he's a divorce lawyer, and he's advising me to get a prenup straight away. Doesn't he know I only ever have prenups? I haven't exactly made it to après-nup yet, have I?'

Genevieve shook her head and her lips quirked in a faint smile. 'I don't know what to do. What does Hayley say?'

He opened her message and read it aloud. '*Finlay!!!!! What is going on????*' He paused and raised an eyebrow. 'Why does she need three hundred question marks?'

'What else is she saying?' Genevieve leaned forward and Finlay read on.

'*Is this for real? You and Genevieve? I didn't even know you knew her that well and I always got the feeling she didn't like you that much – I don't need to remind you I felt the same way about you and Elise. Please call me and tell me how it happened. You both look ridiculously happy. I want to kid myself on that you were just fooling around but it looks so real. Will she go to Dubai with you? And the ring. You gave her THE RING! I guess she really is all that. So hope this is it this time. Just scared it's happened so fast... again xxxxxxxxx.*' He frowned. 'Now we have three-hundred kisses and hearts. So that's it. I *am* going to look like a right prick.'

'Oh god,' Genevieve moaned. 'This is not good.'

He pulled open the message from his mum. 'Mum says: *Oh my darling, darling boy. Please tell me this girl is a good one. I know her as Hayley's friend and she's always been a nice girl. But why now? I hope she's not playing some game with you and this turns out to be her idea of a joke. I'm sick of women using my precious boy like this. Please call me and tell me this is all ok and she's really worthy of you. You're such a darling. I hate the way Gabby and Elise treated you. Let's hope this is third time lucky. No one deserves to be happy as much as you, my love.'*

He glanced up at Genevieve and pulled a face. 'Well, you go tell my mum it was all a mistake and I'll go tell yours.'

She shook her head. 'We're totally up shit creek. Everyone is going to think we're awful. It's going to take months of damage limitation on my socials. And I know it sounds frivolous and silly, but it's my job.'

'I'm not laughing. I don't think it sounds silly. It sounds impossible.'

'What are we going to do?'

'I really have no idea.'

Chapter Eleven

Genevieve

'Congratulations.' Geoff Harrington said, jumping up from the bar stool at the kitchen island and dashing towards Genevieve and Finlay.

'Good morning, sleepy heads,' Hilary added, beaming like they were precious little three-year-olds who had slept in after a birthday party with too much cake.

Stupid as it may seem, Genevieve kind of felt like that, though cake hangovers weren't as painful as prosecco ones and they rarely led to marriage proposals.

Her mum was hugging her and as she pulled away, Genevieve spotted her dad shaking Finlay's hand vigorously and clapping him on the arm. Her dad wasn't stiff or dry when it came to emotions, but he usually held himself together around her boyfriends and showed more of his business side than the dad-side he used at home. Why then did it look like his eyes were a little shiny?

Could those smiles get any wider? Genevieve couldn't stop herself from smiling back at both her parents. She should be reminding herself this wasn't real and that she and Finlay needed to look for an escape clause. No way should she be enjoying it, but her mind drifted into a fantasy where this was real. Something about it made her lightheaded and bubbles fizzed in her chest. A happy anticipation crackled around her, but she had to shut it out.

Not real.

None of this is real.

But how could they get out of it? They still hadn't thought up a way. She'd lose face if she confessed to her followers it was all drunk nonsense and Finlay's family would be furious with her for playing with him. Plus, he'd have to suffer yet another failed engagement. Was all of that inevitable? Shouldn't they just nip it in the bud right now?

'Now...' Geoff clapped his hands together. 'I'd like to get you both something to celebrate. Not just a candle holder or a sandwich toaster, something meaningful that will be useful.'

'No, really,' Finlay said. 'That won't be necessary.'

'Don't be silly. Of course it is.' Geoff led him to the kitchen island and indicated for him to sit.

Finlay threw Genevieve a look, as if begging for help.

'Listen, Dad, this is all just a...'

Geoff smiled at her expectantly and Finlay's eyes widened. She couldn't say this was all a joke or a mistake. Her parents thought her whole life up to this point a joke and a mistake. If she burst this bubble now, how could she bear the fallout? Her gaze connected with Finlay's and he mirrored her helplessness.

Where was the escape route? What should they do?

'Just a what?' Geoff said, glancing between her and Finlay.

'Just a bit overwhelming,' Finlay said. 'The reaction. We had quite a lot to drink last night and didn't mean…'

'To record it live,' Genevieve added.

'Ah, yes.' Geoff nodded.

'We did wonder,' Hilary said. 'I mean, the engagement itself doesn't surprise me at all. I could tell the moment I saw you together you were made for each other.'

Genevieve's eyes caught Finlay's again and they shared a silent moment. If only this space-age house had been designed with ejector pods. They could sure use one around about now.

'I was surprised that you chose to make the event public,' Hilary went on. 'But then I suppose if I were you I'd want to shout it from the rooftops too. You've made such a good catch.' She sidled up beside Finlay and put her hands on his shoulders, her gaze soft and full of admiration.

'Um… yeah.' He glanced at her and smiled.

'So, we need to think of a gift,' Geoff said. 'And I'll need your input on what would be most useful. Also a party. Now we can do you something like we had yesterday, or I'd happily take a function room at a hotel or restaurant. There's the Loch View Hotel or the Cross Keys.'

Finlay blanched and Genevieve knew exactly what he was thinking. A few short weeks ago, he'd had an engagement party there with Elise, and she'd pulled the plug on their relationship.

Genevieve had been there, watching them. She tried to bully her mind into going back there. She'd spent the evening trying not to look at Finlay but failing miserably. When she'd heard what Elise had done that night, it had taken every last vestige of pretence to remain on Elise's side and not cut ties with her for how she'd treated him.

No chance could she make Finlay relive that by going there again. If her dad threw a party for them, how could she fake her way through it? Every second they prolonged the lie, they were making things worse.

'Listen, Mum, Dad, we can get back to you on the gifts and the party. My head isn't there yet and I'm sure Finlay is the same.'

'Yeah... I, um, need to...' He seemed to be grasping for words.

'Get some air?' Genevieve suggested. 'To help clear our heads.'

'Exactly that,' he said. 'And thank you for all your hospitality.'

'No problem at all,' Hilary said.

'Well, I need to walk Mitzi.' Genevieve checked the time. 'So, we can get back to you about... everything.'

'Of course, of course,' Geoff said. 'There's no rush. Oh, but you need to call James Charlton. He was looking for you yesterday. I think he's going to offer you something big. You don't want to miss out.'

'Really?' Genevieve sucked on her lip. Hopefully it was something to do with business and not personal. She didn't need two proposals on the same weekend.

'Don't you want some breakfast?' Hilary asked.

'We could take some toast with us,' Genevieve said. 'I'm not sure my stomach can take much more.'

'Yeah,' Finlay agreed.

'We could have the wedding here,' Hilary said to Geoff as she fetched some bread. 'In the rose garden.'

'That would be very fitting. Are you a churchgoer?' He asked Finlay.

'Um... not really.'

'I'm not either but Hilary is very involved in the church. Would be lovely to have you married in Glenbriar Church, such a pretty place.'

Finlay smiled at Geoff before switching his focus to Genevieve and pulling a face that clearly asked, *what should I say next?*

'We'll take the toast outside,' Genevieve said.

A few moments later, toast in hand, she and Finlay took Mitzi up the path towards the woods. Geoff and Hilary had brought her and the labs into the house after all the other guests had gone. Presumably when Genevieve was wasted in the bed beside Finlay. What had got into her? Too much alcohol, for starters! Plus, she'd been high on the fact she'd squeezed a kiss out of him. Somehow, a few glasses had turned into several too many and the kiss had turned into a proposal.

'What the hell are we going to do?' Genevieve said.

'I have no idea, but this is awful.' Finlay nibbled on the end of his toast.

'Should we just suck it up and tell everyone the truth?'

He groaned and rubbed his forehead. 'I'm going to look like a total and utter idiot, but let's face it, I do anyway. After Elise, everyone thinks I was stupid to rush in there. It's my M.O. I can already hear everyone commenting behind my back on how idiotic I was to do it again.'

'The thing is, whenever we do it, we're going to look stupid, unless...' Genevieve's phone buzzed in her pocket. 'I need to turn this to silent.' She pulled it out and her heart sank further. Elise.

'Oh Christ,' Finlay said, glancing over. 'Things can't get any worse, can they?'

Raising the phone to her ear with a sigh, Genevieve braced herself.

'What is going on?' Elise said.

'Meaning what?'

'You know exactly what I mean. Since when are you and Finlay a couple? I saw you yesterday afternoon, and you didn't even want to get in the car with him. You hate him. Everyone knows that. You're always so standoffish with him. But now you're engaged. It's so obvious it's fake. But why would you do that?' her voice sounded shrill and on edge.

'It's not what you think.'

'I know exactly what it is. And, Genevieve, I'm so sorry for you. Please don't do this.'

'What are you talking about?'

'I never thought Finlay would do this, but clearly the split has hit him hard and now he wants revenge. On me. It's the only reason he'd have done something like this. Please, whatever he's said to you, walk away. I know you want to find "the one", but don't do it like this. I'd hate you to get hurt.'

'Look, that's not—'

'I know I'm a fine one to talk. I never set out to hurt Finlay. When he came along, he was such a friendly, steady guy, I thought I could make it work and he'd help me get over Aidan. And it worked for a while. Obviously now, it looks like I used him and he feels the need to hurt me in return.'

'No, that's not what he's doing.'

'Oh god. This is worse than I thought. How can you not see it?'

'Because I know the circumstances.' But did she really? Wasn't it so much more likely that Elise was right?

'Remember James Charlton?'

How could she forget? 'Why are you bringing that up?'

'It's James all over again. You're making up your own little love story and hoping you can turn it into something real.'

Fuck it! This was when she wished she hadn't confided everything in her best friends. Elise was so damn right. But Genevieve had never let on he was the only man she'd ever slept with. Sex didn't equate with feelings for most people but to her it did. No matter how much she psyched herself up on dates, she couldn't do it. James was a nice enough man, gentle and unthreatening, but he'd been fine with casual sex, not taking it to mean anything. While they'd 'dated', it had been nothing but a show for their respective parents. Genevieve had played the game, pretending he was 'the one', until James had walked away from the arrangement, unable to keep up the pretence any longer. Their families believed they'd split amicably but didn't know they'd never really been a real couple at all. Elise was right, Genevieve was great at making up her own reality and now she was at it again.

'Genevieve, please,' Elise said. 'Listen to me. I'm only saying this for your own good.'

'I know, but don't worry. Everything will be fine. You'll see.' If Elise thought she looked stupid and gullible now, just wait until thousands of people discovered this was all a mistake.

She ended the call and half closed her eyes. 'Did you hear all that?' she muttered.

'Some of it,' Finlay said.

'Elise knows it's all fake, only she thinks I've been duped into it by you, so you can get revenge on her.'

Finlay shook his head. 'One day she'll discover the whole world doesn't revolve around her. I kind of wish I could be there to see it.'

Genevieve put her phone on silent and thrust it into the back pocket of her tight jeans. 'This is all such a mess.'

'You're not wrong.'

Elise's words burned in her ears. She'd known Elise for a long time. They'd shared so much. It made sense just to tell her this wasn't real and put her mind at rest but a selfish part of Genevieve didn't want to. Why should she give up on Finlay? She'd liked him longer than Elise ever had and she didn't want to treat him in the same way.

'I need to get back to the flat,' Finlay said. 'I've got loads to do.'

The words brought reality raining down on her. He was packing to leave. 'We should confess...' Her eyes met his and that spark of something she'd felt ever since yesterday afternoon reignited. For her, it had always been there, but now it had intensified and was even more potent because it seemed to exist for him too... Though that could be her imagination playing tricks on her.

'Yes. We should.' He kept his gaze on her for a few more seconds, then turned away with a sigh. 'I'm sorry I've messed up again. But this wasn't real, was it? So it'll just disappear as a silly prank, won't it?'

'No doubt.' Her focus slipped to the ring on her left hand. It really was beautiful and fitted her so perfectly. She tugged at it and for some unknown reason, a lump rose in her throat and tears threatened. Mastering them, she pulled the ring from her finger and held it out to Finlay.

He stared at it, and for a second, she thought he was going to refuse it. But he put out his hand, and she dropped it into his palm. His fingers closed around it and his Adam's apple bobbed like he was also swallowing back a lump.

'I guess it wasn't third time lucky, after all,' he muttered.

Chapter Twelve

Oliver Wright crossed his arms, leaned on the doorframe between the hall and living area of Finlay's flat, and stared at Finlay. 'I honestly don't know how we're still friends.'

Finlay snorted and shoved the empty kettle under the tap.

'Seriously, Fin, you're setting yourself up to be one of my best clients in the future.'

'Chance would be a fine thing.'

Oliver's ribbing was nothing new, but Finlay couldn't imagine ever needing him in his professional capacity. Why would he require a divorce lawyer? It wasn't like he ever got further than the engagement stage.

'I think you must have missed a few crucial lessons in dating and relationships.' Oliver strolled up to the kitchen island and leaned his forearms on the bare work surface. Only the essentials were left in the flat now, and it was as sad and empty as Finlay himself.

'And you think you're the one to teach me?' Finlay arched an eyebrow as he chucked a teaspoon of instant coffee into a mug. 'The man who "doesn't do long term".'

'That's my choice,' Oliver said. 'But it's not the point I'm making for you. How do you manage to go from hardly knowing someone to engaged in the space of a few hours?'

'We were drunk.'

'You didn't look drunk in that film.'

'Which is a miracle in itself. I can't believe you watched the bloody thing. We were definitely drunk. I don't really remember what made me do it. We were fooling around and—'

'You mean you were at it in the garden? In public?'

'No,' Finlay said. 'Just kissing. I think. Argh.' He facepalmed. 'I really don't know what we were doing.'

'That much seems clear. And why do you keep choosing your sister's friends as dates? Of all the people you should be steering clear of.'

'Why?'

'It's not exactly putting her in an easy position, is it?'

'I guess not.' Finlay turned his back to Oliver to pour the water into the mugs. Oliver made a good point. How did this affect Hayley's relationship with her friends? First Elise and now Genevieve? Why hadn't he thought of that before?

Add selfish to his list of failings.

'It's an unwritten rule. Don't date a friend's sibling. Far too complicated.'

'A sibling's friend, don't you mean?' Finlay handed Oliver a mug.

'What?' Oliver frowned, then gave a brief headshake. 'Yes. Both, in fact.'

'Well, whatever. It's not like it matters now.'

'Why? What exactly is happening with you and Genevieve?' Oliver sipped his coffee, peering over the mug almost like he wasn't sure he wanted to know the answer to his own question.

'Nothing. She gave me back the ring. I told you. We were drunk.'

'So, it's not real?'

'Na.' He made it sound as aloof as possible but a stabbing pain in chest prevented him saying anything else.

'Have you told everyone that?'

'Just you. It only happened last night. I haven't had a chance to speak to anyone else.'

Oliver raised his dark eyebrow. 'And what about her? Has she made another live appearance telling everyone it was a silly drunken moment and you're not actually engaged?'

'I don't think she's done it yet.'

'Why not?'

'I don't know.'

'You better get her to do it soon.'

'You think? I'd quite like to slip off to Dubai and be there when the shit hits.'

Oliver sent him a stern look. 'Like that's going to work. If you go off to Dubai alone, everyone will wonder why she isn't going with you. You made a mistake. Suck it up and move on.'

'Yeah, yeah. I will.' But it hurt. The whole thing was a sore spot. On top of the breakup with Elise, it made him look like such an idiot. He'd thought Genevieve would do it straight away, especially with Elise breathing down her neck, panicking that he was using Genevieve in the same way Elise had done to him. Ugh. Did she think everyone was like her?

The front door buzzer rang. Oliver glanced into the hall. 'You're not expecting viewers, are you?'

'No. It might be Hayley. She hinted she'd drop in.' No doubt she thought she could get a better story out of him in person. Hell knew how she would swallow the truth.

Oliver looked on the verge of rolling his eyes, but his expression stayed impassive. If Finlay hadn't known him for a long time, he would probably have missed it.

'What do you have against my sister?' Finlay muttered as he made his way into the hall. 'She's the nicest person on the planet.'

'I don't have anything against her.'

'Hmm.' Finlay didn't believe him. Oliver had never warmed to Hayley, which seemed bizarre. Everyone liked her. She was that kind of person. He pressed the answer button on the intercom and the screen woke, displaying not Hayley's face as he'd expected but Genevieve's. 'Er... Hello. What are you doing here?'

'I don't have your number and I need to talk to you.'

'Ok.' He glanced sideways, then leaned closer to the microphone. 'Oliver's here too.'

'Who?'

'My friend, Oliver.'

'The lawyer?'

'Yes.'

Genevieve looked around like she was thinking. 'Can you come out here then? I need to speak in private.'

'Ok. Hang on.' He switched off the screen and returned to the living room. 'I'm just nipping downstairs for a minute, back in five.'

Oliver looked at him, his expression loaded with curiosity. He was sharp and Finlay was aware of how totally suss this must look.

'If it's your sister and you want to talk to her without me, I'm happy to make myself scarce.'

'It's not her. Five minutes,' he said, heading straight for the main door. He nipped down the stairs and out the back.

Genevieve stood fiddling with a bracelet and tapping her toe. Mitzi sniffed around the path near the wheelie bin on her long lead.

'Hey,' Finlay said, and Genevieve turned swiftly. Mitzi scuttled over to him and he gave her a quick tickle. 'What's up?' Finlay straightened from patting Mitzi and frowned at Genevieve.

'Oh my god, Finlay...' Her expression was tense. 'I don't even know where to start.' She shook her head dramatically.

'Uh-oh... What now?' Could anything worse have happened? If his new employers had got wind of the video, would they have contacted her? Or had he actually slept with her and she was pregnant? But she couldn't know that after only a few hours. His mind did a hundred-mile-an-hour sprint through several wild ideas before she spoke again.

'I need you to help me with something.'

'Ok. What?'

'Are you still free next weekend?'

'Still free? Why? Did we arrange to do something I've forgotten about?'

'Not exactly, but apparently you told my dad you were free nearly every weekend of the summer holidays except the Highland Games weekend, so you'd be available for a game of golf.'

'Oh shit. So, he wants me to play a round with him?'

'Ha! If only. It's worse than that.'

'Um... how?'

'He asked me if I was free and stupidly I said yes before I realised where it was going.'

'And where is it going?'

'He wants us to spend a weekend in a castle.'

'What? Have I slipped into the plot of *Scooby Doo* somewhere along the line?'

She let out a sigh and shook her head. 'No, nothing like that.'

'Then what? Is it some kind of initiation test your father subjects all your suitors to?'

A small smile played on her lips. 'No. The castle belongs to a friend of his. She wants us to preview her couples' retreat weekend. We'll get a top-class room and free meals.' She pulled a little face like she hoped that might be the clincher.

'Hold up a minute. This sounds remarkably similar to yesterday.'

'Yeah. And that reminds me. Can you also give me the ring back?'

'Why?'

'Because we have to pretend we're still a thing.'

'Wait, what?'

Mitzi jumped at his leg and yelped. He bent down to scratch her ears and she instantly dropped onto her back, throwing her legs in the air so he could tickle her tummy.

Genevieve let out a groan. 'It's a total nightmare.'

'I still don't get exactly what's going on. Why do we have to do this? Have you still not learned to use that little word? You know the one that starts with N and ends with O?'

'I can't this time. Let me explain properly and you'll see why.'

'Ok, shoot me with the worst.' He let out a sigh.

'Remember Flora MacDonald?'

'Are you on something?' He crossed his arms. 'First a castle, now Flora MacDonald? You mean the Skye boat woman?'

'No, the lady who owns Storminch Castle.'

'Who? Oh...' A memory stirred. 'Is that the lady who likes rugby?'

'Yes. She's loaded and always giving money to worthy schemes. My dad's been courting her as an investor for years and she's invested in small-scale projects, but he's desperate to get her on-board with a big project he's doing.'

'Still don't see what this has to do with me and you.'

'I'm getting there. Before she started talking to you, she was telling me about this couples' retreat she'd set up at the castle. I thought she was mentioning it as something I might like in the future, but no. She's already been in touch with Dad and he wants me to do it ASAP. He thinks if we go along, try it out and I promote it on all my socials, she'll reciprocate by agreeing to an investment deal.'

Finlay half-closed his eyes. 'Seriously?'

'Yes. Don't you get it? They all think we're engaged and we'll be jumping at the chance to have a free romantic weekend in a luxury castle. My dad reckons the deal's already in the bag. If I back out, he'll go nuts.'

'Haven't you told your parents the truth?'

'Have you?' Her eyes pressed for an answer.

'Well, no. Not yet.'

'Have you told anyone?' she asked.

'Just Oliver. I told him when he arrived.'

'Well, go and tell him not to say a word. You have to do this.'

'Why? I'm sure it wouldn't be that bad if we said no.'

'Well, she's also going to put money into your junior rugby team to make sure it lasts for another three years at the very least.'

'What?' How could he pass that up? The team was already on the verge of going under with him leaving, but if someone was willing to subsidise it, he could throw them that lifeline and not feel as bad about abandoning them.

'That's what she said. So, will you do it?'

Just call me Finlay, the sucker for the sad case.

He needed to learn to use the word 'no' too, but he couldn't, not now when he had the chance to save the junior rugby squad. 'This could get really messy, you realise that?'

'It could, but it gave me another idea that might be the answer.'

'Not another one.'

'This one is good.'

He arched an eyebrow. 'How good?'

'How about we say I'm going to Dubai with you, then at the last minute, I'll get cold feet, say I can't bear to leave Mitzi and that we split for the best?'

'Hmm. Can't you take dogs to Dubai?' He wasn't sure, but part of him preferred her idea to confessing to a moment of drunken stupidity.

'Maybe, but she doesn't like it when it's too hot, so taking her to a desert country would be cruel.'

'Oh man.' Finlay raked his fingers through his hair.

'What else can we do? My parents are so nuts about you it's impossible to tell them. They asked where the ring was and I lied that you'd taken it to get it engraved. It's getting worse already, but I can't stand letting them down so soon. They'll think I'm even more in need of their matchmaking services and never stop shoving people under my nose. I can't stand it.'

Finlay groaned and cocked his head. He understood how she felt, but with every move they made they were making this worse.

'Finlay! Genevieve!' A voice called and they both turned. Hayley came bounding towards them, her long dark hair bouncing over her shoulders. 'Oh, my god. You beautiful pair. Come here.' She grabbed them both and pulled them into a hug, almost breaking Finlay's neck in the process as she attempted to make him the same height as her and Genevieve. The hug threw him closer to Genevieve and his body woke to memories of Saturday. Very pleasant memories of roses and kisses. He'd kiss her again in a heartbeat, which couldn't be a good sign, could it? An undeniable attraction existed. Why had he never noticed it before?

'Let's see the ring then.' Hayley beamed, and Genevieve's cheeks turned pink.

'Oh, I've got it to get it engraved,' Finlay said, his eyes meeting Genevieve's.

'Ah, I see.' Hayley smiled between the two of them. 'This is so exciting. Unexpected but exciting.'

'Isn't it?' Finlay said.

'Why are you out here?' Hayley asked. 'Are there viewers inside?'

'No, just Oliver.'

Hayley pulled a face. 'Oh, him.'

'What is it with you and him?' Finlay muttered.

'He's such a grumpy guts,' Hayley said.

'He's not that bad.'

She looked at Genevieve as if to say, 'Oh yes, he is,' and Finlay shook his head.

'Shall we go in?' Hayley said.

'Oh...' *Fuck*. He'd have to grab Oliver and tell him not to say anything to Hayley, or anyone, about the engagement not being legit. Oliver's reaction was not going to be good.

Hayley and Genevieve were on their way up.

Shit.

'Hold on,' Finlay said, jogging past him on the stairs. 'I... um, need to unlock the door.'

'What? It's already open,' Hayley said, laughing. 'I can see it.'

'Oh, so it is.' Hell, was there no way of getting to Oliver first.

As they entered, Oliver came to the living room door and looked into the hallway. He scanned over the three of them. As soon as his eyes landed on Hayley, he said, 'I better go. You've got enough people here.'

Hayley huffed an impatient sigh.

Oliver frowned at Genevieve for a second, then glanced at Finlay, his partially raised eyebrow asking why she was there.

'I'll see you out. I need to show you something.' Finlay practically shoved Oliver out of the door.

'I thought you said it wasn't your sister at the door. And why did she bring *her*? Is she totally insensitive?'

'Hayley didn't bring her. Genevieve came around herself and then Hayley turned up too. Listen, there's been a development.'

'What development?'

'Genevieve and I are going to keep the engagement going until I leave for Dubai. That's the official line, so don't go telling anyone what we spoke about earlier.'

'Are you insane?'

'No. She's come up with a plan for us to end this more amicably and not make me look like someone who gets engaged for a hobby, or her someone who needs her parents to find her a man pronto. It's just another three weeks, but it'll soften the blow for our families, so please, don't blab.'

'I won't say a thing. I'm not a gossip.'

'Yeah, I know. And thanks. You're a good mate.' Finlay clapped his shoulder.

'So are you, but sometimes I think you need your head examined. Do you have any idea how crazy this is?'

'Yup. But you try living my life for a bit and it'll make more sense.'

'No thanks. I'm fine as I am.'

Finlay leaned his elbows on the rail and watched Oliver go down the stairs. His friend had a point. He massaged his forehead, pressing deep, trying to coax some sense out of this situation. Just three and a bit weeks. He could do this. Except he still had a flat to sell and now a weekend at a castle to get through... With his fiancée, who wasn't really his fiancée at all.

A fiancée who was in his flat with his sister. He went back in and found the two of them chatting at the French windows. Hayley pointed towards something on the other side of the river and they both laughed. Even if they hadn't already been friends, this wouldn't have been an unusual sight. Hayley was good with people and always had a knack for making people smile. Everyone except Oliver.

'You managed to scare Oliver off again,' Finlay said.

'Nothing to do with me.' Hayley pulled a face. 'He's such a grouch. He's got a face that could curdle milk. I'm not sure why you stay friends with him.'

'Because I like him. We've been together through some tough stuff and I know he's always got my back.'

Genevieve smiled at Finlay. 'You're such a sweetie.'

'Am I?'

'Of course.' She moved closer and winked. 'Why else do you think I'd want to marry you?'

He held back a snort. 'My good looks? Charm? Exceptional bedroom skills.'

'Finlay!' Hayley gaped at him. 'I'm here, remember, and that is not something I want to think about.'

He smirked but his eyes were still on Genevieve. Weird maybe, but would it be so bad if this was real? That look on her face held so much. Some of it he'd got to know already, but there was more to unpack and he wanted to do it. But three weeks wasn't really long enough.

'Just wait until next weekend,' Genevieve said with a wink. 'For when we're at the castle.'

'Ah, yes. The castle.' Finlay rubbed the back of his neck.

'It sounds awesome,' Hayley said. 'You're so lucky.'

It was on the tip of his tongue to say she could go instead of him if she was that interested, but that would give the game away. He had to act like this was an exciting event in his calendar.

'I can't wait,' he said.

Chapter Thirteen

Genevieve

The windscreen wipers rushed back and forward so fast Genevieve could hardly see a thing.

'Storminch Castle, huh?' Finlay said, leaning forward in the passenger seat and peering into the thunderous rain. "Stormy Castle" would hit nearer the mark, I reckon.'

'You're not wrong.'

'This has to be an omen, right? I mean, it's been a pretty good summer so far, but it looks like November out there now. Does this place have its own weather system?'

Genevieve smirked.

Bushes swayed wildly at the side of the road and the low cloud was so thick and dark it was hard to believe it was just past midday.

'Is this a haunted castle?' Finlay asked.

'Aren't they all? Isn't that part of the charm?'

'Charm, huh? This is probably the spirits coming out to warn off people approaching under false pretence. Like a couple arriving for the couples' retreat when they're not actually a couple at all.'

Genevieve didn't dare take her eyes off the road, but she smiled. The ring was back on her finger; Finlay was at her side. Everything was good.

Except he was right. This was all a charade.

Flora MacDonald always seemed like a pleasantly eccentric woman, but she was also shrewd in business. If she wasn't, she'd already have bent to Dad's courting and given him the money he wanted. She was clearly still sizing him up. This may be entirely unrelated... Or it could be a test. Genevieve was used to getting free products and experiences in return for publicity, but her dad was convinced this was all part of Flora's scheme.

'There's no way she'll find out we aren't a real couple,' Genevieve said, telling herself as much as Finlay. 'Unless Oliver has called her up and told her.'

'He wouldn't do that. The only people who can make her think that are us. So if we want to fool her, it's up to us.'

'I think we can do it.' They had to because if she learned they'd come under false pretences, she might back away from dealing with the Harringtons or think they set up the charade to get her backing. And she might think Finlay too was out for nothing but money to save his rugby team. 'We need to make sure this doesn't look like a setup – something my father has sent me to do or something you're only doing for the money. I really don't want to fail. It'll cause so many problems if I do. This could be a good opportunity for both of us.'

'I can't deny I'd love to save the rugby juniors, and I get that you want to do this for your dad, but how is it an opportunity for you otherwise? More freebies?'

'If it leads to her making a deal with my father, it'll feel like I've really achieved something.'

'I don't get it,' Finlay said. 'You've achieved loads, haven't you?'

'Not really.'

'What about all the social media stuff?'

'But that's nothing compared to my brother and sister.'

'Why do you have to compare yourself to them?'

'I don't.' But that wasn't really true. All her life she'd been compared to them one way or another. Whether she liked it or not. There was no getting away from it. 'I'm so used to being the baby of the family, Rafe and Cressida's little sister. You know at school I actually had teachers say to me, "You're not as good as Cressida was at this" and, "Haven't you learned anything from your big brother? He was exceptional in this class". I was never as good at anything as them.'

'You're more famous than both of them now. Lots of people know about you and watch your cookery stuff. Look at all the people who watched our proposal.'

'Yeah. But my family don't think it's a real job or a real thing.' They'd already achieved so much. How could she do anything they hadn't already done? If she could secure this deal, it would feel like a big win.

'You should have more pride in yourself. Even I've tried one of your recipes.'

'Seriously? Which one?'

'The creme fraiche tomato pasta chicken.'

'Always a winner.'

'So easy, but tasty.' He put his hand on her knee and gave it a little pat. 'I think this is it. Isn't that the sign up ahead?'

'Yes, it is.' Genevieve turned through the pillared gates. They weren't palatial but were too ostentatious for a normal house. The drive was fairly short and lined with trees all bending and creaking in the wind. Her dad had been right; it was a completely underwhelming building. The original castle looked like it had been eaten by a truly ugly extension resembling a school or some other municipal structure.

'Ok... This is an interesting castle,' Finlay said. 'That looks like the outside of the monkey house at the zoo.'

'It wouldn't surprise me if she kept "exotic pets".'

'Now you're scaring me. If there's a leopard or something wandering around, I'm out of here.'

'There's something at the front door; it might have claws for all I know.'

'Very funny. Is that Flora?'

'Sure is.'

She stood just inside the thick wooden door frame of the old part of the castle, wearing a dress that looked like it was made of pure gold. It shimmered in the wind.

'I'll get the bags,' Finlay said. 'And leave her to you.'

Genevieve pulled into a space next to a low wall. As soon as she was out of the car, she bolted towards the castle door. Rain battered her. *Bugger.* Her hair would be ruined.

'Inside, inside,' Flora said. 'Is Finlay ok?'

'He's fine, just getting the bags.'

Flora rubbed her hands together and smiled. 'Good. Though you'll only need clothes. Everything else is provided. Wait until you see it.'

Finlay jogged over, carrying two bags. The second he was inside, Flora pulled the door shut and bolted it. Genevieve had an odd feeling that she'd just been locked into a quest and the only way to escape was to pass a series of tests. Was that stupid? Or more realistic than it should be?

'Pleased to meet you properly,' Flora said. 'We weren't fully introduced at Geoff's last week. I'm Flora MacDonald, and before you ask, not the one who helped Bonnie Prince Charlie flee after the Battle of Culloden.'

'Right. I did wonder when I first heard your name,' Finlay said, raking his fingers through his hair and shedding a few drops of water. 'You couldn't have reincarnated from her spirit or anything?'

Flora chuckled. 'Possibly so. It's certainly a fun idea.'

He shook her hand with a smile. 'I'm Finlay. And I can't thank you enough for the offer to help with the rugby club.'

'Oh, I'm delighted to help. It's one of my passions. Now, in you both come, and I'll show you around. You can leave the bags here while I show you the public areas downstairs.'

Finlay stowed the bags next to a huge empty fireplace in the circular room they'd stepped into. Genevieve shivered.

Why did I wear such a lightweight outfit?

The cream palazzo jumpsuit was great for elegant casual, but she could do with a wrap. Hopefully the other rooms had central heating. It might be July, but this place was Baltic.

'Cold?' Finlay whispered, moving closer and putting his arm around her. His warm palm landed on her upper arm. 'We can't have that.'

Heat started to return to her body and beyond. It filtered into her soul and she rubbed the ring on her engagement finger. If a genie popped out of it, she'd ask him to make this fairytale be real.

What actually happened on the night they got engaged was still a blur. Genevieve kind of remembered telling Finlay she'd always fancied him but she wasn't sure if she actually had. She also wasn't sure if it was something she wanted him to know or not. It might be easier if he didn't, then when the split came, he wouldn't have to feel bad for her. She could carry on being serenely indifferent on the outside and let her heart break inside.

'My plan is eventually to have more than one room available, but the one you'll be testing is the deluxe room.'

Finlay glanced at Genevieve and whispered, 'Testing?' as Flora opened a heavy studded oak door.

Genevieve shushed him but she'd already given many thoughts to their sleeping arrangements. Considering they'd already technically shared a bed overnight, they could do it again. Couldn't they? Flora had promised complimentary champagne. If they drank enough of that, they'd be sure to forget who they were sleeping next to anyway.

Flora led them through the grand, ornate doorway into what could almost pass for the heart of a centuries-old Scottish castle. If it wasn't for the regimented line of boxy windows, the massive dining area could have fooled most people. But the poor building design gave it away. The décor was amazing though. The warm, flickering glow of chandeliers lit the area and long oak dining tables stretched out, each adorned with fine china, crystal glassware, and silver cutlery. A fireplace occupied one wall and had a very elaborate flower display cascading along the mantelpiece. Paintings of the countryside and lavish still-life scenes adorned the walls.

Flora grinned, her gold dress shimmering under the lights. 'What do you make of it, darlings?'

'Stunning. Is it ok to walk around later and make some films?' Genevieve asked.

'Absolutely. Though if you wouldn't mind sticking to the rooms I show you.'

'Of course.'

'This is where you'll have your evening meal. I plan to hire a chef once we're up and running, but for now, we have Ann the housekeeper and she's a very good cook. Do either of you have any dietary requirements?' She turned and looked suddenly serious.

'No,' Genevieve said. 'Unless you include Finlay eating like a horse.'

'Hey,' he said, mock outraged.

'Exactly. Hay is for horses, after all.'

'I adore the two of you.' Flora chuckled. 'And if we have no dietary issues, I'll tell Ann to make the pheasant for this evening. It's a speciality of hers and I think you'll love it.'

'Sounds good to me,' Finlay said and exchanged a glance with Genevieve. 'But then, I pretty much eat anything and everything.'

'And we wouldn't have it any other way,' Genevieve said.

'You're a cook yourself, aren't you?' Flora asked her.

'Not exactly, but I enjoy filming easy-to-make recipes for busy single girls.'

'And they work for single guys too,' Finlay said. 'But now we can eat them together.'

'Indeed, we can.' Genevieve nudged him playfully and he tightened his grip on her arm.

Flora chuckled at them. 'I should tune in and have a proper look at the recipes. Now, follow me, little ducklings. This here is the breakfast room.' She opened another door to a bright, airy room with a cottagey feel to it, a cosy space with windows over-looking the castle's private gardens. White tablecloths covered the round tables and one had a large vase of flowers in the centre.

'Come morning, you'll get a range of local delicacies. I've sourced as much as I can locally.'

'Sounds wonderful,' Genevieve said. If her father's deal rested on her enthusiasm, she should put on a good show.

'Now, back through this way,' Flora said. 'Here we have the lounge.'

They entered what seemed to be a large conservatory. Rain pattered on the windows, but even through the gloom, the loch was visible. Plush sofas and armchairs surrounded a central coffee table, also adorned with fresh flowers. 'This, my lovelies, is the perfect place for stargazing; should you happen to be up late with nothing else to do... Though I'm sure that won't be the case.' She gave them a wink and moved further into the room.

Genevieve stifled a laugh at the politely horrified look on Finlay's face.

They returned to the cold entrance room and collected their bags before Flora led them up a spiral staircase, which opened up to reveal a spacious and elegantly furnished bedroom. A massive four-poster bed, draped in rich, deep-red fabric, took centre stage. A small, modern and obviously fake fire provided a cosy touch. This curious tower room was pleasantly warm compared to the rest of the place.

'The design of this castle is very unusual,' Flora said. 'It was a ruin up until the nineteen-seventies. Instead of restoring the whole thing the owners restored this one tower and built a modern "castle" around it. These days it would never get planning consent. It's a talking point if nothing else and that mixture of old and new means we can have a beautiful vintage bedroom like this and right through the door... Voila... a modern bathroom like this.'

Genevieve's eyes almost popped out. The bathroom was as big as the bedroom and had an enormous sunken bathtub in the centre. One wall had a huge walk-in shower and on either side of it were two doors.

'These,' Flora said, opening one of the doors, 'are the toilets. A his-and-her toilet, completely private with their own basin and nicely out of the way of the personal oasis,' she declared with a wink in the direction of the bath.

Large voile curtains hung across a wide window and rather theatrically Flora looped them back. 'Tada!'

The view to the loch was stunning but Genevieve was completely distracted by the fact that it wasn't merely windows behind the curtains but a large private balcony with a hot tub. Steam rose from it and the rain pattered on the covered roof.

'Wow,' Finlay said. 'That's unexpected.'

'And you like it?' Flora asked.

'I can honestly say I've never tried a hot tub before.'

'Well, you can remedy that straight away.' Flora smiled between the two of them and chuckled warmly. 'So, darlings, do you want me to leave you to it?'

'If that's what you want,' Genevieve said. 'But I don't want you to think we're shooing you away.'

'Not at all,' Flora said. 'I'm happy to go, so you can start enjoying yourself.'

'Thank you so much. I'll get as much on the socials as I can.'

'You'll find chocolates and champagne on ice in the bedroom too.' She gave them another wink and a wave and left them to it.

Finlay went to the door of the bathroom where they were still standing, somewhat dumbstruck, and checked she had definitely gone. 'This place is utterly insane,' he said. 'What's she going to charge for it?'

'Thousands I imagine.'

'What's the bath all about?' He gaped at it.

'It's romantic.'

'Is it? You ever tried... You know, getting it on in a bath? Water isn't actually that easy for body mechanics.'

'I said romantic, not necessarily sexy.'

'Yeah, but the way she kept winking. I think she expects us to be christening every square metre of this place with some action.'

'She obviously thinks you've got some staying power.'

'Maybe I do.' He mimicked Flora's wink, then shoved his hands into his pockets and strolled onto the balcony. 'Fancy a romantic soak in the rain?'

'I suppose I should test it.'

'If you're filming all of this and putting it online, does that mean everyone will see me again?'

'No, I'll just film the rooms and not have either of us in it. I'll comment as I walk around. That kind of thing.'

'Fair enough because I'd rather not appear online in my birthday suit. My new employers won't appreciate that.' Finlay returned inside and pulled the French doors shut. He headed back into the bedroom and Genevieve followed. 'Here's the champagne. And these look nice.' He picked up a neat little box of what appeared to be handmade chocolates. 'Want one?'

'Let me get a photo before you open it.'

'Ok.' He replaced it and moved to the dressing table, where a white basket was filled with bottles and toiletries.

Genevieve took some photos of the champagne and chocolates then hit record. 'Guess where I am?'

Finlay turned, but she put her finger to her lips and filmed the room, then panned around to the champagne bucket, deliberately going the opposite way to where he was looking through the basket.

'Oh good god,' he muttered.

Genevieve hit stop – thankfully it wasn't live. 'What is it?'

'There's a packet of condoms in here. What is that woman like? I think I should check the room for hidden cameras. Maybe she's set it up as her own little peep show.'

'Don't be ridiculous. She's sweet.'

'If you say so.' He pulled out the mirror on the wall and checked behind it.

'Finlay, what the…?'

'Have you never seen the film *Sliver*?'

'Um… no.'

'Well, if you watch it, you'll understand.'

'Look, even if she had installed hidden cameras, or whatever it is you're looking for, it's not like we'll be putting on a show for her, is it?'

'Obviously, but what if that show is what she wants in return for handing cash over to your dad and my rugby club? She might be suspicious if we don't, you know…'

Genevieve sat on the end of the bed and smirked. 'Finlay, you're a funny guy. You really are. But do you really believe that?'

'I'm not sure I believe anything that's happened to me in the last few weeks. My normal life seems to have left the building and some other bizarre existence has taken over.' He leaned over and toyed with the champagne bottle. 'Shall we crack this open?'

'Do you think that's a good idea this early? The last time we did that… well, you know what happened. Why don't you go and try the hot tub or something and let me get a film in here before you eat the chocolates and drink the champagne?'

'Yes, we better take care. Because after I've sampled the food and drink, I might be tempted to try the heather body wash and the bluebell candle before I get testing the vegan, natural-feel, pleasure condoms.'

Genevieve held her hand over her mouth to cover her laugh. Honestly, it would only encourage him. He was so full of nonsense, but in an endearing way. Most of the guys she'd dated before were so much more serious. She'd never have felt comfortable asking them to do anything like this. Even James. Which reminded her she still hadn't heard what the big deal was with him. She hadn't reached him when she'd called and was still waiting for a call back. Maybe it hadn't been business at all. Had he been trying to get back together but since he'd heard about her engagement backed off?

With a sheepish look, Finlay held up his hand. 'I'll go play quietly in the bathroom while you get your footage.'

'Thanks.'

She got out her phone and made some films, talking through where she was and gushing about it. With Finlay out of the way, she chanced going live; it was quicker than uploading later. When she'd done the bedroom, she glanced into the bathroom. He was standing on the balcony, looking out at the dreary weather.

She snuck up behind him and tapped his shoulder.

He jumped. 'Want to give me a heart attack? I thought it was Flora sneaking in to find out why we're not tangled in the sheets.'

'Well, I am a tantric temptress after all.'

'So you keep telling me. It's about time you produced the evidence.'

'You wish.' Or more like she did – and wished that he wished. 'Would you mind stepping back into the bedroom and I'll do a quick film in here?'

'Sure.' He saluted her and headed back inside. Genevieve went around the bathroom waxing lyrical about the place and trying not to let go of the thought of how this would feel if it was real. Stripping off and jumping into the bath, the hot tub, and the bed with Finlay really would be top priority then. As it was, they were going to spend the afternoon with her faffing about on social media and him doing whatever he'd brought with him to do. Hardly the romantic retreat she'd have if she could.

Chapter Fourteen

Finlay

Finlay lounged back on the giant four-poster bed. This place was unreal, so far above the kind of place he'd usually choose to stay. He was more likely to be in his one-man tent after a long bike ride or in a cheap B&B close to his latest Munro. Being in Dubai was going to be a big culture shock and he hadn't really prepared. Doing this kind of thing pushed him deeper into denial when he should be making plans. But he'd applied for the Dubai job when his life was in tatters... Now it was bizarre and he didn't quite know what to make of it.

Genevieve's muffled voice was still talking in the bathroom. Finlay's hand hovered over his phone. Would it be weird to open her page and have a look? He kind of wanted to see what she was saying without opening the door and butting in.

As he decided to check, the doorhandle clicked, and she entered the room. He stupidly dropped his phone like he'd been caught doing something he shouldn't.

Genevieve raised an eyebrow. 'What are you up to?'

'Nothing,' he said, in what turned out to be a really guilty sounding tone.

'Oh yeah?' She looked completely unconvinced. 'Watching something naughty.'

'Excuse me?' He narrowed his eyes. 'I'm not sixteen.'

She smirked. 'Do you want to come downstairs with me? I'm going to film those other rooms Flora showed us.'

'Do I have to be utterly silent?'

'Preferably.'

'Then wouldn't it be better if I stayed here?'

'Suit yourself,' she said. Her expression was nonchalant, but was that a hint of disappointment?

'Actually, I'll come. It'll be boring sitting here.'

They made their way out of the room onto the spiral staircase. Genevieve led the way, taking the steps tentatively in her glittery trainers. The long cream jumpsuit she had on looked oddly like a wedding dress and Finlay swatted away all the thoughts of rings and marriage. Not to mention every reminder of what they were doing.

'I genuinely think this place is haunted,' he said. 'I can almost feel the spirits of the dead.'

'Are you having a laugh?'

'You said it yourself; castles usually have ghosts.'

'And you believe they're real?'

'Doesn't everyone?' he said, keeping his tone as serious as he could.

Genevieve stopped, turned around, and gave him a stern look. 'You don't actually believe in ghosts, do you?'

He gave a little shrug. 'Not big marshmallow-type ones, no. But both my mum and Hayley are very into spiritual type stuff. They've both had strange occurrences happening.'

Genevieve frowned. 'I remember Hayley telling me about that. Like they've messaged each other at exactly the same time or suddenly remembered something and a few seconds later had a call to remind them... like they read the other's thoughts.'

'Exactly. My mum said I used to be freaky as a kid. Apparently, I used to tell her all sorts of bizarre stories about places I used to work and my brother who died in the war and stuff like that.'

'Are you serious?'

'Yeah. I don't remember any of it now. It was when I was really tiny, but she thought I was connected to a past life. I think I just had an overactive imagination, but who knows?'

'So, should I pay attention to these spooky vibes you're getting? Because I don't fancy running into anything scary.'

'Ah hello, I thought I heard voices,' Flora said at the bottom of the stairs and they both jumped. 'Didn't mean to startle you,' she said.

'It's ok.' Genevieve massaged her chest. 'Finlay was just telling me ghost stories and... Well...'

'You thought I was a ghost?' Flora chuckled.

'Not really, but my brain was playing tricks on me.'

'Is the castle haunted?' Finlay asked and Genevieve threw him a look of disbelief. He winked at her.

'Good question,' Flora said. 'There are definitely a lot of odd noises in the night, which is why I want to push ahead with renting out some of the rooms. It can be very lonely.'

'I bet,' Genevieve said. 'Doesn't the cook live here?'

'No. She lives in a village a couple of miles away. I live here all alone.'

Perhaps it was because they'd been talking about supernatural things, but Finlay thought he caught an aura of sadness coming from Flora despite her cheery smile and jaunty outfit.

'Now, is there anything I can do for you?' she asked.

'We were going to get some pictures and maybe films of the dining area.' Genevieve glanced around the hallway. 'Would that be ok?'

'Of course,' Flora said. 'You're very busy though. I want you to have a relaxing time, so don't feel that you have to go over and above. Feel free to unwind, just take pictures as you go along.'

Finlay tried not to let his mind wander into thoughts of Flora spying on them again. Was she aware most couples would come here not only to relax but to jump each other's bones as soon as they could? Perhaps something of his thoughts showed on his face because Flora cast him a knowing look.

'I don't mean *that* kind of picture.' She cocked an eyebrow. 'Nothing too personal needed, but you're such a lovely couple. People will like to see you. In fact, I wonder if I could get a professional photographer to take some pictures of the two of you around the place. You'd be quite a poster couple.'

Finlay smiled, hoping it would cover the terror inside. No way could they be photographed. He didn't want a lasting memory of his third failed engagement. Not when he needed to sweep it under the carpet and make it go away.

'Sounds like a lovely idea,' Genevieve said. Her acting was more convincing and Finlay only heard the note of uncertainty because he was looking for it. 'Though I'm sure you could find better models than us.'

'It's hard to find people with the right look,' Flora said. 'The two of you have exactly what I want. You're both good looking, you're newly in love, so you have that sparkle in your eyes, and you're real. I don't want models who don't even know each other rocking up and posing. It's fake and doesn't give off the right vibes.'

Finlay's insides cringed. She had to be kidding, right? They looked real! Nothing could be further from the truth. He wanted to catch Genevieve's eye but at the same time didn't think it was a good idea to give away his discomfort.

'I...' Genevieve started. 'Finlay's a teacher. I'm not sure modelling fits with the code of conduct.'

'Oh, don't worry,' Flora said. 'It would all be very tasteful. I wonder if I could persuade my friend Louis to do it. He's very skilled with a camera and he might be free.'

'You want to do it *this* weekend?' Finlay said.

'No time like the present. And the two of you are perfectly dressed for it.'

Finlay's neutral outfit of black trousers and a white shirt now looked like dressed-down groom's attire next to Genevieve's dress. They were going to look like a couple straight from a wedding. He internally groaned.

'I...um... Well, I'll get the dining room pictures,' Genevieve said.

'Go right ahead,' Flora said. 'I'll go and give Louis a call.'

Genevieve almost dragged Finlay into the dining room.

'Oh hell,' she muttered. 'How can we get out of this?'

Finlay folded his arms. 'This is all your fault, so you better think of something.'

She moaned and fake cried. 'This is a bloody nightmare and I have no idea what to do.'

'Still haven't learned that little word, have you?'

'You heard her. I tried.'

'You did.' He let out a sigh. 'Then let's hope Louis isn't available at such short notice. Surely, he won't be.'

'That is a bit ridiculous but maybe they're close and he'll do anything for her.'

'Don't say that.'

'Ok, let's keep our fingers crossed he's busy.' Genevieve opened her phone. 'Now, you be quiet for a bit and let me get this film.'

'Yes, Miss.' He saluted her and drew back into the shadow around the heavy, dark oak door. When had his life taken such a surreal turn? Things hadn't been easy the past few months, years even, but this was ridiculous. Maybe he should just embrace it in the spirit of fun. The last hurrah before he left the country. If pictures of him appeared in a brochure for this place, then so what? All it would be was a lasting monument to a completely insane phase of his life. Maybe in decades to come, his grandchildren would find the photos and speculate about who Grandpa's mysterious friend was and why they'd been snapped posing like that. None of them would ever guess the truth. Far too absurd.

When Genevieve was done chatting to her phone about the dining room, they went back into the hallway.

'I don't know how you do that,' Finlay said. 'When I had to record lessons during the lockdown, it was a nightmare. I always sounded like someone else or a robot. You sound so natural.'

'If you imagine you're talking to a friend, it's easier. I try not to think about how many people might be watching and just focus on chatting to one imaginary person.'

'I still don't think it would work that well for me.'

'When I was little, I always pretended I was on camera. My mum used to laugh because she was always walking in in the middle of docu-dramas about my dolls and their life issues.'

'I remember you and Hayley doing stuff like that.' Finlay let out a laugh. 'You've been training for a long time. You used to always be narrating stuff in her bedroom. I could hear you through the wall.'

'You could?'

'Not what you were saying exactly, but it always sounded like you were pretending to be on TV.'

'We were.' Genevieve laughed. 'Hayley would do my hair and pretend she was a famous stylist, then I'd do her make-up. We used to spend hours at it. If Elise was there too, she'd pretend to be cabin crew and we'd play we were going on holiday.'

'Those were the days, huh?' Now, he'd messed up the friend-ships good and proper.

Flora emerged from a side room and both Finlay and Genevieve fell silent, waiting for her to drop the bomb.

'Louis isn't answering. I'll try again later.'

Their collective relief made them sag against each other and Finlay put a bracing arm around Genevieve. Flora smiled indul-gently.

'Why not have a quick drink with me?' Flora asked. 'While you're here. We can sit in the conservatory.'

It wasn't like they could refuse. The rain had stopped and blue sky was appearing through the clouds. Genevieve and Finlay sat beside each other on a wicker sofa, while Flora opened a drinks cabinet and read out various labels.

They both decided on a small port liqueur while Flora took a rather large glass of sherry.

'What made you want to open a couples' retreat?' Genevieve asked as Flora handed her a small glass full of the deep burgundy liquid.

'Good question.' Flora passed Finlay his glass, then raised her own. 'Slainte.'

Finlay and Genevieve mirrored the move, then took sips. Port liqueur wasn't a familiar drink to Finlay, and it was a little sweet, though quite pleasant.

'You know I'm a strange lady,' Flora said, taking a seat.

Finlay furrowed his brow at her unlikely self-assessment, even though he didn't doubt she'd been called that many times behind her back.

'I'm under no illusions about what names people have for me. I embrace it rather than get upset by it.' She smiled at him. 'I'm utterly fascinated by romance. I read way too many romance books and I've probably seen every romantic movie there is to watch, but with all that said, I'm not romantic in myself. It's not something I've wished for. That's not to say I don't value friends and companionship, but I've never sought a romantic relationship.' She sipped on her sherry. 'Growing up, I was often ridiculed and name called. Even latterly, people call me all sorts of names and cast barely veiled insults at me. I'm not deaf or stupid, but like I said, I don't let it bother me. These days there are all sorts of labels for young people who feel like I did. They're allowed to choose any or all of these things and if it saves them from going through what I've been through, then I'm happy for them. For my part, I don't feel like I want to assign a label to myself. I've grown into my own skin and I'm happy to be here. The couples' retreat, I suppose, sprung from my fascination with romance for others. When I started thinking about letting rooms, I kept coming back to that. So I decided to do it. It's the same with anything in life. If you want to do it, go for it. Don't wait until tomorrow. There may not be a tomorrow or tomorrow might be too late. Do it now. As you get older, you realise the importance of that.'

Finlay had almost finished the little glass of port liqueur when Flora stopped talking. He hadn't expected quite so much personal information, and it seemed Genevieve hadn't either, as she looked strangely lost for words. Flora simply smiled, however, and took another sip of sherry before continuing.

'I think because people have always found me a little eccentric, it's made me cautious. I don't care what they think of me, but I don't like it when they assume eccentric equals stupid. I'm actually very intelligent, even if I say so myself. I've been blessed with a lot of money in my life and I know how to make it work for me. I always like to get to know people before I enter into business with them. Your father is one such example.'

Finlay glanced at Genevieve. His heart hurt seeing her looking so uncomfortable. Why did she have to do the dirty work for her father?

'I'm sure my father doesn't think badly of you. He always talks highly of you and invites you to his parties.'

Flora laughed a little. 'Yes, he does. And he's a generous man in that respect, though many people butter me up in an attempt to part me from my cash.'

'I hope you don't think I did that,' Finlay said.

'Not at all. You didn't even know who I was when we spoke about the rugby club, did you?'

'No, I didn't.'

Genevieve put her glass on a side table with a sigh. 'I'm sorry if my dad has done that. I'm not a businessperson as everyone knows, so a lot of his dealings are lost on me.'

'You are a businessperson, Genevieve,' Finlay said, surprising even himself. 'You just do a different kind of business. Don't undervalue what you do.'

'I couldn't agree more,' Flora said. 'I know a lot of people look down on what you do, especially people of my generation who think it isn't a real job, but it's very shortsighted. Jobs and business evolve daily.'

'That's so true,' Finlay said. 'We discuss this at school all the time. We're training and preparing kids for the world of work, but the jobs a lot of them will go into don't even exist yet.'

'Yes, exactly that.' Flora pointed at him then turned to Genevieve. 'It wouldn't surprise me if you get some lucrative sponsorship deals in the future. I'll even invest in return for the publicity here, so don't put yourself down. And if your father dismisses your job, that's very shortsighted of him because you and people in your industry are very well placed to promote businesses like his.'

Genevieve smiled and gave a little headshake. 'I'm not sure he sees it like that, but I appreciate you saying it.'

'Not at all. I'm just delighted to see you here enjoying yourself. Call me an old fool, but I'm always suspicious and I couldn't help but wonder if Geoff had pushed me towards you in an attempt to win my backing. You wouldn't believe the elaborate schemes people have come up with in the past.'

Uh-oh... Just how elaborate?

Had anyone ever faked an engagement before? Finlay suspected not. His sixth sense had kicked into operation again and he felt waves of discomfort flowing from Genevieve. He didn't feel much better himself. They were here under false pretence and not only that; it *was* a ruse to get her to bend to Geoff's wishes. Now Flora was talking about sponsorships and she was funding his rugby club. Could it get much more awkward?

Finlay put his hand over hers and gently pressured it. The gesture meant solidarity. But there was no getting away from the fact they were sitting in a very precarious place and all the escape routes were blocked.

Chapter Fifteen

Genevieve

'Ah, it's Louis.' Flora picked up her mobile and got to her feet. 'I'll take it out here and leave you two lovebirds in peace.'

The second she left the conservatory, Genevieve turned to Finlay. His hand was on hers but she barely registered it as ice was flowing through her veins. 'Oh god,' she said. 'What if he says he can take the photos? We might be stuck as the poster couple forever.'

'We'll just say we'd rather not do it. I mean, it's not unreasonable to say we're not comfortable with it.'

'But she knows it's the kind of thing I would normally jump at.'

'You already said it wouldn't sit well with my job. I'll just play that up. She's a nice person, she'll understand.'

She groaned. 'So much for us coming here to relax.'

'Well, she admitted she's an odd woman. Maybe she is, only not for the reasons she thinks.'

'I didn't expect such an outpouring.'

'Me neither.'

'I feel a bit sorry for her. She sounds really lonely.'

'She does, but why buy a castle? Wouldn't it be better to live in a flat surrounded by people if you were lonely?'

'I don't know. Maybe she's lonely but likes living alone... Does that make sense?'

'Kind of. But none of this really makes sense, does it?'

Flora re-entered and Genevieve sat up, trying to look casual and at ease.

'Louis can't do any photos this weekend, but he's going to get back to me with dates.'

'I don't really want to be in any photos,' Finlay said. 'The idea of it is lovely but I don't think I want pupils of mine seeing me on things like that. You know how high school pupils would make fun of it.'

'Ah yes. I see your point.' Flora sipped some sherry. 'I should leave the two of you alone. You'll be wanting some time without my interference. Why not make use of the hot tub now the weather's a bit better?'

'Good idea,' Finlay said. 'Thanks for the drink.' He got to his feet and Genevieve followed.

'We'll see you at dinner,' she said to Flora as she passed her.

'Yes, indeed. Now go and enjoy yourself.' Her eyes flashed rather wickedly and Genevieve was glad to leave the room in case her cheeks had gone red.

Finlay marched to the staircase like he was on a mission.

'I'm not joking about those hidden cameras,' he muttered. 'And if she doesn't have them, she'll be hanging around listening at the door or out in the field with binoculars, checking what we're doing in the hot tub.'

'Stop it,' Genevieve said, giving his arm a fake slap.

'Well, really, if we were actually a couple, she's a bit of a passion killer. I mean, she's a nice lady but I wouldn't want to do anything. I'd be too freaked out she was going to appear with her cameraman.' He pushed open the door to the room. 'Are we really going to test the hot tub?'

'Sure... We can always do it individually.'

Finlay half snorted a laugh. 'God knows what she'll make of that.'

'She won't know.'

'I bet she will,' he said darkly.

'I just hope she isn't annoyed with us saying no to the photos and doesn't use that as a reason to say no to my father.'

'Look, your dad can't hold you responsible for that. He's a businessman and should use more appropriate methods. He shouldn't expect you to do his dirty work.'

'It's easy to say that, Finlay, but you don't have to live with it. He always says that in business you have to think out of the box, take risks and do things differently. He won't see this as anything more than a different method.'

'Hmm, well, it's not a very ethical method. And I can't have her taking those photos. It's not just the pupils. My new employers in Dubai have very strict social media rules for staff. It wouldn't surprise me if there's something in the contract about public photos too.'

'Well, we'll just have to be extra good from now on.'

He huffed out a laugh and started unbuttoning his shirt. 'Can we do that?' He undid another button. It seemed unlikely he was doing it to silence her, but it had that effect. She watched as he slowly made his way down, then tugged it off. The last time she'd seen this, she'd been too hungover to pay proper attention. This time, she was fully alert. His contoured chest was covered in a smattering of hair, tapering into a thin line leading to his waistband.

He cleared his throat and Genevieve met his eyes. 'Nice acting,' he said. 'Just watch Flora doesn't pop in to wipe up your drool.'

'Excuse me? You think I'm drooling over you?'

He undid his buckle with a flourish and a pronounced wink. 'Aren't you?'

'Of course I'm not.' Though she kind of was. 'And you're the one doing the striptease.'

'Oh yeah, that's exactly what I'm doing.' He raised an eyebrow. 'But now you mention it... In case she's listening.' He climbed onto the bed, knelt on it and put his hand on the headboard, then pumped it against the wall a few times.

'Oh, stop that,' Genevieve said. 'You really are awful.'

'Ok. Two of the worst things you could say right there if we're trying to be authentic. You should be saying "don't stop" and "you are *sooo great* at this".'

'Ha, ha, ha,' she said, making sure he got the large dollop of sarcasm. She looked away and marched over to her case, pulling out her bright fuchsia bikini. Glancing into the mirror, she saw Finlay climb off the bed and drop his trousers. His gaze landed on the skimpy bikini in her hand.

'Whose turn to drool now?' She smirked as she looked around.

'Very amusing.' He made quite a meal of searching his bag for his trunks, then put them on facing away from her. She had a nice view of his rear before he pulled up a pair of baggy board shorts. Maybe they were a deliberate choice. They certainly hid any evidence that he found her skimpy swimwear a turn on. Not that she was in it yet. Getting a jumpsuit off was never a gainly sight.

With a slight shake of his head and a quirk of his lip, he left the room for the bathroom, and Genevieve wriggled out the top half of her jumpsuit and pulled off her bra. Freeing her breasts to the cool air made them jut out, her nipples peaked, pointing straight at the door Finlay had just gone through. How could she deny how much she craved his touch? She tossed her hair over her shoulder and tied on her bikini top. Quickly she tugged off her jumpsuit and her knickers, replacing them with the bikini bottoms that were little more than a triangle of fabric.

The French doors were open and Genevieve headed outside. Finlay glanced up from his position deep in the bubbly water of the hot tub. 'This is surprisingly relaxing,' he said. His eyes roamed over her and his facial muscles seemed to tighten a little. 'I thought we were doing this individually.'

'Really? Can't you handle this?'

'Handle what exactly?'

She raised an eyebrow and climbed into the warm water. 'Still you drooling, I'd say.' She settled opposite him, letting the straps fall from her shoulders.

'Has the tantric moment arrived?' Finlay said, his gaze meeting hers.

'Maybe.'

'Oh god, this is so good,' he groaned and Genevieve gaped at him. He grinned. 'Just making it sound genuine, in case you-know-who is listening,' he whispered.

Genevieve rolled her eyes. 'Right. Well, from what I've heard, getting frisky in a hot tub is never as romantic as it is in the movies. Not that I've tested it.'

'I think it's all about the foreplay. You know, a bit of kissing, some caressing and cuddling? A few well-placed nuzzles, a bit of exploration, and when we're fully ignited, we nip into the bedroom and let loose the fireworks.'

Genevieve sucked on her lip, not sure whether to laugh or to move in beside him and let him do everything he'd just said. She settled on a smile and asked, 'Are you an expert in such things?'

'I told you, I've never been in one of these things in my life before. The principle seems clear enough though.'

'Maybe we should test it. That's what we're here to do, after all. Your tantric mistress is looking for a master.'

He raised his eyebrow. 'Are you mad?'

'I don't think kissing you in a hot tub is worse than pretending to be engaged. People hook up all the time at parties.'

'Yeah, I'm not sure that's a road I want to travel.'

Genevieve watched him, dying to ask him why not. But she wasn't sure she really wanted to hear the answer. Was it he just didn't like her enough or was it because he felt more for her than he should? She could relate to the latter. Much as she'd love to get closer to him, she wasn't sure she wanted to move things any deeper. It would be hard enough ending this when the time came without any added emotions. Or should she not give any of that a second thought and do what Flora said – do what made her happy today, right now, as there may be no tomorrow?

'Why are you moving to Dubai?' she asked.

'Isn't it obvious?' He stretched his arms along the side of the tub and Genevieve tried not to let the sight of his broad chest have any effect on her. Why should it? Apart from the fact it was gorgeous.

So near yet so far.

'Because of Elise, I guess,' she said.

'Spot on.'

'But why Dubai?'

'They're always looking for teachers and the pay is great. Much better than here.'

Genevieve rested her head back and let the warm water soothe her. 'It's not a place I ever fancied going to,' she said. 'I know a lot of people love the scene there, but it intimidates me for some reason.'

'Why? Because you're not allowed to kiss in public?'

'All the rules scare me.'

'They've relaxed a few of them, but my employers are very strict, which is why I was panicking about that video. Technically, an unmarried couple aren't allowed to share a room in a hotel in Dubai. It would be a grey area for me to move into my accommodation with a fiancée.'

'But I'm not actually coming.' Had he forgotten?

'What? Oh, yeah, I know. I just meant how it'll look from their perspective.'

'Won't it be a really big culture shock? What if you don't like it?'

He ran his hands through his hair, leaving a slightly damp trail. 'I'm trying not to think about it like that. I've committed to a three-year contract, so I can't back out now.'

'You're very brave.'

'You think?'

'Definitely. I admire anyone who wants to live in another country. I'm not sure I could even manage another town. This is where I've always been and it's never bothered me.'

'I thought you'd travelled quite extensively.'

'I have, but only on holiday.'

'Maybe that's the best idea. I'm sure I'll find out, come the end of the summer.'

'Mitzi can't go anywhere like that. She really struggles in the hot weather. I have to leave her with Mum and Dad if I travel.'

'Aw, bless her. The poor wee pup.'

She smiled across at him, restraining all the urges to jump into his arms. The port liqueur wasn't enough to send her over the edge like prosecco. She was mistress of this and could handle her feelings as she always did. But her heart still niggled away like she had palpitations, shoving wishes and desires to the surface, begging him to stay, to notice her and to make this real. Only she couldn't. Because pretending love wasn't the same as real love. And what about her relationship with Hayley? Would that suffer when this ended? Hardly a reason to keep it going indefinitely. That day would inevitably come anyway.

'I'm shrivelling up,' she said. 'I think I should get out.'

'Me too,' Finlay agreed, looking at his hands. 'We can warm up in the bedroom. I'll rattle the headboard some more and you can ooh and ahh a bit.'

'Shut up.' She flicked some water at him as she stood up.

He turned away to avoid it and laughed.

As she made to climb out, her foot slipped and she wobbled. She grabbed the side for security at the same time as Finlay's hand landed on her back. He was standing behind her.

'Are you—'

He didn't finish the sentence. He lost his footing on the same slippery patch and grabbed hold of the back of her bikini top as he splashed into the water.

'Bugger,' he said.

The ties came apart and the top slipped off, leaving her fully exposed.

'Bloody hell,' she said. 'Just as well no one *is* in that field.'

'You hope.' Finlay stood again, grabbing the edge and climbing out, obviously determined there would be no more slip-ups.

'There are more subtle ways to undress me.' She pulled the soaked top back up.

'Are you questioning my technique?'

She raised her eyes to him and her body clenched in response to the look on his face. Nothing could hide the hunger. She shivered.

'It's cold, let's get inside.'

'Shower?' he said, raising his eyebrows. 'In the large-enough-for-two wet area.'

'Whatever,' she said, trying to sound like it was of no concern.

He smirked and went inside. She waited for a moment, the cool breeze playing on her skin, flushed and warm from the tub. The sound of the shower burst into action, water splashing onto the tiled floor. She moved to the door, her heart racing. Finlay had his head back as he rinsed himself down. Fully naked now, she saw his blurred shape through the frosted glass. No way could she go in there with him. She would definitely do something she regretted. He moved towards the opening and lifted a towel. She had a brief full frontal before he pulled the towel around his waist.

'I'm done,' he shouted.

She held back, out of sight, so it didn't look like she'd been watching. When she went inside, he was still in the bathroom.

'I left it running. I was waiting for you.'

'You seriously think it would be a good idea to share a shower?'

'No. I think it would be a very bad idea. Very bad indeed.' He sat on a white wooden chair beside the bath.

'What are you doing?'

'My turn to watch.'

'What? No way... I didn't—'

'Oh yeah? You sure about that?'

'Get out. Go on.' She flapped her hand at the door.

With a low rumbling laugh, he did.

She stepped into the shower, hoping it would wash away her deep embarrassment.

Shit. Shit. Shit.

He knew she'd been watching.

Chapter Sixteen

Finlay

Finlay buttoned up his shirt and adjusted his cuffs. Maybe Genevieve's usual boyfriends would have whipped out tuxedos or kilt suits for dinner, but he wasn't in that league. Sure, he owned a kilt made in the finest McBride tartan, but the rest of the ensemble was pricey, and he'd never invested in any of it. He rented the jacket and shirt from the kilt shop in the town whenever he was invited to a wedding and borrowed his dad's shoes and socks. His grandmother had given both him and his cousin Aidan kilts for their twenty-first birthdays. Such was the forgiving nature of kilt design that even if he and Aidan had a middle-age spread at some point, the kilts would still fit. But Finlay hadn't changed a huge amount in size or bulk since he was twenty-one. Anything he'd put on was muscle built from the cycling and sports he loved doing. The kilt was more likely to get an outing alongside a t-shirt at the Highland Games or if he went to watch Scotland in the rugby.

The bathroom door clicked open and Genevieve entered the bedroom. Finlay's jaw dropped, possibly for real, though he tried to hold himself together. It wasn't easy. She looked utterly stunning in a floor-length chiffon dress in a delicate soft green. Her long hair cascaded over her shoulders and around the halter neck. The air seemed to shimmer around her and she floated rather than walked to the bedside stand where she opened a small jewellery box.

'You look beautiful.' He'd said something similar when they were going to Geoff's party and it was true. Whatever she chose to wear she looked stunning, but when she dressed up she was off the charts gorgeous – walking perfection.

'Thanks.' She glanced up in the middle of lacing a sparkly bracelet around her wrist. 'You look pretty good yourself.'

'You think?' He wished he'd made more of an effort. There hadn't been a lot of time, but if he'd just hired a Bonnie Prince Charlie shirt even, he could have worn his kilt and looked a bit more suitable.

'Yeah.' She smiled. 'Understated elegance.'

He chuckled. 'Nice. Understated, that's me.'

'Actually, it is.' She closed the lid of the jewellery box. 'You have that way about you.'

'How do you mean?'

'Well, you're kind of always there in the background, sensible and steady. You don't push yourself forward, but once people get to know you, you're... well, different.'

'Am I?' He kind of wanted to hear what else she had to say, though he knew what she meant, and it was a fairly accurate description. In so many ways, he'd lived in the shadows of people more out-there than him. His parents were both sociable people. His sister definitely was. His cousin Aidan had obvious looks and an aura of quiet power around him. Oliver was a brain box and had always been top of every class. Finlay was good at sport but rarely took part in the most popular one – football. He'd never joined the team, always preferring rugby and cycling. Wherever he went and whoever he was with, he was like the wingman rather than the lead. And he wasn't complaining. Often it was nicer to let others shine and easier to bask in their glow than make light of his own.

'You're a really funny guy,' Genevieve said. 'Your sense of humour is so dry, but it makes me laugh. I imagine a lot of people don't get it or don't notice.'

He nodded. 'Maybe just as well.'

'Maybe.' She smiled at him and her eyes sparkled as brightly as the ring still adorning her left hand. A powerful wish to make this situation real surged through him but that was madness. He'd committed to going to Dubai and she'd made it quite clear she couldn't go there because of little Mitzi. And really, was there actually the possibility she liked him enough? Sure, they were getting on and having fun, but only because they were safe in the knowledge this wasn't real. It didn't mean she felt strongly enough to marry him. And he didn't want to marry her, did he? She was another Elise – beautiful, but with her own agenda. Hadn't she demonstrated that by talking him into going to her dad's party and refusing to deny the engagement until she'd wrung all the usefulness from the situation? He couldn't afford to fall into that trap again. How gullible had he been with Elise? He'd believed all her lies right to the end. Not this time. He'd play along for now because it was going nowhere in the long run.

'Shall we go?' He held out his elbow like a Victorian hero in one of those period dramas his mum loved. Genevieve looped her hand into it. Every time she was close like this and her perfume soared into his consciousness, a powerful awakening of his senses took place. *Ignore it.* This just demonstrated what an easy guy he was. Flash him a smile, waft some perfume under his nose and he'd follow like a sad puppy.

'Do you think Flora will eat with us?' Genevieve asked.

'I expect so. Part of her reason for opening the place up like this seems to be to get company.'

'Maybe she should have made it a single person's retreat.'

'Ha,' Finlay huffed out a laugh. 'That gives off all the wrong vibes though. It would be almost impossible to market that without getting a whole lot of people showing up, thinking it was the place for an easy lay. I doubt that's the kind of thing she wants.'

'True. And I suppose with her fascination with romance, that's what she wants to promote.'

They reached the dining-room door and Finlay hesitated. 'Should we just go in? Or knock?'

'Open it. She said we could go anywhere as long as it wasn't her private quarters.'

'Wonder what she has in there?' he whispered.

Genevieve threw him a look. 'Nothing bad, I'm sure. But who would want guests nosing around?'

'Still can't help wondering.'

'Stop it.' She fake-slapped his arm. 'She's nice really.'

'Doesn't mean there aren't skeletons lurking in her cupboards.' He pushed the door.

'Should we just sit?' Genevieve said. 'Seems odd that she's not here.'

'Burying the remains of the last ones out the back before she gets to us.'

'Finlay.' She glared at him.

'Sorry, bad joke.' He put up his hands, but she smirked.

Three places were made up at one of the tables. Two beside each other and one opposite. For all Finlay might have joked, he liked the fact Flora had gone for small tables and not one long one. If he'd come here when other couples were also in residence, he wasn't sure he'd want his romantic weekend shared with everyone. He'd like to wine and dine his date in private, not sit with everyone else while Flora held court at the top. Maybe others wouldn't mind but it seemed intrusive to him.

'Apologies, mucho apologies.' Flora bustled in behind them, dressed in a very bright red and black layered dress that reminded Finlay of a Spanish dancer doll his mum had bought his sister when they'd been on holiday in Torremolinos as kids. 'I got caught up on a call. Now take a seat. Ann has everything ready and will be bringing it up shortly.'

Finlay pulled back the seat for Genevieve and she bowed her head slightly as she took it. 'Thank you, kind sir.'

'Oh you are wonderful,' Flora said. 'Ah. Here's the champagne.' She lifted a bottle from a cooler on the thick oak sideboard.

'Let me get yours too,' Finlay said, skirting the table and pulling out her seat.

'What an absolute charmer you are.'

He caught Genevieve's eye and tried not to laugh.

Ann, the housekeeper, arrived with a catering trolley laden with silver dishes. She crossed to a sideboard and lifted them on to it, then removed the lids. One by one, she ported plates to the table.

'We have a mini tower of haggis, neeps and tatties and I also have cock-a-leekie soup. It's all in small portions, so you can enjoy both if you like,' Ann said, resting a plate in front of Finlay.

'This looks really good,' he said.

'Let me get a photo,' Genevieve said. 'I love the towers. So cute.'

Cute was one word for it. Hopefully the main course would be larger. Finlay could eat this in one mouthful – though obviously he'd been brought up with better table manners. His mum would murder him for even having such a coarse thought.

'Guess what I've been doing while the two of you have been having fun upstairs?'

Finlay stopped chewing, not wanting to look at Genevieve. Was this where Flora confessed to having spy cams, after all? Had she seen them mucking around? Him rattling the headboard and accidentally pulling off Genevieve's bikini top?

'I've been stalking you.'

Finlay gulped his food and almost choked. 'Pardon?'

Genevieve was looking at her, a frown growing on her otherwise smooth forehead.

'Online, of course.' She grinned, took a sip of champagne, then chuckled. 'I'm not *that* odd. Listening at doors and peeking through keyholes is hardly my thing.'

'We didn't think that,' Genevieve said, not looking at Finlay. 'Though you had me worried for a second.'

'What did you discover online?' Finlay asked, not sure he really wanted to know.

'Many things. Your proposal was very romantic. The rose garden was such a stunning backdrop. I think I'd like to have a rose garden here. Very romantic.'

'That clip isn't still there, is it?' Finlay said to Genevieve.

'Not on my feed but someone might have saved it.'

'I have my ways,' Flora said. 'I was looking you up, Finlay, and I fell down a rabbit hole when I realised you were related to Hayley McBride.'

'You know Hayley?'

'She works at the salon in Glenbriar. I've been having my hair done there since the year dot. Hayley isn't usually my stylist but the last time I was in, she dyed my hair pink for a charity event I was attending because poor Amber was ill.'

'Ah.' Finlay knocked back some champagne. 'And did Hayley have that film on her social media?'

'A very short clip. How nice for her to have her brother and her friend get together.'

Finlay was going to kill her. Not that she'd get why. He hardly ever looked at his social media sites but he could imagine Hayley writing a gushing congratulations message to them both. Why hadn't Genevieve spotted it and asked her to remove it? The second he thought it, he knew why. She couldn't ask that without confessing none of it had been real.

'It's all happened so quickly,' Genevieve said. 'I've hardly had time to thank people for all the messages. I've probably missed lots.'

'I had a strange memory though,' Flora said. 'I'm sure Hayley told me her brother was engaged to her friend before, when she was doing my hair. She was telling me about an engagement party she was invited to. But that can't have been you if you only just got engaged. Do you have another brother?'

'No,' Finlay said, his shoulders sagging. 'It was me.'

'But not me,' Genevieve said.

'I was engaged to another of Hayley's friends.'

'But this was only last month sometime.'

'I know.' His voice was quiet and flat. How could he escape the fact that stuff like this would forever punctuate his life? Very soon he'd be defending himself on his second failed engagement to one of his sister's friends and the third in his life. Hardly something to be proud of.

'Oh dear,' Flora said. 'I'm not sure whether to be intrigued or worried.'

'He didn't cheat on anyone, if that's what you're thinking,' Genevieve said. 'We'd obviously met before. I've known Finlay for years, but we didn't start dating until after.'

'You can't have been dating long before the engagement.'

'No,' Finlay agreed, not looking at either of them. 'When you know, you know.' His words were flat and he realised it sounded a bit sarcastic but there was no getting them back.

'But I guess you didn't always know,' Flora said. 'Or wouldn't you have got together long before now?'

'Well...' Genevieve frowned and her eyes met his. 'I always liked Finlay. When we were younger, I didn't think he'd notice me or look at me as anything but one of Hayley's friends. When he left school, I didn't see him much. We only really reconnected when he started dating Elise, but obviously I didn't act on my feelings or anything then. She's my friend too. But when they split, I didn't want to wait any longer. I'd waited long enough and if it was ok for Elise to date our friend's brother, why not me?'

Finlay's gaze never left hers as she spoke. Her words sounded true, but she was just making that up, right?

'Seems a real shame you didn't notice her long ago,' Flora said to him.

'Yes. It is.' Still not moving his focus from her, he sipped his champagne. Why hadn't he noticed her before? Was she telling the truth? She'd always seemed so cold.

Ann arrived with the trolley laden with more silver dishes. She laid them on the sideboard, then cleared away the starter plates.

'Who's looking after your adorable dog this weekend?' Flora asked Genevieve.

'My mum and dad. Mitzi loves their dogs, so she'll be very happy.'

'Wonderful. I'm considering getting a dog myself. Would you recommend French bulldogs as a breed?'

'Definitely,' Genevieve said, and she looked delighted and re-lieved to engage Flora on a safer topic of conversation.

Finlay leaned back as Ann laid a plate of smoked venison and honeyed shallots before him. It looked utterly delicious but his stomach felt tight and unsettled. As he cut a section of meat and placed it in his mouth, his thoughts roamed away from the canine conversation and back to what Genevieve had just said. Were there other forces at play here? Was this 'arrangement' more than a ruse to get Flora to make a deal with Geoff? Another memory stirred in the back of his mind; he couldn't quite place it and he wasn't even sure it was real. Had Genevieve not said something like that to him before? Had they had a similar discussion in the past? But when? A realisation slapped him like someone had upended the champagne cooler over him. The evening he'd proposed. They'd been so drunk but words had been said, not just by her. Some of it was caught on film, the end of what had been a night of confessions and kisses. But that was just drunken ramblings... Wasn't it? None of it was real. It mustn't be. He couldn't afford it to be.

CHAPTER SEVENTEEN

Genevieve

Genevieve scooped a layer of cream from the tiny goblet of cranachan in front of her. Ann, the housekeeper, had done an amazing job of preparing some traditional Scottish dishes and presenting them perfectly. Genevieve had splashed them all over social media with gushing comments. Hopefully this would be enough to make Flora want to back her father, though it didn't seem that Flora had much interest in her father's business.

How annoying will it be if Flora says no to Dad after all this?

Genevieve caught Finlay's eye and he gave her the same look he'd been giving her ever since she'd confessed to always liking him. She could tell he wasn't sure if she was serious or not. What if later she told him it was true? Would it make any difference?

Not if he doesn't feel the same.

After the meal, Flora plied them with liqueurs and talked until Genevieve felt almost too drowsy to reply, not because she'd had too much to drink or was particularly tired but the conversation wasn't something she could get into. Flora knew so many people and very few of them were familiar to Genevieve. She lost the thread of where the conversation was going or what she was even talking about. Finlay was nodding along and hopefully in the right places.

'They have a stand at the Highland Games every year. Your father usually has one too, doesn't he?'

'Um... Yes.' Her ears pricked up at the mention of her father. He'd not be impressed if she couldn't remember some important detail that might get him in Flora's good books. 'He doesn't work on it himself, but he'll have someone there.'

'I thought so. I might have a chat with him about the games. The committee this year has been full of bickering. Some new committee members have caused a bit of a rift. They want to keep it very traditional while others want to modernise things. I'm not really sure where I stand. I suppose modernisation is fine, but I wouldn't like to lose any of the traditional stuff.'

'Me neither,' Finlay said. 'I do the tug of war every year and it's great.'

'The tug of war is so much fun,' Flora said. 'And I adore the team leader, Brann the builder.'

'So do all the girls,' Finlay muttered.

Flora laughed. 'I imagine they do. He is very ruggedly attractive, I suppose, but he's also a genuinely nice man. I've had him up here doing repairs many times and he's an absolute gentleman.'

'I've never been to the Highland Games,' Genevieve said.

'Really?' Flora looked shocked.

She shrugged. 'It never crossed my mind to go.'

'But there's a dog show, nothing like Crufts. It's just for fun. You should go and get your lovely little pooch in it.'

'Yes, I should.'

'And you'll have to go and support Finlay in his tug of war.'

'Yup, my farewell to Glenbriar. The final tug before I fly. When I come back in three years, I might be too old and creaky to get back in the team.'

'What do you mean?' Flora asked.

'Oh.' He gave a fake cough, and Genevieve wanted to sink into her chair and hide. 'I, um, am going to Dubai to work for three years.'

'You never said. What about the rugby team?'

'That's part of the reason it's going to fold, because I'm not sure they'll get another coach, but funding will help with that.'

'Hmm,' Flora said with a frown. 'Are you both going?'

'Yes.' Genevieve pulled a smile. 'Though I'll have to leave Mitzi, which will be devastating after I waited so long to get her.'

'Can't you take her with you?'

'She doesn't like too much heat,' Finlay said.

'Well, if you want someone to care for her while you're away, I'd be happy to do it. I had no idea you were planning this.'

'That's very kind. Thank you.' Genevieve looked at Finlay, then checked the time on her phone. 'Would you mind if I went up? The food was delicious, but it's made me a bit sleepy.'

'Of course, on you go,' Flora said. 'Goodness me, I've kept you far too long. Sorry, sorry. I always talk too much when I'm in company. Bear in mind when I actually open up the retreat, I won't dine with the guests, but they'll be welcome to join me after for drinks and chat should they want to. I only dined with you so we could talk things through. I hope I didn't spoil it for you.'

'Not at all,' Genevieve said.

The spiral staircase was cool and a little eerie, with fake candles on sconces to light it.

'We are so screwed,' Finlay said as they entered the room. 'I didn't mean to mention Dubai, but it slipped out. All this making stuff up and pretending is doing my box in. I can't remember what's real and what's not.' His eyes flashed red as he kicked off his shoes. 'We need to stop this.'

'Right now?' Something rippled through her stomach, setting her on edge.

'I don't know. It's all so fucking awkward. And if I lose that funding now, right after I thought I'd secured the future of the club, I'll be letting down so many people.'

'I'm sorry.'

'It's not your fault. I'm the idiot who proposed in the first place. Why did I do that?'

Why indeed? She wanted to believe that somewhere deep down it was because he really liked her, but that was silly. She was making up her little stories again.

'Because you were drunk. I don't think me asking you to do this was a good idea either though. We should just have told everyone and have done with. If my parents were upset I should have sucked it up like I usually do.'

He sighed. 'Yup. But it's too late for that now, isn't it? Is it going to be any different if Flora turns up at the Highland Games expecting to see us together? If we tell her it was all fake, won't she think it was your dad setting things up to try and con money out of him? It could ruin his reputation as well as ours.'

'Oh god.' Genevieve sank onto the soft bed and put her head in her hands. 'You're right. This has snowballed out of control.'

'Not completely, but we're going to have to stick with the plan and make this last until I leave for Dubai. Otherwise Flora will think it's all a setup and I don't want your dad blaming that on you. I also don't want to lose the funding. Only three more weeks, then you can tell everyone you like Mitzi more than me, which probably won't be too difficult for people to believe.'

Her heart compressed. She loved her dog dearly, but the way she liked Finlay was different. It was all too raw to analyse and part of her didn't want to think about how deep her feelings for Finlay were. If they were too strong, how could she bear the parting? Because bear it, she must. He would be gone from her life in just over a fortnight. She really couldn't go with him because she didn't want to leave Mitzi – that much was true. And he wouldn't stay. Not for her... Just like James hadn't. Why should she expect anyone to play along with her?

'So, ready to spend our second night together?' he said. 'I wonder if we'll have better memories of it this time.'

'Any memories,' she added.

'Precisely.'

She turned to look at him. He pulled off his shirt and tossed it on a seat near the door. Was he always this cool about people seeing him naked or only her? Why should she be anyone special? He had a good body, so no need to be worried about anything. Strange how so much of this felt genuine – like how natural it was being around him. Seeing him undressing was undeniably hot, but it wasn't awkward. His presence was like a warm blanket she could slip into and feel safe and happy. Even when he was grouchy or being sarky, he was still loveable and she couldn't imagine him ever being anything other than completely trust-worthy. That thought made her want to kick Elise. What a silly woman, treating someone like him the way she'd done.

'Are you sleeping in your dress?' he said.

'No.' She got to her feet. 'I was just thinking.'

'What about?'

'Elise.'

'Oh please. That's not someone I want to think about right now.'

'It's just that I hate what she did to you. She's my friend and it hurts to say it, but what she did was wrong. I don't want you to think that's what I'm doing.'

He furrowed his brow. 'You mean using me to get at someone else?'

'That is what I'm doing, isn't it? I'm using you to get something from Flora.' She shook her head. 'I'm just as bad as Elise.'

'No, there's a difference. At least you're admitting it. She duped me into believing she cared. You were upfront from the start. We can view this as a business transaction. No hearts hurt in the process.'

Ha! Just like James, and look how that had ended. And it was worse this time because Genevieve *did* care... for real. One heart would be hurt very soon. At least it wouldn't be his this time. She could spare him that, if nothing else. As for herself, she'd go on as she always had, and no one need ever know. Except they would. Or they'd know she'd split with her fiancé. Well, at least she could make her heartache look authentic because it would be very real.

'Hey,' he said. 'I don't mean I think you're heartless or anything. You're a good person.' His eye contact was strong and he seemed to be puzzling something out. 'I think I will actually miss you when we split. This has been a wild rollercoaster but a lot of it I've enjoyed.'

'Me too... probably more than I should.' Her gaze met his, straying down to his broad chest then back to his eyes before dropping to his lips. 'What if I wanted to use you for something else?' she whispered. The words pushed their way out before she could censor them.

Holding his arm across his body, he ran his hand around his jaw, not looking quite as sure of himself as he had done moments before. 'Use me for what exactly?'

'Oh, you know? Just my little joke,' she said, and her voice cracked a little, sounding more high-pitched than she meant it to.

'No, no, no.' He shook his head and leaned across the bed. 'You're so not getting away with that. What did you mean?'

'Well...' She looked him up and down. 'You're a half-naked man in my bedroom. What's a girl to do?'

'Seriously? You want to use me for sex?'

'Sounds a bit crass when you put it like that.' And just because he might want to sleep with her didn't mean he had feelings for her – she had to remember that.

'But you're talking about hooking up for the night?'

'In theory. But I was only joking really.' She needed to backtrack. He looked more shocked than interested.

'Shame. Because you're a very attractive woman.'

'Thank you, but...'

'No need to thank me or deny it. It's true.'

Now she was far too hot. 'I was going to say, I...' If she said the words she wanted to, she'd sound ridiculous.

'You what?' He peered into her eyes like he was x-raying her, and she wished she hadn't opened her big mouth. Curse her body for feeling this way and wanting physical contact. She was so starved, so rusty. But using Finlay was all wrong.

'I don't know.' She turned away and started unfastening the side zip of her dress. A lump was swelling in her throat and she wanted to cry. She'd messed with this situation enough. She really was doing exactly what Elise had done – she had her own agenda and was ready to do anything to satisfy it. But she couldn't do anything that would hurt him. An hour or so of pleasure wasn't worth it.

'Hey, Genevieve. Are you ok?'

'Yeah, fine.' Unwanted memories flooded back from when she'd been with James – it felt like another life. He was the only man she'd been with and it had never been her who initiated anything... Maybe she shouldn't even have tried this time. Sex didn't equal feelings. It wouldn't for Finlay. She was setting herself up for a fall.

Just stay calm.

'I'm not completely against the idea of you and me hooking up for the night,' Finlay said. 'I'd be a liar if I said I didn't find you attractive. I suppose I didn't expect you to say it outright. But I want to know what you were going to say after.'

'Well, if you must know, I was going to say it's been a long time.' She kept her back to him. Not looking at him made it easier to say. Her heart was thumping a little too fast.

'What has?'

'Since I... properly hooked up with anyone. I just... No one usually... I'm fussy, I guess.' Hooked up! Who was she kidding? She'd never done that, even though she made out that she did.

'And do I stand up to your specifications?'

She glanced around at him. It wouldn't be a good idea to let him know how much. 'In the absence of any other competition, you'll do.'

A little smirk played on the corner of his lips. 'Oh, I get it. Right time, right place.'

'Just as I engineered it.' And maybe that was closer to the truth than it should be.

'How can I refuse?'

'Why not use the benefits of a fake fiancée?' Wouldn't be the first time she'd played a game like this. She'd done it with James hoping it would lead somewhere, but it was always just business for him. Something felt different this time.

Finlay moved closer and she held her breath. Now he looked too hot and too fit with that bare chest in full view. His eucalyptus scent brought tingles to her nose, and they darted through her body. 'I'd quite like to help you take this off.' He slipped his hands down the sides of her dress. 'If you'll permit me.'

'Ok,' she breathed, her lower body clenching at the heat.

'Because you really are very beautiful.'

'Am I?'

'Of course. And sweet and funny.' He leaned his head closer, so his words fell softly on her neck. 'Not to mention a pleasure to be around. As if I'd engage myself to anyone less.'

'Says the man who's already been engaged twice.'

'Thanks for reminding me.' He gently tugged her closer and placed a soft kiss on her neck. 'We'd be stupid to waste an opportunity like this, wouldn't we?'

'And you don't mind digging us in deeper?'

'We're in pretty deep already, no?'

'Yes.' She just got the word out, even though her brain had jammed as he kissed her again. The dress wasn't the easiest to get off with the halter neck, but she wanted out of it. The promise of skin-to-skin contact was driving her crazy. Stepping back from his hold, she slipped out of it and let go. Only a strapless bra and her lacy knickers covered her. It wasn't much different from the bikini she'd had on earlier. Plus, he'd seen her without any clothes on before. Jeez, he'd stood beside her while she threw up naked just over a week ago. But she still felt almost shy.

'You're so beautiful,' he said.

'Do you say that to all the girls?'

'Only the ones I like.'

'And have there been many of them?'

'One or two, but none quite like you.'

She slipped her hands around his cheeks, gliding them over his neatly trimmed beard. It suited him, keeping him rough around the edges, but not scruffy. 'I quite like you too.'

'Good, because right now, I want to do some other things with you. Things that are only suitable for people that I particularly like.'

'Such as?'

'For starters, I'd quite like to kiss you.'

'Then what are you waiting for?'

He tilted his head slightly, still in her hands, and leaned towards her. She pulled him the rest of the way and their lips came together forcefully, and oh so satisfyingly. No more waiting or playing. Not tonight anyway. She slipped her tongue into his mouth and he met her with a hunger she hadn't expected, but it sent bolts of lightning through her. If he was acting, this was an award-winning performance – so convincing. A rush of joy and warmth flooded through her, almost like the man she'd dreamed of from afar actually felt the same for her. He was definitely hot for her, and that made her smile into the kiss.

Soon all the remaining clothes were on the floor, and they lay naked on the bed, locked in a tight embrace. Finlay's warm weight and his firm touch melted her and set her alight at the same time. Nothing was enough, though, at the same time, it was almost too much. She moaned as he moved his kisses from her lips to her cheeks, to her collarbone.

'This is all very nice, isn't it?' he mumbled, running the tip of his nose towards her breasts.

'It really is.'

He worked his way down her body, kissing her everywhere until she hit a new level of ecstasy. How good at this was he?

'Where's that basket?' he said, stroking her hair as she rested back on the pillows, breathing heavily, still not sure why it had never felt this good with James.

'Windowsill.'

'Flora really is a well-prepared and sensible woman,' he said, crossing the room in the semi light and raking through the basket of toiletries. His naked silhouette was stunning, and Genevieve watched shamelessly as he put on a condom and returned to her. 'I really must thank her in the morning. It's not every day a guy is treated to such a delectable layer of protection.'

Genevieve laughed. How did he manage to bring humour to every situation?

He lay alongside her again and she wrapped her legs around him, pushing him onto his back so she was on top. She'd never been this daring before, but it felt right.

'Nice,' he said, running his hands down her body to cup her bottom. She leaned over and pressed her lips onto his.

He moved inside her exquisitely, his soft groan making her clench. This wasn't something he could fake – and she didn't have to. As their movements got quicker and more intense, sensations she hadn't achieved with anybody else washed over her, making her breath catch in the back of her throat. Finlay moved faster like he'd lost all control and his breathing changed to a rasping pant. The intensity of the moment overwhelmed her, and she was overcome with dazzling sparks. She wanted to cry.

Why am I so emotional?

Finlay jolted beneath her with a long groan and she rested her hands on his shoulders as the aftershocks rolled over her.

Now it was done she wasn't sure what to do. Despite them being so close, joined together, she felt suddenly alone.

She moved off him. Should she get dressed and go sit downstairs or something? Would it be weird to stay here? This was just a hookup after all and that was what happened, wasn't it? She didn't want to admit how miserably ignorant she was about what to do next.

'Genevieve,' he said in a low, quiet voice. With what seemed like a big effort, he pushed himself up, so he was sitting beside her and wrapped his arms around her. The instant warmth removed the lonely feeling, but the desire to cry rushed back tenfold. 'Let me get this off and then can we cuddle for a bit? Or do you not like that?'

'I...' She didn't really know. When she'd been with James, he hadn't been a cuddler, or not with her anyway, and she'd resorted to wrapping herself in lots of blankets and assuming it was normal. 'I'll wait here.'

'Ok.'

It wasn't long before he returned. 'So, do you want to cuddle up or just go to sleep?'

She rolled over, so she was reunited with his heat. 'Cuddle.'

'Good.' He brushed her hair from her forehead and then kissed her just above her eyebrow. 'I love to cuddle. Best way to end a weird day and a hot evening.'

She smiled and held back a lump in her throat. The tears were desperate to get out, but now she realised it wasn't because she was upset, but because she'd not been this happy in a long time.

CHAPTER EIGHTEEN

Finlay

Finlay ran damp fingers across his hot brow. The water in the bath must be close to boiling, much like his blood when he looked at the woman next to him. Over the years he'd trained himself not to look at Hayley's friends or, if he did look, not to *see* them properly. Now that rule had gone well and truly out of the window. Not only had he crossed every possible line with Elise, but now he'd repeated it with Genevieve. Make that exceeded it.

How was one night with Genevieve better than months with Elise?

Genevieve rested her head back on the edge of the giant sunken tub and rubbed a lather up her arm with the heavily perfumed soap. The erotic possibilities for this bath had multiplied since last night. Drying her hand on a fluffy white towel, she picked up her phone.

'Are you recording this?' he asked.

'I could do a quick live from the sunken bath.'

'And get me fired before I even get there?'

'True. I won't.'

Finlay smiled and lazed back. 'What would you say to your followers if you went live?'

'Tell them this retreat is stunning and the possibilities of this bath are... Well,' – she raised an eyebrow – 'that would be telling.'

'Would it?' Finlay rolled his head to look at her.

'It certainly would.' She stood up and rinsed the soap from her naked body with a very provocative slide of her hands over her breasts.

'Stop it, you tease.'

She ducked down again and sidled up to him. 'Maybe you should help me wash. Seems like I'm in a filthy mood.'

He shook his head, barely holding back a laugh. She was so different from her public persona. It would almost be funny if she'd left her phone recording and her followers heard this. With a moment's unease, Finlay glanced at it. 'That's definitely not recording, is it?'

She pulled it towards her and checked. 'Definitely not.'

'Then come here.' He pulled her close, cupped some soapy water from the tub and ran it over her upper arm.

'And can I help you?'

'I'm counting on it.'

She put her hand under the water, keeping her eyes on his and gently touched him. He could take a lot more, but the lightness of her touch was thrilling and teasing. Who'd have thought washing someone could be so seductive?

Soon the kisses started up again. Their mouths had been apart too long and needed each other. His body desperately desired to reconnect with hers.

Soapy suds dripped off them as they clambered out of the bath and grabbed towels before heading back to bed.

'This headboard is actually very well screwed,' Finlay commented as they rolled on top of the covers, his hands aching to touch every inch of her beautiful bare skin.

'So are we,' Genevieve added.

With a smile, he moved on top of her, and she wrapped her legs around his back.

Five stars from me for this romantic retreat.

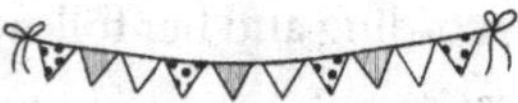

'Is Flora expecting us for breakfast?' he asked half an hour later as they lay side by side, Genevieve stroking a rhythmic line down his chest with her fingertip.

'She didn't give us a time, and she keeps telling us to have fun, so she can't object.'

'Very true.' He tightened his hold on her a little. Life was busy and people didn't make enough time to appreciate moments like this. When he was with Elise, he definitely hadn't. Neither of them had. They'd never woken up on a Sunday morning and done anything like this. She'd get up early to go to the gym and meet friends while he'd gone off running or cycling. Maybe his bad feelings towards her since the breakup were causing this line of thinking, but he couldn't imagine wanting to do this with her. Their physical relationship had been ok. Elise was an attractive woman, but she was cold. Now he knew why. She'd never really fancied him. Maybe he'd never properly fancied her. The chemistry was missing.

Something odd was going on with Genevieve though. For something that was meant to be fake or a brief hookup, it felt strangely real, intimate, almost loving. He'd thought her cold too – before the proposal – but she wasn't. This definitely wasn't cold. Warmth spread between them and he was sated with a deep, happy sensation he didn't remember experiencing for a very long time. Last night, there had been a brief moment straight after their explosive climax, when she'd gone silent and icy. He'd thought she was on the verge of tears, maybe about to run away, but she'd curled up in his arms and everything seemed fine again. Not that it should be. Maybe her initial reaction had been the sensible one because Finlay couldn't bear to analyse this situation too much. All he knew was he shouldn't be feeling this good about something that wasn't going to last past the end of the month, but at the same time, he didn't want to let the sensation go either.

Genevieve's finger tracing changed to making a figure of eight across his chest. With a contented sigh, he tilted his head and placed a kiss on her brow.

'We've definitely given this place a good test drive.'

'Haven't we just. Flora will be overjoyed when she sees how many condoms are missing from that packet.'

Finlay chuckled. 'Oh god, I never thought about that. Maybe we should take the whole box.'

'She might wonder why we came so unprepared.'

'We were just making use of the facilities and besides, she provided the vegan, natural-feel, pleasure condoms, when I would have gone with everyday value. It's a no brainer.'

'You're a madman.' Genevieve prodded his chest.

'I think we're both a bit mad.'

'What do we do after today? I mean... If we're still keeping the engagement story going, we should at least arrange to see each other,' she said.

'In what way? Do you mean you want to keep having this kind of hookup or you want to meet up twice a week for tea and biscuits while we pretend to be getting ready for Dubai?'

'Whichever.' She gave an almost petulant shrug – as though it was of no real concern to her, but her expression had dropped and her hand stilled.

'Well, I really am packing up for Dubai, so you can come and help me with that if you want. I'm still trying to sell the flat. I have the tug-of-war practices to attend every Tuesday, but that's about it. The rugby coaching is only during the school term and all I need to do is see if I can persuade one of my colleagues to take it on.'

'Won't you miss all this stuff?'

'Maybe. But I'll be trading it for a whole lot of new experiences, which can't be bad.' That was what he'd told himself ever since getting this job and that was the line he was sticking to. It wasn't like he could go back now. He'd signed a contract. And why was he even considering anything else? He didn't want to stay here, not with the shitstorm surrounding his breakup with Elise and the one that was going to explode around his engagement to Genevieve. He wanted to be far away when that blew up. But he wasn't that great at change either and a sick, nauseous sensation came over him every time he thought about Dubai. He pushed it away.

'We should get dressed,' Genevieve said, shifting away from him.

He supposed so but it would be much nicer to lie like this for the rest of the day.

The breakfast room had a table set up when they arrived downstairs, though ten thirty was maybe too late to expect service.

'Should we help ourselves?' Finlay asked.

'But what can we have? Dry cereal?'

'Good point. There's no milk, is there?' He perused the sideboard that had a covered plate of pastries, some cereal containers, and a selection of jam. 'Croissants and jam?'

'Hello, hello,' Flora said from behind.

Finlay resisted the urge to jump comically and pretend to be ultra-shocked, but really, she had a habit of jumping out of nowhere. And how did she always know where they were? Spy cams! Maybe not such a joke after all.

'Morning,' Genevieve said. Her cheeks were slightly pinker than usual, even under her make-up. Maybe it was his imagination, but the bare skin on her chest under her delicate scooped-neck top looked flushed. Was she still basking in that post-coital glow?

'Good morning,' Flora said. 'I hope you slept well.'

'Very well,' Finlay said, and it wasn't a lie. In between the fun, he'd slept like a log.

'Excellent.' Flora clapped her hands together. 'I've been looking at all the posts you've put up.' She winked at Genevieve. 'Happy to see you enjoying the facilities.'

Finlay glanced away. Uh-oh. What on earth had she put up? Hopefully nothing too suggestive. But even if he wasn't in the clips, anyone who'd seen that engagement clip would know who she was here with. And had they been a real couple, then big deal, why should he care? But they weren't and every move they made added to the wall he'd have to climb to get out of this mess in a few weeks' time. People were going to find it more and more disturbing that a couple who were all loved-up at a romantic retreat were splitting up and going their separate ways. People like his mum, his sister, his friends, his former workmates, his tug-of-war teammates – people who cared about him.

'I'll get you some breakfast,' Flora said. 'If you want anything cooked, just let me know.'

Finlay could eat his body weight in food at this point but part of him just wanted this trip to be over. If Flora didn't want to work with Geoff after this, it wouldn't be for lack of effort on Genevieve's part. She might not see it like that, but he'd vouch for her. Sleeping with him was above and beyond... Not that it had been necessary, though it had been nice. He took his seat, his eyes on Genevieve, his mind rewinding to all those hot moments they'd shared in the past twelve hours.

She blinked before catching his eye. 'We need to have a plan,' she said when Flora left the room. 'If people are going to believe I'm considering going to Dubai with you, I have to at least look like I'm doing that.'

'So what do you propose?'

'I'll leave the proposing to you. You're the expert, after all.'

'Very funny.'

'I've been thinking for a while about moving, so maybe I should put my house on the market too. It would go along with the story and then, after you've gone, I can sell it and move somewhere else. I've always fancied living near the river.'

'I think I said this before, but you can buy my flat.'

'I would. I love that place.'

'Well, it's up to you. If you want to put your house on the market, go ahead.'

'I'll call the estate agent tomorrow. That'll look realistic and won't be a lie, because I really don't want to make up too many lies.'

'It's not like we have to now, is it? I mean, we did actually get engaged and now we've consummated the relationship good and proper, so who's to know it's not real?'

'Who indeed?' she said, looking down at the table.

'This is as real for you as it was for Elise,' Finlay said.

'Meaning what?'

'Well, we were engaged, occasionally slept together and she planned to sell her flat and move in with me too. And that was it. She didn't have any deeper feelings than you.'

Genevieve fiddled with the ring on her left hand. 'I see what you mean. I guess the difference is that you loved her, whereas with me... Obviously you don't.'

'Obviously.' He dusted the front of his jeans. Of course he didn't. That would be stupid. He liked her, sure, but love... 'To be honest, I'm not sure I loved Elise. I loved the idea of her.' What guy wouldn't want someone that stunning in their life? And he was flattered to think she liked him. That was the kind of idiot he was. Just like he'd been flattered by Genevieve admitting she was attracted to him physically and wanting to take that further. And he had. It had made for a pleasurable few hours, but it didn't mean he loved her. Love was something else. According to Oliver, it didn't exist, not for extended periods anyway.

'Well, that's fine. Maybe you can love the idea of me too and that'll be enough.'

He cocked his head and frowned. Sure, he loved the idea of her. After last night, the idea of her would be on his mind an awful lot. But something niggled at him. Would it be enough for what? That question was much harder to answer and when he searched for a response, his brain fogged over, refusing to look too far.

'Here we go.' Flora returned to the room with the chef trolley Ann had used the evening before.

'Thank you,' Genevieve said. The pink glow on her skin had faded and she looked much more like the cool woman who'd turned up on his doorstep with Elise not so long ago, the unflappable friend of his sister's, not the passionate loving woman he'd got to know since.

He'd like to find that woman again but that wouldn't be wise, not when in a few short weeks he'd have to say goodbye to her. And that was ok, right? Because that was the plan and exactly what he had to do.

Chapter Nineteen

Genevieve

Genevieve didn't have to put much effort into tidying her house. It was always social media perfect to the point of looking unlived in. She'd taken Mitzi for a brisk walk and settled her in her basket. Now, everything was ready to be photographed. Emelie Bright, the estate agent, was someone she'd met occasionally before. She'd handled property sales for Geoff, and Genevieve knew her to be efficient and timely. She'd unofficially nicknamed her Bright by name, bright by nature. Finlay would probably call her something similar and his voice seemed to say it in her mind, tinged with his wry tone.

She adjusted two cushions and stepped back to examine the effect. Why could she think of nothing but Finlay? Her followers were wild with excitement about her reels from the retreat and Flora had already had dozens of people calling her, asking to book the castle. Hopefully that would coin some favours for her dad. But it didn't solve the biggest problem, the one she hadn't shared with anyone except Mitzi. And even then, she could hardly bear to talk about it because it hurt so much. Lovely as it was having everyone telling her what an amazing catch she'd made, they didn't realise how every word cut her deep. Finlay wasn't hers. Not really. And no matter how much she wished he was, she knew it wasn't going to happen. He was sticking to his plan and going to Dubai.

The doorbell rang. Emelie was early, but that was good. It would get this part out of the way. Genevieve's stomach was tugged by irrational nerves. She'd never done anything like this before, not without support from her parents. She hadn't wanted to ask them this time because they'd wonder why Finlay wasn't around to help. Mitzi lifted her head, but was too tired to do anything else. Genevieve pulled open the door and stepped back in surprise.

'Finlay. What are you doing here?'

He ran his hand around the back of his head and ruffled his hair. 'Thought I'd drop by in case you wanted moral support. I got the impression you weren't that thrilled about being here on your own.'

'Did I give that impression?'

'Subtly.' He raised an eyebrow. 'Though I'm not sure why. You're the queen of real estate, remember?'

'How could I forget? But it's easier to be objective about other people's property.'

'This place is like a show home. It's not like you've got anything to worry about.'

She stepped back to let him in and Mitzi came bounding up for a tummy rub. Genevieve understood that feeling all too well. She'd happily lie back for him too. When they'd been together at Flora's castle, he'd opened doors to new possibilities that were hard to walk away from.

Discipline.

If she could just control herself for the next few weeks, he'd be gone from her life and she could start rebuilding it without him. He was a blip and she'd get over him. It was just a game after all.

He strolled into her hallway and looked around. Her resolve faltered. When he was so close to her, she wanted to yield to the comfort of his arms, even if she knew it couldn't last and it wasn't real.

'I'm not going to add anything to the décor, am I?' He squinted into the living room. 'I hope I haven't left footprints on the rug.'

Genevieve couldn't help herself from checking. He chuckled and she threw him a look.

'Got you,' he said.

'Please behave, especially when the estate agent is here.'

'You know me. I'm always on my best behaviour.'

'Yeah, sure you are.'

'Smells nice in here.'

'That's my wax melts.' The bell rang again before she let on how much she loved that fragrance – eucalyptus and mint – because it reminded her of him. She opened the door to a neat young woman in a sharp suit, holding a folio under her arm. Her poker straight auburn hair sat perfectly trimmed on her shoulders.

'Genevieve, hi, nice to see you again.'

'Hi, Emelie. How are you?'

'Excellent, thank you.' She glanced around. 'You've got the place looking stunning. I don't think we'll have any problems selling it. I'll need to have a proper look and get some measurements and pictures, then I can give you an idea of market prices and once the surveyor has done the home report, we can set the asking price.' She made her way into the living area and came face to face with Finlay. 'Oh... Are you the surveyor?'

'No. I'm Finlay. Genevieve's...'

'Oh, you're together. So sorry.'

'It's fine,' Genevieve said.

'So, do you both own this house?'

'No. I have my own house.'

'Is it on the riverside?'

'Yes.'

'I remember valuing it a few weeks ago. So, do you have your eye on somewhere together?'

'Nothing yet,' Genevieve said.

'Well, if you want any recommendations, you know where to come.'

'We will.' Finlay sat down and rested in a perfect manspread. Mitzi lay down at his feet and he tickled her. Genevieve sat beside him and Emelie took the other sofa, opening the folio on her lap.

'Now let's go through the questionnaire,' she said.

Having Finlay beside her was like having an invisible force field. He said nothing and sat quietly tickling Mitzi. Genevieve couldn't explain why his being there was any better than being alone but it was.

After answering all Emelie's questions, Genevieve caught Finlay's eye and he smiled at her. She'd miss that smile. His thigh brushed against hers and the sense of familiarity struck her. Soon she'd be alone again and this fake reality would be nothing but a memory.

'If you don't mind me getting some pictures and measurements now,' Emelie said.

'Of course.'

Genevieve got to her feet and Finlay followed, chivvying Mitzi into the hallway while Emelie photographed the living space.

'We're back to selling houses and being all domesticated,' Finlay muttered.

'You're the one who chose to come.'

He smiled. 'Glutton for punishment. That's me.'

But she had the impression he quite liked it. Maybe he liked her company. Why else would he have come?

The doorbell rang again and Finlay shook his head. 'You're very popular.'

'Tell me about it.' She turned to the door and opened it. A spasm of tension gripped her chest at the sight of the two people on the doorstep. Hayley and Elise. 'Um... Hi. Why are you two here?'

'We need to talk,' Elise said.

Hayley smiled. 'I'm just here to see you're ok. I've hardly seen you and...' Her eyes darted to Elise and Genevieve guessed she wanted to say some hard words. Hayley was there to soften whatever it was.

'Hayley.' Finlay stepped up behind Genevieve, placing his hand on her shoulder and she was enveloped by his soothing fragrance. 'And...'

'Me,' Elise said.

'Listen, this isn't a good time, girls.' Genevieve looked behind into the lounge. 'I've got an estate agent here to value the house.'

Elise folded her arms and stood her ground. 'We'll wait because this is important.'

Genevieve let out a sigh and Finlay's grip tightened on her shoulder. 'Whatever it is you want to say to Genevieve, you can say it in front of me too,' he said. 'I'm not going away so you can slag me off.'

'Like I'd do that,' Elise said. But Genevieve would be shocked if she didn't say something about him.

Hayley held out her hands and shared a helpless glance with her brother.

'Well, I assume Hayley's only here to stop you saying anything too upsetting to Genevieve and I'm not going to let you do that either.'

'Why would I do that?' Elise said. 'I don't want Genevieve to get hurt. She's my friend, so I wouldn't say anything with the intention of upsetting her, but what about you?'

'What about me?'

'Can you honestly say you don't want to hurt her?'

'Just butt out, Elise,' he muttered. 'I've never in my life wanted to hurt anyone.'

'Let's all be nice,' Hayley said. 'How about we wait out here until you're finished with the estate agent? We're just here for a friendly chat, that's all.' Hayley linked her arm through Elise's and pulled her away.

Genevieve closed the door and stared at Finlay. 'What are they playing at? How embarrassing when Emelie is here. I hope she didn't hear that.'

'She's in the kitchen, so I don't think she would have.'

'I know Hayley is off on Tuesdays, so maybe they just want to see me, but they could have let me know.'

'Excuse me for not trusting Elise, but it unfortunately goes with the territory.' Finlay huffed out a low growly sound and mussed up his hair.

'Let me handle her, ok?'

'Yeah, yeah, ok.'

Genevieve grabbed his arm. 'I mean it, Finlay. I can handle her. She's here to see me, not you.' And while she appreciated him standing up for her, she had to face this.

'I'm aware of that, but I know firsthand how cruel she can be towards people who think she cares about them.'

She swallowed at the look of hurt in his eyes. This was why he was leaving and going somewhere he wouldn't run the risk of bumping into her again.

A slight cough caught their attention. 'I have everything I need,' Emelie said, folio under her arm. 'I'll be in touch shortly once we have the floor plan and the sales page made up. Hopefully, the surveyor will be around this week and we can get the home report sorted and check the valuation.'

'Thank you,' Genevieve said. 'That's great.'

'No problem.' Emelie put out her hand and they both shook it one after the other. 'And if you need any help with the house hunting, drop me a message.'

'Sure will,' Finlay said, leaning on the living room doorframe, with his arm up high, in the same casual way he'd done in his flat on the day the fake engagement started.

Genevieve walked Emelie to the door and followed her out. Close to the fence, Hayley and Elise stood side by side. Hayley looked like she was trying to show Elise something in the garden but Elise was stoney faced.

Emelie Bright climbed into a gun-metal Hyundai Tucson and drove off with a brief wave. Elise wasted no time in marching over.

'Oh my god,' Elise said. 'Genevieve, are you ok?'

'Of course I am. Why wouldn't I be?'

'Because this engagement isn't real.'

'Pardon?' Genevieve stared at her.

Hayley looked away and picked on a nail. 'Do you realise how insulting this is to my brother?' she muttered.

'I'm sorry, Hayley,' Elise said. 'And I don't mean it to be at all insulting. Finlay's a good guy and I was awful to him. I'm not denying any of that, but what he's doing to Genevieve is just as bad.'

'He's not doing anything to me.'

'He's using you to get at me.'

'No, really, he isn't.'

Elise gave her an almost pitying look. 'It's so obvious. Why won't you believe me? Why else would he get engaged so soon after me? Why propose to you on the same day you came to his flat with me? I saw the two of you together and there was no clue that he even liked you. So, I guess the two of you must have got completely rat-arsed, and he proposed for a joke or a dare or whatever. Why the hell did you say yes though? I don't get why. Are you that desperate?'

'Not nice,' Hayley said.

'You know what I mean,' Elise said. 'Not desperate as in you'll settle for anything but desperate to be engaged. And if you said yes because you were drunk, why go along with it now? You're even selling the house. Does that mean you're going to Dubai with him?' She held up her hands like she was grappling with something. 'I have so many questions.'

Genevieve gave a little shrug. How could she begin to answer them? Elise made some good points.

'Elise,' Hayley said softly. 'Finlay is nice. He always has been. There's no reason why Genevieve shouldn't like him. I know you and him didn't work out and you didn't actually love him, but you liked him. You knew he'd be trustworthy.'

'I did,' Elise said, and her expression drooped slightly. 'That's why I don't understand why he's doing this.'

Is it so hard to believe he actually likes me?

Yes. Because it was all a lie.

Having Hayley list all the reasons Elise had chosen him for her deception in the first place knocked a guilty nail into Genevieve. He had a good nature and a soft heart – so easy to take advantage of and to hurt. She almost berated herself for doing the same thing, only this time Finlay understood the rules.

'I still don't get it,' Elise said. 'Why are you going along with this?'

'Because...'

'Finlay might be good, kind or whatever,' Elise added, 'but he's also—'

'Standing right here? Listening to every word?' Finlay's voice said from the door.

Genevieve barely turned around, only enough to glimpse him casually leaning on the doorframe with his arms crossed.

Elise shook her head. 'This would be better without you.'

'Oh, I'm sure it would be,' he said, making his way over. 'But I'm not going anywhere unless Genevieve tells me to go.'

'She calls the shots, does she?'

'She's my... partner,' Finlay said, putting his arm around her shoulder. 'I'll do what's right for her and whatever she needs me to.'

Elise shook her head. 'I have no idea what game the two of you are playing, but I really don't get how you went from nothing to engaged in one day. Someone's going to get burned really soon. I just don't want anyone else to get hurt.'

'How noble,' Finlay said. 'Because you would know nothing about hurting anyone.'

'I didn't set out to hurt you.'

Hayley pulled a helpless face at Genevieve and reached out to pat Finlay's arm. 'I'm so happy for you both. If you say everything's fine, then I believe you. I also understand your misgivings, Elise. I know it's been sudden, but sometimes it happens.'

'What does?'

'Love at first sight.'

'But Finlay's seen Genevieve loads of times. It was hardly first sight.' Elise's jaw set and it looked like she was working hard not to say something else, but her resolve obviously cracked when she added, 'It's not like this is the first time you've done something like this either, is it?'

'Pardon?' Genevieve glared at her.

'Well, you pretended to be with James Charlton to get your parents off your back and then you tried to draw that out into something that it wasn't.'

'Um... What?' Finlay said.

Genevieve slowly raised her gaze to him.

'Didn't you know?' Elise said.

'This is different,' Genevieve said.

'And real.' Hayley smiled.

'Look, I don't know anything about this James person,' Finlay said to Elise. 'But you're right, it wasn't love at first sight. That would be insane because I first saw Genevieve when she was roughly twelve and I was seventeen – she definitely didn't float my boat at that age. But after you left her at my flat that afternoon, we had a realisation.'

Hayley smiled and cocked her head like this was the sweetest thing she'd ever heard.

'Really?' Elise said.

'Yes. I realised I'd been attracted to Genevieve on some level for a long time and when she invited me to go to the party with her, it was clear she liked me too. Things were so easy between us, there didn't seem any reason to wait any longer.'

'Right.' Elise arched an eyebrow like she didn't believe a word of it. Genevieve didn't blame her. It sounded pretty ridiculous, but her heartrate sped up at the thought that Finlay's words might be close to the truth. Could he have been attracted to her for a long time? Almost instantly, she dismissed the idea. As if. He was making up bullshit to throw them off the scent. His physical attraction to her at Flora's castle had been real, but that was just sex, right?

'Listen, Elise, give them a break, ok?' Hayley said. 'Not everyone's relationships will be the same.'

'Sure. I'm sorry if I've upset you. I can just see this going all wrong. I'll message you,' she said to Genevieve. 'And I truly didn't mean to offend either of you. I just... Oh, never mind. Whatever I say, I look like the bad guy.' She turned and marched off. Hayley followed her and said something before returning to Genevieve and Finlay.

'I'm not going back with her. Can I come in for a minute?'

'Sure,' Genevieve said.

'Are you going to get on our case too?' Finlay said.

'Yes, but about something completely different.'

'What now?' he asked.

'Mum wants to know why you haven't brought Genevieve around yet or invited her to meet the two of you together. She doesn't want to invite herself either, in case she looks too pushy.'

Genevieve led them into the house and gestured for them to take seats. Mitzi pounced on Hayley, who laughed and tickled her.

'Your mum has seen me before,' Genevieve said. It was one big difference between her parents and Hayley's mum. While Geoff and Hilary Harrington took very little interest in their children's friends, Lisa McBride liked to know everything about everyone. More often than not, Genevieve and Elise had ended up at Hayley's house as teenagers. Lisa was the mum who taxied the friends everywhere and would dot in and out of Hayley's room, bringing them snacks and drinks, pretending to hang up laundry or put things away, when really just wanting to be part of everything. They'd learned to not stop talking and to let her in on the chats. Maybe that was another reason why crushing on Finlay as a teenager had been something Genevieve had to keep locked away. Lisa might not have minded, but the embarrassment would have been horrible. Even now, her face and neck felt hot at the thought.

'Of course she's seen you,' Hayley said, still scratching Mitzi's tummy. 'But she wants to see you together. She's already upset that she hasn't seen you, Finlay, for ages and you're going away soon.'

He dropped his head into his hand and sighed. 'Yeah, I know. I've been so busy.'

'So's she. She's hoping to cut her hours at work, but you know what she's like. She's been saying that ever since we were at school.'

'Does she still work at the Drip Drop Coffee Shop?' Genevieve asked.

'Yes,' Finlay said. 'She's in with the woodwork there.' He glanced at his phone, then at Genevieve. 'I'll message her and see when she's free this week, then we can go see her.'

'Sure.' She swallowed back her trepidation. Yet another awkward meeting.

Hayley gave Mitzi what was obviously meant to be a final scratch and sat back in her seat. Mitzi, however, was having none of it and sat at Hayley's feet, staring up at her. Hayley beamed at Finlay, then Genevieve. 'I just can't get over the two of you. Of all the people I'd never have put together.' She gave a little flick of her hands. 'And you know how much I love setting people up, but I'd never thought...' She was still smiling like it was the happiest mistake of her life. Genevieve inwardly gave herself a pat on the back for hiding her crush for so long from one of the nosiest people on the planet.

'Well, you know me,' Finlay said. 'I always like to stand out from the crowd and bring something new to the party.' His tone was sarky, like he was known to be the most boring man on the planet. Genevieve narrowed her eyes slightly as she took him in. Her biased brain told her he was handsome and sexy. Maybe not everyone would agree with her but if they thought him dull and average, that was their own problem – she knew otherwise.

'How true,' Genevieve said with a smile.

'Perfect,' Hayley agreed. 'Speaking of parties, you can bring Genevieve to Dad's birthday bash.'

'What?' Finlay glared at her. 'You are kidding, right?'

'Why would I be? Dad will want to meet her too.'

Genevieve tried to read Finlay's expression. She knew their dad lived in Dundee and Finlay didn't see him often, but something in his face said that he either didn't want to go to the party at all or he didn't want her with him.

'Great,' he said. 'Let's add that to the calendar of fun events to tick off my bucket list before I... we leave for Dubai.'

Hayley smiled but her face was a little tense. 'I'm going to miss you two so much. This has all been so sudden and I' – she covered her mouth like she might cry – 'I'll miss having you both around. Now it's not only one of my favourite people I'm losing, but two.'

Genevieve's insides coiled and Hayley gave her a fond smile. How would this conversation go in a couple of weeks' time when Finlay had jetted off to Dubai and Genevieve was still here... Would she still be one of Hayley's favourite people then?

CHAPTER TWENTY

Finlay

Finlay staggered back and wiped the sweat from his brow. His hands were raw and his muscles aching from almost an hour of tug-of-war practice.

'Come on folks,' Brann, the team leader, said, dusting his hands together. 'This is like the dress rehearsal. We've only got two weeks left.'

Like they didn't know that already, which was why this extra Saturday afternoon practice had been squeezed in. Brann, a builder by trade, was usually easy-going but when it came to the tug-of-war he transformed into a warrior-like competitor. He'd insisted on them all wearing their kilts and 'Brawny Briars' t-shirts so they could get the feel of what it would be like on the day. Maybe it was sensible; there was a lot of new blood on the team, one of the newbies being Aidan, Finlay's cousin. Since the Elise debacle, things had been cold between them even though there had been a recent thaw. Logan was also there with a stunning blue-haired cousin of his. She was the only woman on the team and despite looking slim, she was as tough as the guys and possibly even more competitive, high-fiving Logan every time their side won.

Aidan moved in beside Finlay and put his hand on his shoulder. 'I don't know what possessed me to sign up for this,' he said in his famously deep voice. 'I feel like we've been put through the wringer. Is it always like this?'

'Brann likes to win,' Finlay said. So did he, but he wasn't obsessive about it. Perhaps taking part in so many sports had taught him you couldn't win at everything all the time and that learning to cope with defeat was part of the process.

'Don't we all,' Aidan said. 'I hear you've got engaged again. That was quick.'

'My speciality, isn't it?' he said dryly, knowing only too well how Aidan had felt when he and Elise had got engaged so soon.

'I hope this one works out for you.' He clapped Finlay's back. 'Solidarity, Fin. We've both been burned by the same woman. I'm lucky to have found Lilah; I hope this girl's the one for you and we can both shove Elise into the history books where she belongs.'

'Yeah, let's hope.' He couldn't muster any enthusiasm into his words because in a few weeks' time, everyone would know Genevieve wasn't 'the one' and he'd be dumped again.

'One more time, folks,' Brann said. 'Then you can all bugger off back home for your dinner.'

Finlay took up the rope and anchored his hands on it. This year's team was looking good but there were always better teams comprising guys who looked like professional wrestlers. The Highland Haulers were usually the favourites and were very hard to beat.

Brann took his place and gave the shout. The scuffle began. But half the team tugging against the other half wasn't a true representation of how it would be once they were in the games arena up against the other teams. Finlay remembered the helpless feeling of being dragged over the line by a stronger team, knowing that no matter how much personal effort he threw into it, they were going down. Why did that feel oddly similar to his life right now? He was clinging to a rope dragging him towards Dubai, away from all his friends, his family... and Genevieve. They weren't even a real couple. He gave a tremendous tug on the rope and let out a roar. In front of him Logan and Cha, the blue-haired woman, also let off shouts and heaved. The rope moved their way, and they dragged the other side across the line. Brann shouted for them to stop.

'Well done, this side.' He pointed to Finlay's side. 'And well done, everyone. We'll still have Tuesday's practice, but we can't do next Saturday as a few people have other engagements.'

Me! Finlay always had other engagements, it seemed. Engagement was his middle name. And next Saturday he had the unenviable delight of taking Genevieve to his dad's sixtieth birthday party – a rock 'n' roll dress-up karaoke event in the function room of a riverside hotel in Dundee. It didn't take a brain surgeon to work out it would be a hideously garish shindig compared to the refined social events Genevieve was used to. Finlay often wondered if he was adopted – made sense in so many ways. If he discarded the family resemblance, it was easy to think he must come from different genes. Both his parents and Hayley were so much more 'out there' than him. He couldn't imagine ever wanting a rock 'n' roll dress-up karaoke for a birthday. His father's latest girlfriend, Liz Brown, was number goodness-knows-what since he'd divorced their mum when Finlay was twelve and Hayley was seven. They'd grown up being introduced to new stepsiblings, even going on holiday with them sometimes, only for his dad to split up with whoever she was. Hayley was good at keeping in touch with some of them. Finlay didn't bother. Their mum moaned about Dad and 'all his women' but she'd had a fair few boyfriends herself. Maybe this was where genetics played their part. Finlay was serially engaging himself to a string of women – not that unlike his dad then.

'See you at your dad's party next week,' Aidan said as he and Finlay packed up their kit bags. 'Are you wearing fancy dress?'

Finlay pulled a face. 'Hayley's got me a leather jacket. That's as far as my rock 'n' roll style goes.'

Aidan chuckled. 'Yeah, I haven't a clue what to wear. Lilah's sorting it. She's going for the full rockabilly look.'

'I literally have no idea what that means.'

Aidan pulled out his phone. 'Look at this.' He swiped through some pictures until he landed on one of his girlfriend. Finlay peered at the photo. She had her red hair pulled into a ponytail with a headscarf knotted on top of her head and wore a green dress covered in huge white polka dots, tight at the top that flared into an A-line skirt.

'Ah. I get the idea now. Like *Grease*.'

'Yup.'

Finlay let out a sigh. He'd told Genevieve about the dress code and she'd probably chatted to Hayley about it, but he couldn't imagine this kind of thing would be her taste at all. She was always so chic and glam. Then again, so was Hayley, and apparently, she had an outfit already. Maybe he was worrying about nothing.

'You're quite the celebrity these days, aren't you?' Logan said, passing him on the way out.

'How do you mean?'

'Eleanor follows your fiancée on the socials. Your proposal was quite something, I hear.' He waggled his eyebrows.

'Seriously?' Finlay shook his head.

Logan clapped his shoulder. 'All good fun.'

Finlay jammed his remaining stuff into his bag. This was when social media was bad. Only the fact it was Genevieve's job meant it was impossible to escape. For now anyway. Just a couple more weeks and he'd be old news. He said a quick goodbye to the team and headed home. He couldn't hang about as they were going for tea with his mum later. His life had snowballed into madness on top of madness. So much for a quiet break before heading off to Dubai; he'd never had such a busy summer holiday in his life.

Genevieve's car was outside when he pulled up at his flat. Odd. He was supposed to be picking her up later. Why was she here already? She knew the code for the key box, so he wasn't surprised to find the door open.

'Hey.' He bent down to greet Mitzi, who started snuffling around his ankles the second he opened the door. 'What are you doing here?' She carried on wriggling about excitedly.

'Hi.'

He glanced up. Genevieve was at the door into the living area, the bright light from the French doors setting her in silhouette.

'Is everything ok?' He dumped his bag on the floor, suddenly aware he hadn't bothered changing out of his kilt and t-shirt. He probably smelled dreadful.

'Fine. I just wanted to see you.'

'I've been at the tug-of-war practice.'

'You took longer than I expected.'

'That's Brann's fault. He's obsessed, not that it'll make any difference on the day. The Highland Haulers are too strong. What do you want to see me about?'

She gave a little shrug. 'I'm just nervous, I guess. It's weird because I know your mum but this feels so... I don't even know how to describe it.'

'Wrong?' he said.

She let out a sigh. 'Yup.'

'It's only another couple of weeks. Then you can tell everyone it didn't work out. You can't bear to leave Mitzi.' His chest tightened at the thought. With all the crazy shit going on, he'd not really given himself a moment to think about the reality of starting a new job – a new life – in another country. It was getting so close and so real. 'After that, all this will become a distant memory.'

'Are you sure it won't be a lasting monument to our idiocy?'

He huffed out a laugh. 'I can't promise that but time has a way of covering up stupidity. Life will go on and we'll pick up the pieces and go with it.' Would you listen to him, making a speech like he was on the playing field, psyching up his rugby team?

'You make it sound so easy.'

'I didn't mean that, but it's what we signed up for. If you want to back out now, then fine. Let's split up and be done with. We can still use Dubai as a good reason, only you've had your realisation a couple of weeks early.'

Her eyes never left his and, like ice was slowly slipping down his windpipe and into his chest, his words settled on him.

Let's split up and be done with.

'I'm not ready yet.' Her voice was quiet.

Me neither. But he couldn't bring himself to say it aloud. It was like confessing to something he didn't want to own. Maybe he didn't want to split up with her at all. But that was mad. He raked his fingers through his hair. They had to split up and now he knew Genevieve had a history of this kind of thing, it only cemented the fact that this was a game. Elise had let slip about how she'd done something similar with someone else. Finlay hadn't quizzed her on it. He didn't need to know. It wasn't like he had a clean slate when it came to his dating record. He'd been stupid to propose so many times… Genevieve liked pretending. And she was good at it. Too good. Convincing even.

'I need to have a shower before we go to Mum's,' he said. 'That was a gruelling practice.'

She moved from the doorway with deliberate steps, looking almost like a catwalk model as her hips swayed. 'Do you need someone to wash you?'

'Is that why you're here?' Still playing the game.

As she reached him, he put his hands on her waist and pulled her close. If this was what she wanted for the next two weeks, he could bear it – for authenticity purposes, of course.

'Maybe,' she said, running her hands over the words on his t-shirt. 'The Brawny Briars.' A smile played on her lips. 'Very apt.'

He dipped in and pressed a kiss on her lips. She responded hungrily and when their tongues touched, familiar heat roared through him.

He was ready, so ready. He pulled back, crossed his arms over his chest and whipped off the t-shirt. Genevieve opened the bedroom door and almost shoved him in, closing it on a somewhat depressed looking Mitzi.

'Sorry, pup,' he muttered. 'But this is not for your eyes.'

He helped Genevieve out of her floaty white gypsy top, lowering her bra straps and drinking in the sight of her pale skin warmed by the flush of arousal across her chest and the top of her breasts.

'If you come into the shower with me, this is all going to get messed up before we get to my mum's,' he said, running his fingers through her long, perfectly straightened caramel locks.

'Then you can have your shower after.'

'Are you serious?'

'Don't you know refined women like me always fantasise about hot sweaty men?'

He chuckled and unbuckled his kilt. 'That's all I needed to hear.' He let the heavy kilt fall to the floor and the buckle made a loud thump. A moment of deep male satisfaction ripped through him as he watched her avid eyes skim over him. She'd seen it all before but it hadn't diminished the attraction. In fact, it had forced her back for more. She was on him before he could think of anything else and he lifted her short floaty skirt, putting his hands under her bottom and hoisting her up. She wrapped her arms around his neck and they fell into another long hot kiss.

'You are so hot,' he said, lowering her to the floor, taking a condom from his bedside cabinet and placing it on the windowsill. He sat on the chair he usually used to drape clothes on. 'Come, sit on my lap.' He patted his knees.

With a grin, she straddled him and draped her arms over his shoulders. He snaked his arms around her, pulling her close. This position was intimate, even more so when she looked at him like that. Her pupils were wide and her irises glinted. Leaning in, he kissed her and the fires ignited. Both of them moaned and Finlay kept a tight hold on her as her fingers roamed into his hair, across his cheeks and around his neck. Her breasts bumped against his chest and he freed one and touched it, looking into her eyes. She threw back her head and smiled. A true smile that lit her eyes even more. No more serene Genevieve. The curtains were wide open and daylight streamed into the room, making this feel really wicked and kind of daring.

He smoothed his hand around her hips, lifting her skirt at the hem.

'So beautiful.'

She bit into her lip, still smiling, as he traced his finger up her thighs.

'And you're still hot and—'

'Sweaty?'

She trailed her fingers across his right pec and a bolt of arousal zipped through him. Raising her eyes to meet his, she smiled. 'Sexy.'

'Christ, you're killing me,' he said with a smile. 'I love it when naughty Genevieve comes out to play.'

'Do you think people can see us?'

'I doubt it. We're two floors up. What will they see anyway? Nothing I'm ashamed of. A beautiful woman having hot sex with her boyfriend?'

'A sexy man making love to his girlfriend?'

'I can do that.'

She squealed as he shifted under her, finding her most sensitive place and kissing her. His tongue made its way into her mouth. Their bodies rocked together, and everything became urgent. Greedy hands raced over his body and he groaned, drawing away from her kisses. He bent his head lower, trailing kisses over her breasts, sucking and licking until she squealed again.

He lifted her skirt and slipped the scrap of fabric to the side. Once that flimsy barrier was out of the way, he touched her until her moans filled the room. He had a vague thought about whether or not the neighbours might hear and what the hell they might make of it before she came undone. Her heavy panting filled the air, and she flopped into him, boneless and flushed.

He held her close, recovering his breath. When he drew back a little and focused on her face, her eyes met his and his heart leapt. That look. What did it mean? Was it admiration? Pleasure? Or more? Something like what he was feeling perhaps? That unnamed feeling he hardly dared entertain but in intimate moments like this, it was hard to ignore. His head was still riddled with a mess of doubts. But those thoughts could fuck off. Now was not the time.

'I need that condom.'

She pulled it from the windowsill where he'd put it and helped him put it on. Watching her fingers in action made him stop breathing. When she moved back into position, she was smiling again.

'Ready for more?' He stroked his hand down her cheek.

'For you? Always.' The cheeky look was still there, but was there a hint of something deeper? Sex and happy hormones were probably making him imagine it but it was almost like she was serious, like she needed this as much as food or drink to stay alive. He felt the same way. He swallowed, holding back for a second as another unwanted thought assailed him. A thought of him sitting alone in his accommodation in Dubai... And not just for a few days. For three years. Three long years. He couldn't exactly expect her to wait for him. A wave of emotion burst through him. He wanted her so badly and not just in this moment. But these moments were all he had left and he had to make the most of it.

She lowered herself onto him and he pulled her close. *I love you so much*. The words hurtled through his head as he thrust into her, keeping his eyes on her. He didn't dare say anything aloud, but he wanted her to know, to understand, and to feel the connection both physically and emotionally. She might be pretending, but he wasn't.

He didn't waste time in the shower. He couldn't afford to. Spending intimate time with Genevieve hadn't been in the afternoon's plans, not that he was complaining. No time spent with her could be considered a waste, not when he had so little of it left.

When he emerged from the en suite with his towel around him, he heard her somewhere else, talking to Mitzi. Maybe just as well. Her attraction to his naked body seemed as strong as his was to hers and if she saw him like this, she might jump him again and he was too weak to refuse. *Yes, you sad weak man,* he chivvied himself as he threw off the towel and grabbed some clothes from the wardrobe.

Ten minutes later, they were in the car and heading the short distance to his mum's house. They could walk it but as they'd left it so late, it was quicker this way. His mum's house was on the hill, as most of the houses in Glenbriar were. The town perched around a hillside at the neck of Loch Briar, where it joined the River Briar. They drove up a steep road that bent around past some old Victorian terraced houses. Aidan's mum lived in one of them with Aidan's loud-mouthed half-sister, Scarlett. As Finlay was related to Aidan through their fathers, he was quite relieved not to have to see Scarlett often. But his mum and Aidan's mum had stayed friends after both their marriages had fallen apart. Even after 'Elise-gate' they'd managed to cling to the friendship and Finlay half wondered what his mum really made of him and his choices. Did she worry to her friends about him? Did they take her worries and spread them on as gossip?

He and Genevieve pulled up in front of his mum's neat little bungalow and Genevieve smiled anxiously.

'My grandma lives not far from here,' she said. 'I should have brought some more food for her. She'll be thinking I'm neglecting her but this past couple of weeks have been mad.'

'They really have.' Finlay unbuckled his seatbelt.

'How was your mum with Elise when she first met you and her as a couple?'

'Like she usually is.' His mum was like Hayley. She liked everyone and rarely had a bad word to say about anyone. 'Why?'

'I don't know. Just nerves.'

'It'll be fine. Mum likes you, there's nothing to worry about.'

'That is what worries me. I hope she doesn't think I'm taking advantage of you.' She looked him up and down, then added quietly. 'Because I kind of am.'

He winked. 'Well, you can take that kind of advantage any time you like.'

'As long as it's within the next two weeks.'

'Yeah. Exactly.'

They fell silent, not meeting each other's gaze until Finlay opened the car door. The garden around the bungalow was a riot of summer colours, but everything was neat and well-kept. His mum enjoyed gardening and, since he'd left home, she paid neighbouring kids to cut her lawn as it was one job she wasn't keen on. Beside the driveway, that was comfortably big enough for two cars, was a rose hedge. Gorgeous red blooms covered it and the scent was immediate and almost overwhelming. Finlay was reminded simultaneously of Turkish delight and sitting on a bench with Genevieve.

'*I was that girl, Finlay.*'

'*What girl?*'

'*The one who pretended to hate the guy she fancied.*'

He frowned and rubbed his forehead. Had she actually said that? When he was a teenager in this house, had she liked him even then?

'*This is fate. You and me. This is the lightning bolt moment. I am "the one".*'

'*I know. It was always you.*'

What? It was the roses. The smell. They reminded him of that drunken night but had she actually said those things? Maybe he was imagining it because he was home and his brain was shoving mismatched things together and trying to make sense of them.

His eyes landed on her. She looked back at him and something intense struck his insides. Was she remembering that night too? Or other things? Maybe childhood memories... Had she really always liked him?

Was it really *always him*? And did that change anything if it was? Or was it just one other thing they had to get over and leave behind?

CHAPTER TWENTY-ONE

Genevieve

'Hello strangers.' Finlay's mum, Lisa, appeared at the door with a broad smile, dusting her hands down the front of a neat, figure-hugging blue dress. She was always immaculately turned out and so like Hayley. She almost looked more like an older sister than a mum. In fact, it was hard to believe she was old enough to be Finlay's mum. She must be in her late fifties, but you could easily knock ten or fifteen years off if looks were anything to go by. In all the years Genevieve had known her, she'd hardly changed.

'Hi, Mum.' Finlay stepped forward, hugged her, and kissed her cheek.

'Aw, my best boy,' she said. 'Always my favourite son.'

'Still your only son, Mum.'

She patted his back and leaned around him to smile at Genevieve, who was smirking at Finlay's retort.

'I've been saying that ever since he was born and he's been coming back with that ever since he was able to talk. I'm very glad

Hayley was a girl. Now I can have a favourite son and a favourite daughter without causing any jealousy.'

Genevieve smiled and held Mitzi's lead tight; she was straining to get to Lisa. Lisa didn't look particularly mumsy – more yummy mummy – but she always exuded warmth and her love for her children was almost palpable. Anyone who harmed a child of hers should watch out. That vibe was intense. Genevieve would bet her bottom dollar Elise had never showed face at this house since the breakup. Lisa would eat her for breakfast, despite always having a smile on her face.

'Nice to see you again too.' Lisa opened her arms and hugged Genevieve. 'All very surprising circumstances, but wonderful ones. And hello, Mitzi.' She bent over and tickled Mitzi. 'I'll get a wee bowl of water set up for you. You'll be roasty toasty in this weather.'

'Thank you,' Genevieve said. Would Lisa still think this was wonderful in a couple of weeks' time? How would Hayley feel when both her closest friends weren't welcome at her mum's house because of their awful treatment of Finlay?

'And it's good to see you again too,' Genevieve said. 'You look great as always.'

'Oh, don't,' Lisa said. 'I certainly don't feel it. I'm sure I've put on weight again.'

'Mum, there's nothing of you.' Finlay shook his head.

'Are you serious? Look at this.' She cradled a slightly round tummy, though it was barely there and certainly didn't look bad. Genevieve hoped she looked that good at Lisa's age.

'That's nothing, Mum.'

'Easy for you to say, but I feel a bit bloated. I was on holiday in Fuerteventura with my friends a couple of weeks ago,' she told Genevieve. 'And I ate far too much.'

'Drank too much vino, more like,' Finlay said.

Lisa play-smacked him on the side of his leg. 'You are a very cheeky boy and hardly one to talk.' She stepped back and peered from him to Genevieve. She seemed to be examining them and Genevieve tried to move closer to Finlay without looking like she was moving at all.

'I'm a great believer in fate,' Lisa said, tilting her head and smiling.

'We know,' Finlay said. 'Does that mean you've been to a fortune teller again?'

'Not exactly.' Lisa beckoned them inside. 'Let's sit in the garden. It's a beautiful day and I've made up a tray. Let Mitzi run about if you like. We're all fenced off.'

'Thank you.' They made their way through the very tidy house. Lisa detoured into the kitchen and Genevieve followed Finlay through the living room and out the French doors. She unclipped Mitzi from the lead as they reached the patio. Finlay took a seat at a wooden table in the pretty garden and tapped the one beside him. Genevieve sat and he rested his hand on top of hers. He flicked her a reassuring, if somewhat uncertain, smile. Lisa came out behind them and placed down a tray of mini sandwiches and cakes.

'This looks great,' Genevieve said.

'It's actually leftovers from the café, but it goes in the bin otherwise, so I like to make use of it. Another reason for this.' She patted her tummy again. 'It's hard to resist.' Taking the seat next to Finlay, she lowered large sunglasses over her eyes and rested back. 'Now, what I was saying about fate has nothing to do with fortune tellers. Even though I do like having my cards read. I often get a feeling, you know. Kind of like a sixth sense or a vibe.'

Genevieve smoothed her skirt, trying to act normally. She remembered Lisa talking about stuff like this before. Once she'd told her mum something Lisa had said, and her mum had told her she should 'never mess with the occult'. Now, she wasn't sure if she believed it or not. Sometimes she had strange feelings herself but dismissed it. Could there be more to it?

'Mum, what you do in your alone time is your business. If you get a vibe, then good for you.'

She leaned forward, lifted a sandwich, and shook her head, but she was grinning. 'Finlay, you are a very naughty boy sometimes. He's so cheeky, isn't he?' She looked at Genevieve.

'Very,' Genevieve agreed. 'The sarcasm king, even though he's not sarky at all, apparently.'

'Don't you two gang up on me,' he said.

Lisa smiled and nibbled on her sandwich. 'Yes. I often get a vibe – not that kind.' She narrowed her eyes at Finlay. 'Not that I'd be sharing that info with you anyway. Right now, I have a really good one.'

'Is that like the rabbit or something?' Finlay asked.

Lisa gave him a hard stare and he smirked.

'I mean about the two of you.'

Genevieve glanced at him. He lounged back with an undisguised eyeroll, like he was used to his mum talking about this kind of thing.

'Oh, here. I forgot the drinks,' Lisa said. 'I'll nip in and get them.' She headed back through the French door.

Bees hummed in the colourful pots on the little patio. A lush green lawn surrounded it and even the fences between the neighbouring gardens were decked with hanging baskets overflowing with flowers. Mitzi had found a shady spot near a flowering shrub and was lying in it with her tongue lolling out.

'So far, so good,' Genevieve whispered. She didn't want to say too much, but she was dying to ask if Lisa had 'got a vibe' about Elise too.

Finlay tilted his head and furrowed his brow, raising his hand over his eyes to block out the bright sunshine. His other hand was still resting on top of hers. He gently rubbed his thumb over the soft spot between her thumb and her forefinger. Genevieve resisted closing her eyes and slipping into a dream world. His light touch created powerful tremors inside her, reminding her of what they'd done before they left to come here. Sex mid afternoon wasn't something she was used to. In fact, before Finlay, she hadn't really enjoyed it that much. It was always one of those things you had to do and no matter how she dressed it up or approached it, she couldn't really get fully into it. But with him, it was important. It brought a physical dimension to their relationship, bonded them together, and made her feel good.

Maybe, subconsciously, she was letting herself go because she knew she didn't have to keep it going for too long.

Or maybe you like it – and him – more than is good for you, a sneaky little voice inside her head said.

'When we were kids,' he said, breaking the spell. 'And you used to come around here to see Hayley. Did you...' He stopped rubbing her hand and his face twitched a little like he was trying to figure something out.

'Did I what?'

'Here are the drinks, my darlings.' Lisa reappeared with a tray laden with jugs and glasses. It looked like a proper old-fashioned picnic and Genevieve remembered Lisa doing this kind of thing when they were younger. She'd always been a hospitable mum and Genevieve and her friends had spent more time here than at any of the others' houses. Genevieve had rarely had friends over that she could recall. Her mum was over kids' birthday parties by the time Genevieve came around, having done so many for the older two. Genevieve's parties were always at a venue somewhere. Her parents were there to oversee drop offs and pickups, but for the event, the staff took over. If she and her friends wanted to meet up casually, Hayley's house was the most convenient. With Genevieve's home being further out of the town, it seemed like a long way when usually they were meeting after school or before they were going out.

'This reminds me of when we were at high school,' Genevieve said. 'You always did a good spread.'

'It's not a problem. I've nearly always got stuff from the café to use up. It's part of the reason I love my work.' She took a seat opposite them and smiled. 'I very rarely have to buy food.'

Finlay leaned forward and lifted the jug. 'Is this lemonade?'

'Made by me.' Lisa smiled.

'Awesome. Would you like some?' He eyed Genevieve.

'Yes, please.'

'Oh, that reminds me. I forgot the water for Mitzi.' Lisa jumped to her feet again and bustled off.

'Oh bugger,' Finlay muttered.

'What?'

'I spilled it. Hang on, I'll nip in and grab some kitchen roll, or it'll drip all over the place.'

From inside the house, Genevieve heard Finlay's voice through the open kitchen window. 'I spilled the lemonade.'

'You dafty,' Lisa said. 'There's the kitchen roll. And Finlay, I just have to say I'm thrilled for the two of you. I wasn't joking when I said I get a vibe. The love between you is so obvious. I can almost feel it.'

'Yeah.'

Genevieve sucked on her lip, understanding why he didn't elaborate.

'She's a lovely person. I've always liked her. Those videos she does are wonderful, but I think she's quite reserved really. I get the feeling all that social media stuff is a front.'

Wow. She got that right. One of the only people who'd ever seen the truth of the situation.

'What will happen when you go to Dubai?' Lisa continued. 'Hayley told me Genevieve has already put her house on the market, which is great. It'll be so much nicer for you not being alone. I was worried about you being so far away and all by yourself. Will she keep doing the social media stuff? I guess she can do that anywhere, but isn't some of that stuff censored over there? How will it work?'

'I, um, don't worry about it, Mum. We'll sort things out.'

'I'm sure you will. Love is all that matters in the end. You learn that as you get older. The love I have for you and Hayley, my sister, my brother, my niece, my friends. That's what matters. The loves I've lost are what hurt the most: my parents, my grandparents, even the dog I had when we were little. These are the things that are important. Careers and hobbies are all well and good but they can't beat human connection or even pet connection.'

'You should get together with Oliver sometime. He takes the opposing view.'

'That grumpy guts.' Lisa's laugh tinkled. 'I love him really, but he's such a cynic. Sadly, he'll probably learn the hard way, when he's a lonely old man, that he should have followed his heart and not that brilliant brain of his. But you're distracting me from what I was talking about.'

'No, I'm not. You were telling me about love conquering the world.'

'Exactly. I'm just a little worried that your private life will be splashed all over social media. Is there any chance Genevieve might give all that up? I mean, the proposal was sweet, but I'm not sure I like the idea of footage of the two of you circulating around quite so many people.'

'Yeah, I don't like that either, and I'm sure my new employers won't be impressed. Hopefully, they won't see it. We have to accept it's Genevieve's job and try not to worry about it. I'll establish some boundaries.'

Genevieve held her breath. He didn't have to do that or like it; it would soon be over but she hated the idea she'd hurt him with those silly films. She knew he didn't want a social media presence... especially not if it would somehow jeopardise his new career.

'Well, the good thing is, son, I've always been good at reading auras and situations. Even when she was a child, I always had a feeling she liked you. When I asked Hayley about it, she said no, never any question of that, but I'm not so sure.'

No way! Genevieve's eyes widened and she stared into the garden. Lisa must be a witch. How the hell did she know that? Genevieve had never given anything away, she was sure of it. She'd always been so embarrassed around him and so sure he wouldn't even look at her.

'And I'll tell you something else; I never got a vibe like that from Elise. I got a vibe alright, it just wasn't a good one. Genevieve has always been very sweet, and I think she's exactly the right person for you.'

'Yeah. Thanks.'

'Let's get back out,' Lisa said. 'She'll wonder what on earth has happened to us.'

Genevieve cringed. Lisa's words were astute, kind and lovely except, like everything else for the last few weeks, none of it was real. She didn't deserve any praise. Lisa was right with her vibes and auras. Genevieve had always liked Finlay. The last few days, she'd indulged all her fantasies. With Finlay by her side, she felt whole. Putting the house on the market hadn't been a daunting experience because he'd been there with her, not doing anything more than being present – someone just there for her. He'd indulged all her physical needs and then some. She missed him so much when he wasn't there and that was only going to get worse.

And none of it meant he returned her feelings. Feelings she'd kept wrapped up tightly inside for such a long time.

When he reappeared, he mopped up the dripping table. Lisa nipped over to Mitzi and placed the bowl close to her, cooing a little and giving her a quick tummy rub.

'You ok?' Finlay caught Genevieve's eye.

'Fine.'

'Here's your lemonade. Finally.' He handed her a glass, then poured another two.

Lisa took hers as she returned to the table. 'Here's to you both and a long and happy life together.' She raised her glass, then clinked the edge against theirs before taking a sip.

Genevieve's drink lodged in her throat and it was hard to swallow, even though it tasted cool and refreshing. She wasn't sure she dared look at Finlay.

'When I was in Fuerteventura,' Lisa said. 'I met this man.'

'Is this something we need to hear?' Finlay asked.

'Be quiet and listen. But there's nothing romantic about this story, so no need to worry. He was working at the hotel and he could do this really amazing trick with glasses when he poured drinks.'

'Are you going to demonstrate?' Finlay asked.

'No way. I'd smash them. I filmed it though. Let me look back and show you.' She pulled out her phone and scrolled. She could talk about everything and anything – a trait she'd given to her children. It passed the time pleasantly and, under other circumstances, Genevieve would have enjoyed it. She laughed along with them at the film and joined in with the chat when necessary, but she couldn't help feeling like a total and utter fraud. On the flip side, she now knew Lisa had read her true feelings for Finlay when no one else had.

'Is everything ok?' Lisa asked, her eyes full of concern as she looked at Genevieve. 'You don't seem quite yourself and you seem a bit uneasy.'

'I'm fine, just tired.'

'It's a busy time,' Finlay added, taking her hand again and squeezing it. Was this part of his act? It didn't feel like it. Nothing could be more natural, and he didn't look like he was faking or trying too hard. He was just there, supporting her when she needed it. 'Selling houses is always stressful,' he said, rubbing the pad of his thumb towards her wrist. Every circle sent a wave of calm through her.

'Of course,' Lisa said. 'And this has all happened so quickly. No wonder you're exhausted.' She gave them a sad smile. 'I've really enjoyed having you both here. I'll miss you. Three years is a long time to be without my baby boy.'

'I'm a big boy now, Mum.'

'You'll always be my baby. I'm so glad you're going with him, Genevieve. He is a big boy, but he always does better when he's got someone holding his hand.'

'Mum,' he groaned.

'You know it's true. You've never been big on change. I was so worried about you going but I feel a lot happier now.'

Genevieve glanced at him and smiled. She turned her hand to hold his and he matched her grip with increased pressure, like he didn't want to let go.

His mum knew best and she'd got the measure of him whether he admitted it or not. Maybe that was partly why he'd jumped into an engagement with Elise… *And me!* Because he liked having a partner. Had he once told her that? Maybe that night they got engaged. She remembered talking a lot that night but wasn't quite sure what either of them had said and if any of it had been sensible, true, or just the prosecco talking.

I wish it had been you and not Elise. You're much more my kind of girl.

Those words kept coming back to her. She could swear he'd said that, but even if he had, did he really mean it?

Prosecco had a lot to answer for.

'Look after each other,' Lisa said. 'I know you will.'

When they left her house later, Finlay drove back to his place. Genevieve's car was there, so it made sense. What didn't make sense was how much she wanted to stay with him. Should she ask if she could come in? Did that make her look needy? Or maybe it would seem like she was overdoing the faking… Or using him for sex again.

'You coming in?' he said when they arrived back.

'Do you want me to?'

'Sure. Like my mum said, I'm always better when someone holds my hand.' He reached across to the passenger seat and stroked her cheek with his thumb. 'Especially when it's someone as nice as you.'

She gave him a weak smile but her insides were jumping up and down.

Yay! He doesn't want me to go!

How silly could she get? Because these days were numbered. All she could do was enjoy the ones they had left.

She got out of the car and waited for Finlay as he locked it. He stepped up beside her and took her hand, stroking her again in that way he'd done all afternoon. It drove her wild with desire for him.

'Thanks,' he said.

'What for?'

'Holding my hand. I need it, remember? Just what the mother ordered.'

'Happy to help the vibe along.'

He smirked. 'Have you got one of those rabbit things too?'

She cocked her head and raised an eyebrow. 'What single girl doesn't?'

'Shouldn't have asked, should I?' He held eye-contact for a moment, then stopped stroking her hand and looked down at the ring. 'Tell me... Did you ever have a crush on me when we were younger?'

Heat flared in her face and she hoped it didn't show. He'd raised his gaze to her again and his expression was filled with curiosity.

'You think you're that irresistible, do you?' She pulled on her best attempt at her casual face. 'Why do you want to know? Did you have one on me?'

'Well, no. Like I said before, you were about twelve when I first met you. It might have worked in my favour, an older boy and all that, but when I was seventeen, I wasn't looking at my kid sister's friends as possible dates.'

'Sensible.' Though she didn't bother to mention it had gone on a lot longer than that. She hadn't had a crush that lasted a year. Nope. That would have been easy. She'd probably have forgotten all about it. But this had lasted a lot longer. When Finlay had been off at university, she'd lived for the days he was back and made a point of visiting Hayley on the off-chance of seeing him, but he'd rarely even looked her way. When he wasn't there, Genevieve liked seeing photos of him around the house and hearing Lisa chatting about what he was up to. When she'd dated James, she'd fantasised during their intimate moments that he was Finlay, though the real deal had proved so much better.

'What about you? You didn't answer my question.'

'Wouldn't Hayley have told you if I had?'

'Not if you kept it hidden behind that serene façade.' He put his hands on her waist and pulled her close. 'What's a guy to think?'

'You just like the idea of being a high school heartthrob, don't you?'

He shook his head. 'Oh, Genevieve. You're going to keep me hanging on, aren't you?'

'I can cook us salmon and asparagus gratin for dinner. Ingredients are in the fridge. I brought them earlier. It's one of The Vieve's specialities. Recipes on all my channels, don't forget to hit subscribe.'

He chuckled, then planted a kiss on her forehead. 'For someone who's made their name as a single girl, you sure know the way to a man's heart and...' He drew back and looked at her. 'Well, I'm going to enjoy these days as much as I can and take the memories to Dubai with me.' Stroking his hand through her hair, he let out a sigh. 'Because I'm really going to miss—'

'My cooking?'

'That. And you.'

She returned his smile, keeping her lips clamped shut because a lump was welling in her throat.

'Let's go inside, beautiful, and we can cook this feast together. Mitzi can have some of the treats I bought her. They're about all that's left in the cupboard.' He kissed Genevieve's forehead again and she held her breath. She couldn't afford to let him see how much she loved every second spent with him or how much she would miss him. No one needed to know that. Like always, she'd deal with it alone.

CHAPTER TWENTY-TWO

Genevieve kicked out her hip and rested her hand on it. Finlay's eyes travelled over the incredible outfit, consisting of a dress with a pale pink V-neck top half and a flared skirt covered in pink roses. On her feet were pink Mary-Janes with white ankle socks, white gloves on her hands and her hair pulled back into a long and immaculate ponytail, fixed with a large rose.

'Wow, you never fail to amaze me. That's one heck of a costume.' He smiled, unable to take his eyes from her. She'd even managed to get the make up to look perfect with bright lips and rosy cheeks.

'Glad it's ok,' she said. 'I've never been to a rock 'n' roll party before. Hayley helped me pick this. She's going in a bright red dress that looks so hot with her dark hair.'

'Did you just call my sister hot?'

'Must run in your family.'

'Ha! You really know how to flatter a guy.' He lifted the leather jacket Hayley had got him from somewhere. His otherwise boring outfit of a white muscle t-shirt and black jeans didn't really look much different from how he usually dressed, except he'd turned up the ankles of his jeans and gelled his hair.

'You look damn hot in that t-shirt,' she said, with a flirty wink.

'You think? And you like my hair, uh-huh?' He put on an Elvis voice and ran his fingers through his slicked back hairstyle. Hayley had given him instructions on how to style it with a front flick but he wasn't sure he'd succeeded in doing it properly.

'Gorgeous.'

'Well, we're going to be quite the pair, aren't we?'

'We really are.'

He took her hand and spun her under his arm. 'You're rocking it, baby.'

She laughed. 'Have you seen my socials today?'

'No. Why?'

'I did a "how to"' session on nineteen-fifties make up, using the products I endorse. It's had hundreds of views already.'

'Wow. You're really something, aren't you? A celebrity.'

'Hardly.'

'I mean it. You wouldn't get all these people watching unless they cared what you had to say.'

'Maybe, though there's a lot of hate too. And some stuff that's hard to read.'

Finlay tilted his head and sighed. 'That's cruel. I didn't know that.'

'Oh yes. The haters will always hate, and sometimes, it hurts.'

He gathered her in for a hug. 'I'd like to track them down and give them what they deserve.'

'No point and you'd never find them... But I appreciate the thought. I've been thinking about changing things up for a while. I'm just not sure what else I would do. I don't exactly have a lot of qualifications.'

'Formal qualifications aren't everything and you have many skills.'

She wrapped her arms around his neck and smiled. 'I would kiss you but it might ruin my lippy.'

'Well, I won't insist. Priorities and all that.' With a wink, he dipped in and kissed her earlobe. 'There, that won't ruin anything.'

As there were five of them going from Glenbriar, Finlay had agreed to be the taxi driver. He really wanted Genevieve in the front with him, but she gave up her seat to Aidan, who had longer legs and needed more space than her. Finlay also suspected she wanted to bee-bop in the back with Hayley and Lilah, Aidan's girlfriend. The three of them sat huddled together in their dresses, looking like the chorus line from *Grease* and singing along to a rock 'n' roll playlist on Hayley's phone.

Aidan's eyes wandered constantly to the mirror, where he looked adoringly at his girlfriend. Finlay couldn't help noticing because *he* kept glancing that way too. Only his gaze found its way to Genevieve. Each time she caught his eye, she smiled broadly with her bright lips, looking every inch the sassy rock chick.

When they reached the riverside hotel in Dundee, the old misgivings slipped into Finlay's stomach. Nothing much was wrong with the place aesthetically. It was a very average-looking carvery type of restaurant attached to a modern hotel. But it was nothing compared to the glamour of Genevieve's parents' home. She could probably handle it as a one off, but this was his family and he couldn't – or wouldn't – change it. They were normal people, not rich with big fancy houses, or famous with thousands of followers on social media. Just run-of-the-mill folks.

Everyone got out of the car in a rustle of dresses and a thud of doors. Aidan had longer hair than Finlay and had managed to set it in a quite dramatic high coif that looked a lot more authentic than Finlay's slicked back look. He put on the jacket, wriggling under its uncomfortable weight in the heat.

Lilah took Aidan's arm and he winked at her. Together they looked like they'd walked off a fifties film set.

Genevieve took Hayley's arm, then looped her other one into Finlay's.

'You've got me as the gooseberry,' Hayley said. 'One day I'm going to have a date for something.'

'Why haven't you got a date? What's wrong with all these guys?' Finlay said. 'Should I be threatening them into dating my sister?'

'Aren't you supposed to do the opposite?'

'Na. That's old-fashioned. You can date whoever you want. Well, as long as he's nice.'

'What if *you* don't think he's nice?'

'Good point, but he'd have to be pretty horrible for me not to like him and I hope you'd never be that bad a judge of character.'

'I'd keep out of it if I were you,' Genevieve said. 'My brother wouldn't even notice who I was dating.'

'Your brother is a hottie,' Hayley said.

'Seriously,' Finlay muttered. 'Are you after him? I thought he was married.' He was sure he'd heard that at some point. His mum and Hayley told him stuff about people, but he often forgot or got stories muddled. No way could he keep up with all the people they knew and how much they knew about them.

'He was,' Genevieve said. 'But they split up ages ago. It's Mum and Dad's best kept secret. They don't mention it unless it's strictly necessary.'

Music blared from the function room in the hotel and it sounded more like a rave than a civilised party. Finlay gave Genevieve a sideways glance, but she didn't look bothered.

'This reminds me of that nightclub we went to in Edinburgh,' she said to Hayley. 'Do you remember? It was full of over forties, and we were like only nineteen.'

'Oh god, yes. They were wilder than everyone our age.'

'But some of the guys were still hot.'

'Seriously,' Finlay said. 'Please, don't tell me anymore.'

'You'll be forty in seven years,' Hayley said. 'So don't knock it. Be thrilled she'll still find you hot then.'

'That's not quite what I meant.' Then he weighed the idea. 'But I can live with that.' Except Genevieve would likely be with someone else by then. He swept the thought away and his eyes landed on the scene inside the room. The fifties motel décor was fun, but his dad dressed in a full white Elvis costume, not so much.

'Oh my god… What is he wearing?' Whatever it was, it looked too tight to be decent.

Hayley laughed. 'That's hilarious.'

The suit was cut low and a large medallion dangled at his chest.

'Your dad's a bit of a looker too,' Genevieve said. 'It definitely runs in your family.'

'Have you got some kind of daddy kink going on?'

She chuckled and play slapped his arm. 'No. Of course not. But I've always liked older men.'

'How much older?'

'Five years is fine.' She winked at him and he frowned, but before he could speak, he spotted someone waving furiously at him. Liz, his dad's partner. He clamped his mouth shut, not wanting to risk laughing or making a comment that could be misconstrued. She was dressed as Marilyn Monroe in a red body-hugging dress with a long white stole. Her hair was bleached for the occasion and she smiled with huge red lips, her long dangly earrings flying about and glinting in the light as she greeted people.

'Wow, that's an impressive outfit,' Genevieve said.

'Hmm,' Finlay muttered. 'This is why he's not with my mum anymore. He likes flashy women.' His mum was glamorous but she wasn't showy with it. 'But Liz is nice. I don't mean to sound horrible. She just likes to outshine everyone with her outfits. It wouldn't surprise me if this whole party was her idea. I don't think Dad is into rock 'n' roll especially. He was born in the sixties, so maybe that's the link.'

'Looks more like the fifties to me,' Genevieve said.

'Yeah, true.'

'It was definitely Liz's idea,' Hayley said. 'I think she wanted an excuse to wear that dress.'

'Ah, here they are. My bonnie offspring,' Finlay's dad said, throwing his arms wide. 'And you both look wonderful.' He kissed Hayley fondly then threw his arms around Finlay, giving him a bear hug. 'And who's this lovely lady?'

'Genevieve,' Finlay said.

'I can't keep up with all his girlfriends.'

'*All* my girlfriends? I haven't had that many.'

'Dad,' Hayley said. 'They're engaged.'

'Ha!' He clapped Finlay's back. 'Don't I know it? Doesn't waste time, this lad.'

Finlay held his tongue. Maybe if he spent more time getting to know people before jumping into engagements, he might not be in this mess, but he said nothing.

'Well, it's nice to meet this one,' Liz said. 'We didn't get to meet the last one.'

'Yeah,' Finlay said, leaning in and kissing her cheek. Her perfume was so overpowering he pulled away, feeling like it was clinging to him.

'You look quite stunning,' Liz said to Genevieve. 'And hopefully you'll stick around a bit longer than the last one.' Her voice was low and her tone cheeky, but Finlay ground his teeth. *Nope*, Genevieve wasn't sticking around either. And every interaction he had here this afternoon was going to make him look even more ridiculous than he already was.

'I think I've seen you somewhere before,' Liz added, frowning at Genevieve. 'Are you on the telly?'

'She's the Vieve,' Hayley said. 'Have you seen her on the socials?'

'Oh yeah. I love watching you. That's why I recognise you. I love the cooking ideas and the make-up. Of course I'm not single, but you're so relatable and easy to listen to.'

'Thanks.'

'What will you do now you're engaged? You can't promo the single life anymore, can you?'

'I, um, yeah... I'll need to think of a new angle.'

'Sounds a bit of a pain. Maybe you'd be better ditching this one in the name of the Vieve.' She burst out laughing and clapped Finlay's arm. 'I'm joking of course. Don't look so worried.'

'Me? I'm not worried,' he said. But his chest constricted like someone was tightening a belt around it. Genevieve would be ditching him sooner than they knew.

After breaking away from Liz, Finlay made his way into the room with Genevieve and Hayley, stopping to chat to some familiar people. Hayley was much better at remembering who everyone was than him, so he was happy to hang back and let her rattle on. Genevieve was well-practised at social occasions too and chipped in with comments and asides.

On a table near the bar was a large collection of glasses beside bottles of prosecco and jugs of orange juice. Finlay would be sticking to the latter today. As the designated driver, he had to, and he also didn't want to risk prosecco again. Not after the last time. He didn't want to return to Glenbriar and discover they'd met a minister who'd married them on the spot – or some other similar mishap.

'I'll get some drinks,' he said, recalling the party at the Harringtons when servers had milled around with trays, making sure no one ever had an empty glass. This way wasn't as convenient but it was safer and probably more economical.

He got both Genevieve and Hayley a glass of prosecco. Genevieve eyed it with a half amused look as he handed it to her.

'It's ok,' he murmured, holding up his glass of orange juice. 'I'm on this.'

'Just as well. You never know where we might end up otherwise.'

'The registry office?' He clinked his glass against hers.

She raised an eyebrow. 'I was thinking prison.'

He chuckled and Hayley turned to look at him. 'What are you two up to?'

'Nothing,' he said innocently.

They mingled some more, chatting to old friends of his dad's and meeting some of their children – children who were his age and had children of their own. People he'd apparently met when they were little, but he didn't remember. Something gnawed inside him, pulling at his gut. This was what life should look like for people in their early thirties, if that was what they wanted. They had partners and families, owned detached houses and drove MPVs. Some of them complained about the dull domesticity of their lives, moaned about how their existence now revolved around their kids, and fretted about whether they'd be home before the little ones had a meltdown. They didn't exactly make it sound idyllic, but Finlay wanted a piece of it. That was where he saw himself now, only he wasn't even close. The claps on the back and the congratulations on his engagement may as well be a punch in the face. In two weeks' time, he was leaving for Dubai. He didn't expect to meet a partner out there and by the time he got back to Scotland, he'd be thirty-six. Guys didn't have a body clock quite the same as women but it didn't stop him feeling like a failure. If only he could channel some of Oliver's feelings on the matter. He took a sip of his drink, pretty certain he could never generate Oliver levels of indifference to relationships.

Someone wolf-whistled and Finlay became aware of a ringing sound. On a stage at the end of the room, his dad was tapping a glass with his spoon. Behind him were some lurid blow-up guitars surrounding posters of Elvis.

'Just to say thank you to you all for coming,' his dad said, beaming around. 'It's almost time for food but before that I'd like to give an extra special thank you to Liz.' He took her hand, inviting her onto the stage with him. Finlay held his breath; it looked like the back of her dress might split as she raised her knees high to clamber up the steep step. Liz smiled and waved like she was embarrassed, though she was clearly loving the attention as she winked at friends in the crowd.

'Liz has organised all this,' his dad continued. 'And it's wonderful. Thank you so much.' He pulled her into a clinch and kissed her. Finlay took a large swig of orange juice. This was something he didn't want to watch: Elvis kissing Marilyn Monroe, especially when Elvis was his dad.

He was glad when his dad announced the buffet was open.

'Your favourite thing,' Genevieve said. 'The all-you-can-eat buffet.'

'One of my favourite things.' Right now, she topped the list. She caught his eye and he winked. The look on her face told him she was wondering if he meant her.

'Tutti Frutti' was blasting from the speakers and some of the kids were on the stage dancing and pretending to play the blowup guitars.

A black and white chequered tablecloth, reminiscent of the floors in a fifties diner, adorned the table and Finlay lifted a plate.

'Liz has really outdone herself this time,' he said, running his gaze over the rockin' burgers, rollin' tacos, rockstar hot dogs, twist-and-shout fries in retro-style paper cones and the shake, rattle, and roll salad bar. 'This is pretty cool.' He loaded his plate with a little bit of everything. Maybe he was lucky or maybe it was all the sport he did, but he'd always been able to eat as much as he liked without any change in his weight.

'How long has your dad been with Liz?' Genevieve asked, lifting a mini chicken taco and spooning out some salsa from a guitar-shaped bowl.

'About four years, I think.'

'And will they get married?'

'I don't know. Mum and Dad divorced twenty years ago. They've both had other partners since then, but neither of them seems to want to get married again. Having said that, Liz has been around the longest.'

'Your mum doesn't seem to mind being on her own. She likes her holidays with friends and she said she tries The Vieve's single girl recipes.'

'Yeah.' He let out a sigh. 'I think she enjoys the freedom but I know she gets lonely sometimes.' When she was feeling like that, she badgered him about grandchildren, telling him how she'd love to look after them and have them fill her days. Maybe one day he'd oblige. He knew she did the same thing to Hayley at times too and they'd both moaned about it to each other. What else could they do? It wasn't like they could spring grandchildren out of a hole in the ground. And Mum wasn't mean about it. She just wanted what she thought would make them all happy. No doubt it would, but it wasn't happening anytime soon. Not from him anyway.

When everyone was stuffed with food, Liz called them all to order with another wolf whistle. With the help of one of her daughters, she pulled back a screen to reveal a masterpiece of a birthday cake.

'Happy Birthday, Sam, darling.' She kissed Finlay's dad on the cheek and pulled him over.

The room hushed as Sam made his way to the spectacular cake.

'That's impressive,' Genevieve said.

It really was. Finlay joined her in pulling out his phone and taking a picture of it. The cake rested on a black fondant base that resembled a stage and on top was an edible replica of an electric guitar, its body intricately detailed and shimmering with metallic silver and gold accents.

Around the guitar-shaped cake were vinyl records made of what looked like chocolate. Edible microphones poised at various angles surrounded it.

'All together now,' Liz said, and she held out her hands like a conductor. Everyone began singing 'Happy Birthday' while Finlay's dad smiled with slightly redder than usual cheeks.

'Thank you, thank you,' he said. 'I don't want to waffle on, as speeches are boring at the best of times, but this has been a quite fantastic party, and it's wonderful to have you all here. Let me raise a glass to all my favourites.' He picked up his beer glass and held it high. 'Here's to us,' he said. 'Who's like us?'

'Damn few and they're aw deid,' Finlay said.

'Good lad.' His dad grinned and knocked back his beer.

Genevieve smiled at him. Was she remembering him saying that at her parents' party not so long ago? What else did she remember? He couldn't recall clearly exactly what had passed between them, and he probably never would.

'I'm not sure where to cut this,' his dad said, lifting the knife. 'It feels wrong to butcher it.'

'Just go for it,' Liz said.

He stabbed the knife into the guitar part of the cake and the room erupted in cheers and applause.

'I hope it tastes good,' Hayley said, appearing at Finlay's side.

'There's enough of it,' Genevieve said.

'You think?' Finlay winked at her. 'Looks like a wee snack to me. I'll polish that off, no sweat.'

Genevieve half rolled her eyes at Hayley but it was obvious she was trying not to laugh too much. And it felt good. They were like a real couple, relaxed and safe in the knowledge they had each other.

Only they didn't.

Finlay's dad carefully sliced further into the cake, revealing layers of chocolate and vanilla sponge.

'Let's get some of that and check the old man is feeling ok.'

Finlay collected plates as they approached the table.

'Who made the cake?' Genevieve asked Liz.

'A lovely friend of mine. She's won prizes for her cakes several times.'

'I can see why. It's incredible.'

'I can give you her details.' Liz pulled out her phone. 'She does wedding cakes too and I'm sure she'd love to do one for the two of you. And she's very reasonably priced.'

'Um... Thanks.' Genevieve took out her phone and Liz sent her the info. Another pointless moment. There wouldn't be a wedding. Finlay was on the verge of saying the marriage wouldn't be taking place for a long time because of his Dubai commitments, but why bother? It was all compounding the lie.

Dance music started up as Finlay chatted to his dad until Liz dragged him away. Soon she and his dad were bopping on the floor with wild movements, like they were having the time of their lives.

'Still the king of the dad dance,' Finlay said.

Hayley chuckled. 'Right, my beauties. I love you both so much.' She gave both him and Genevieve a hug like she was leaving for a week. 'But I'm not hanging around cramping your style. I'm off to find some hot teddy boy to dance with.'

'Shall we dance too?' Finlay asked.

'In a minute. Can we get some air first?' Genevieve fanned her face. 'It's really warm in here and I've just seen a message I really should look at.'

'Sure.'

They walked outside where some picnic tables had been set on a grass verge overlooking the wide mouth of the River Tay. Two bridges were visible further up: the rail bridge and the road bridge. Genevieve walked to the edge and leaned on the railings. Finlay followed.

'What's the message?'

'It's James Charlton,' she said with a sigh.

'Who? Isn't he the guy you used to date? Or pretend to date?'

Genevieve's cheeks reddened slightly. 'Yeah, but that's all done with. He wants to meet me about a contract with Duchan Fayre.' She stared at her phone. 'This could be huge. It's a chance to design and promote my own range with them. He says he's been thinking about it for a long time and we could be the perfect partnership.'

'Right. In business or...'

'Oh, just business, for sure.' Her eyes sparkled as she looked at her phone. 'This is so exciting. What a chance.'

A green monster was writhing in Finlay's stomach. Once he was gone, would Genevieve take up with James again? Maybe she'd only been pretending with him before but who knew what might happen now? Finlay wasn't exactly in a position to do much about it. While she and James were here working on contracts, he'd be thousands of miles away – probably forgotten.

'Congratulations,' he said, and he took her in his arms. He wouldn't spoil this moment for her with jealousy. The world righted itself for a moment. Everything was good when they were together. He loved the very masculine feeling of being bigger than her and able to support her physically. But another part of him wanted to shrink into her arms and let her soothe him, tell him everything would work out and that they would be fine. 'I hope it's everything you've ever dreamed of,' he said quietly.

'Thank you.'

Only it wouldn't be anywhere near what he was dreaming of.

He stroked her back, holding her close, drowning in her beautiful rose perfume, then placed a lingering kiss on the side of her neck. 'I'll always love...' His voice faltered, and he stopped himself from adding 'you'. She seemed to freeze in his arms. 'Looking back on these days.'

'Me too,' she said. 'Me too.'

Chapter Twenty-Three

Genevieve

Genevieve adjusted the camera angle, ensuring that the soft glow of the down lights illuminated the scene in Finlay's kitchen just right. With him gone early to the Highland Games, she had a short while to do this before she picked up her granny. She tapped the record button on her phone.

'Hello, everyone. I hope you've got the sunshine today like we do. I thought I'd pop on and show you how to make a delicious meal, perfect for summer, when you're not going to be in all day, but you want to come home to something without having to think too much.'

She wanted to do this for Finlay and herself anyway, so why not record it? Made sense.

'You don't need any fancy equipment except a slow cooker, which most people have kicking around. It's actually an under-used piece in my house, but I'm getting into it more and more.'

She flashed a bright smile at the camera as she lifted the first bowl of ingredients. 'We'll start with some seasonal vegetables.'

She tossed them in. 'I've got bell peppers, juicy cherry tomatoes, and mixed herbs. Like with all my recipes, you can adapt them to your own taste. I've already chopped the tomatoes and given them a really light fry. I find if you don't do that first, they can come out bitter.'

She pulled up the next bowl. 'Next, we'll add some protein to our dish,' Genevieve continued, reaching for a pack of tender chicken thighs. 'I love using chicken thighs in slow cooker recipes because they stay moist and tender, soaking up all the flavours of the dish, but you can use other meat, or meat substitute if you're vegetarian or vegan.'

She seasoned the chicken with a blend of aromatic spices. 'I'm just using a little paprika, cumin, and garlic. Not too much. It smells amazing.' She breathed it in. 'Layer up the ingredients like this,' Genevieve explained, arranging the vegetables and chicken.

'All we need now is the stock which I have ready in the jug.' She carefully poured it over the ingredients. 'Now, put the lid on. I'll set the slow cooker to low and that's it. I've got some big news coming soon...' The contract with Duchan Fayre was already in tentative negotiations. She didn't want to say too much as it would be blatantly obvious she wasn't planning on going to Dubai if she was arranging photoshoots and cooking shows at Duchan. But it occupied her mind better than focusing on the growing chasm in her heart when she thought about Finlay leaving. 'Watch this space. I'm off to enjoy my day and when I come back I'll have something tasty waiting. If you've invested in my range of storage boxes, this is a perfect recipe to store leftovers and reuse for lunches or another dinner during the week. I'll pop the recipe in the comments. Let me know your thoughts and remember to hit like if you enjoyed watching.'

With a wave, Genevieve ended the recording. Right, that was part one of her day sorted. She went onto her laptop, found the recipe she'd typed earlier and pasted it into the comments box beneath the video. Already there were some watchers and a couple of comments. Most people who followed her were friendly but there was always the possibility of a mean comment. She clicked them open and checked. Thankfully nothing bad.

'Right, Mitzi,' she said. 'Let's go get granny and we'll see how Finlay gets on at the games.'

Crunch time was fast approaching, and she had to make the most of every second with him. Making that film was a distraction, if nothing else, something to fill the lonely moments without him. Something she'd soon have to get used to.

Half an hour later, Genevieve manoeuvred her granny's wheelchair through the crowd in the Highland Games field in Glenbriar. The surface was uneven and already well-trodden, though it was early days yet. Mitzi toddled along behind.

'I can't believe I've never been here,' Genevieve said, looking across the arena. A few people on horses passed them by, wearing smart dressage jackets. All around, generators hummed from the food stalls and lucky dips. 'It's quite an event.'

'It's grown out of all proportion since I was last here,' her granny said. 'That was years ago. There was none of this nonsense.' She pointed at a shoot-the-duck stall lined with rows of cuddly toys. 'It was more about the dancing and the competitions.'

Genevieve's shoulders were a little shaky. She wanted to blame it on the exertion of pushing her gran around the bumpy field, but it wasn't that. Her whole body was gripped with an almost paralysing sensation, it was forcing her to take one step at a time and only make the most superficial conversation. If she thought too deeply she'd scream. This was the end and nothing could change that. No superficial films or chitchat. Finlay was competing in the tug-of-war today, then late tomorrow he was flying to Dubai. She was fudging around all the questions about whether she was packed and ready to go too. The game was up.

Everyone believed she was going. But she wasn't.

Nausea rose inside her at the thought.

Her parents had made it worse, or better in their eyes, by inviting her brother and sister over for the weekend. They were desperate for her siblings to meet Finlay and to give him and her a memorable send off. She cringed. This was the brief calm before the shitstorm hit good and proper.

'We're meeting them next to the tractor display,' Genevieve said, checking her phone. 'Rafe's just messaged. They're all waiting.'

'It's over there, I think,' her gran said. 'Near that big green banner thing.'

'I see it.' Genevieve pushed her forward. The crowd parted to let them through and a smiling man in a pale blue shirt and tan chinos waved and approached them. Genevieve raised a hand to her big brother. He looked tanned and healthy as he always did and she imagined how Hayley would fake swoon if she saw him.

'Hello.' He pounced down and hugged their gran. 'You're looking well.'

'Apart from the gammy hip, all's good.'

'You're a trouper, gran, so you are.' He straightened up and beamed at Genevieve. 'And hello gorgeous little sister number two. Congratulations to you.' He pulled her in for a hug.

'I hope she sticks at it a bit longer than you.' Gran prodded him in the leg.

'Yes, yes. Let's hope.' He pulled a please-help-me-get-out-of-this-convo face at Genevieve. After tomorrow, his divorce would be old news. She'd take the family-scandal crown off his head and have it on for god knew how long.

'Is Cress here too?'

'She's over there with Mum and Dad. She and Tina have some big news too.'

'Oh?' Genevieve spotted her older sister alongside her partner, and as Cressida turned to them, Genevieve's jaw dropped. 'She's pregnant?'

'Wonderful,' Gran said. 'Though is it a stupid question to ask who the father is?'

'Maybe don't ask that,' Rafe said.

Genevieve pushed Gran towards them and Cressida hurried over to hug her and Genevieve.

'You kept that quiet.' Genevieve pointed at the bump.

'Much like your engagement and the fact you're leaving the country tomorrow.' Cressida gave her a mock stern look. 'All a bit sudden, isn't it?'

She gave a little shrug, hoping it looked like coy embarrassment.

'Wait until you meet him,' her mother said. 'And you'll understand why it was sudden. He's very handsome and just the nicest man.'

'I still haven't met him,' Gran said with a little pout. 'Though I feel like I already know him from the wonderful video of him proposing.'

'I heard about that,' Cressida said. 'But by the time I went to see it, it had gone from your page.'

'It was a mistake putting it live. He's a teacher, so he doesn't want too much on social media,' Genevieve said.

'Ah, that explains it.'

Rafe had broken away and was chatting with another man. Genevieve's heart stopped when her eyes landed on him. James Charlton. *Shit.*

Cressida rubbed her chin. 'How do you think you'll like Dubai?'

'Oh, I, um... I'm not sure.' Genevieve frowned, still eyeing James.

'Hey, Gen,' Rafe said. 'Look who's here.'

'Hi.' James gave her a smile. 'Nice to see you again after all the emails of the last few weeks.'

'Oh, yes.'

'I hear you're going to Dubai,' he said.

Bloody hell! She'd happily strangle her brother... not that he'd understand why.

'I am.'

'I didn't realise. I'm not sure how that'll work with the contract. I assumed you'd be here.'

Genevieve fiddled with the button on Mitzi's lead. 'I need to work that out.'

'It'll be restricting to schedule events if we're dependent on flights. And costly for you.'

Shit!

'I... er...'

'Don't worry about it just now,' James said. 'We can chat about it another time. Remotely I guess if you're not going to be here.'

Her cheeks heated. How could she admit she wasn't going at all. This was just another game... Exactly like the one she'd played with him. He'd walked away from it and now Finlay would do the same. Her heart hiccupped, threatening to crack her chest open. She buried the sensation deep. *Must be strong. Don't let anything show.*

'I guess,' she said.

'I only found out just now from Rafe you were off to Dubai.' James gave a little shrug. 'In your emails, you agreed to several dates. Some of them are quite soon. This could be tricky. But leave it with me.' He gave them all a friendly wave.

'Do you think he'll pull the plug on it?' Genevieve said, heat and panic rising inside her. Should she go after him and confess? What if he shut it down immediately? Or if he discovered her engagement conveniently ended just in time to take up the contract, would he guess this was her faking it again? Did it matter if he did? Other than adding to the personal humiliation she would suffer anyway.

Rafe patted her upper arm. 'There'll be other opportunities.'

But this one was so perfect.

'When do I get to meet Finlay in person?' Grandma asked from behind.

'Well...' Genevieve pulled out her phone, still in two minds about going after James. 'He'll be with his team. I'm not sure when he can get away, but I'll message him and let him know where we are in case he's free.' She wrote a text but she couldn't send it. All of this had to stop right now. In fact, while they were all here, she could tell them it was finished, then save her contract. She wasn't engaged, she wasn't going to Dubai and that was that.

The text lay flat on the screen unsent and Genevieve stared at it.

GENEVIEVE: Hey, we're at the tractor stand if you're free to meet my gran, my brother and my sister. xx

'Send it then,' Cressida said, leaning over and tapping the send button before Genevieve could stop her.

Great.

'I have to thank you,' her father said, 'and Finlay too. Thanks to you, Flora MacDonald has agreed to funding a large research programme. She was delighted by the two of you.'

'Oh...' Genevieve smiled. 'That's great. We didn't do much... I mean, it was a fun experience.'

'I bet it was,' Rafe said.

Cressida smacked his arm. 'Don't be rude.'

'I'm not.' He rubbed his elbow like she'd inflicted a painful wound. 'But it wasn't exactly a tough brief. Come visit and test the facilities in my luxury couples' retreat. I can't see why anyone would refuse.'

'Unless they haven't got a partner,' Cressida said. 'Like you.'

'Who says I don't? I'm perfectly happy dating the person I'm dating.'

'And who's that? An imaginary friend? You used to have one of them, didn't you?'

Genevieve caught her mum's eye as Cressida and Rafe carried on their banter. Hilary was giving Rafe a somewhat disapproving look. She liked to have the perfect family and she'd succeeded in having three good-looking children, even if Genevieve said so herself, but they'd all swerved off the road to perfection. Rafe's divorce and disinterest in settling down was his defect. Cressida was almost perfect, but wanting to carry on working after she had the baby would knock some points off.

The wheels would fall off Genevieve's cart tomorrow evening.

'Listen, I need to go and—'

'Darling, come with me a moment.' Her mum took her arm and led her away before she could finish speaking. 'I want to show you something. You'll like it.' Genevieve couldn't think why she wanted to show her a large red tractor. Or did she want to have a rant about Rafe? Mum didn't often rant but occasionally she let things get the better of her. She'd once told Genevieve he should never have married his ex-wife and that the woman had been rude to her from the start, but she hadn't said anything because she didn't think it was her place.

'What am I supposed to be looking at?'

'Come around this side.' She led her to the other side of the tractor so it blocked them from view of the others. 'I don't really want to show you anything, but I have something I need to ask you. It's worried me a great deal over the past few days. I wasn't sure whether to say anything but I feel I have to.'

'What about?'

'About Finlay.'

'Oh?' Genevieve blinked and turned her gaze to the shiny red paintwork on the tractor's bonnet.

'When I first met him you told me he was a brother of one of your friends, but you didn't say who.'

'Does it matter?'

'Maybe not. But when Flora came around to talk to your father about the deal, she told me he was Hayley's brother.'

'Yes, I know that.' Genevieve furrowed her brow. Where was her mum going with this?

Her mum ran her hands through her neat caramel-toned hair, so similar to her own, only shorter and a little less glossy. She was perfectly turned out for the occasion in dark brown jeans, hunter boots and a pink shirt, but the outward display didn't fit with the turmoil in her expression.

'Did you also know that only a month or so ago he was engaged to someone else? Someone who's also a friend of yours.'

'Yes. Of course I do.'

Her mum shook her head. 'I like Finlay a lot, please don't mistake me, he seems like a delightful man, but everyone keeps saying how sudden this engagement is. I feel I can't not ask you.'

'Ask me what?'

'If this is all genuine?'

'Why wouldn't it be?' Her heart was pounding a tattoo in her chest.

'I don't mean your feelings aren't genuine. Of course I can see that they are. You obviously care deeply for him and the fact you're willing to sell the house and leave Mitzi with us tells me you're serious about him. But are you sure he feels the same?'

Genevieve clenched her teeth inside her mouth. How could she answer that truthfully? Because she wasn't sure at all. There had been one moment at his dad's party. One heart-stopping moment when she'd thought he was going to say he loved her. Then he'd said something else and the conversation had moved on. They'd never returned to it and maybe that spoke volumes. Finlay had played his part, but that was all he'd done...Wasn't it?

'Genevieve? I'm sorry if I've said something awful. I'm sure he loves you deeply. It certainly seems like he does but I have to ask myself why he'd get engaged to you so soon after someone else. And to a friend of his ex. It seems like the kind of thing someone would do to get revenge and while I want to believe that isn't the case, I also don't want you to get hurt. Oh dear.' She rubbed her forehead.

This was exactly what Elise had said from the start.

'I can see I've hurt you by even suggesting it,' her mum said. 'Please. Forget I said it. Obviously, my fears are groundless. I just couldn't keep it to myself after what happened to Rafe. I can't stop thinking that I could have stopped a lot of heartbreak if I'd told him how his ex-wife treated me right from the start. It felt wrong to say anything, so I didn't and now I've done the opposite and hurt you. I'm so sorry.'

'Don't be.' Genevieve glanced around, willing the tears to stay back. 'I actually couldn't tell you how Finlay really feels about me.' They'd been almost living together for the past two weeks. The days were comfortable and fun. He'd gone off on some cycle runs while she'd worked. They'd even gone running together a couple of times. They'd cooked, cleaned, shown viewers around and everything felt great. At night they shared a bed, came together and enjoyed each other's bodies, kissed, made love and cuddled all night. She'd never had a relationship like it, but ever since day one, it had been pretend. He was just playing the game and enjoying the benefits. Just as James had until it had run its course.

'I'm confused.' Her mum put her hand on Genevieve's shoulder and squeezed it. 'What are you saying? That Finlay hasn't told you how he feels?'

'He hasn't.'

'But... That's just because he's a man, right? And sometimes men don't know how to communicate their feelings properly. It's not because... Well, you don't think he's really doing this to get revenge on someone, do you?'

'No.' She tried to wade through the brain fog descending on her from every angle. It wasn't that. That had never been a factor. It might have inadvertently had that effect, but Finlay wasn't a revenge kind of guy. He'd never have set out to intentionally hurt Elise. *Just like he'd never hurt me.* He'd gone along with every aspect of her plan and never wavered. The reason she felt so shit was because she loved him and he didn't return her feelings. That wasn't new. She'd fancied Finlay for years from afar but she'd never allowed it to bother her. Only that was impossible now. She'd sampled too much of what life could be like. She'd enjoyed it too much. Going back to being immune to it wouldn't work because the fever had got too deep a hold.

'Let's go and find him,' her mum said. 'You can talk to him. I'm sure everything will be fine.'

'No. It won't be. I'm not going to Dubai.'

'But Genevieve, you can't back out of that now.'

'I can. I have to.'

'Is this because of what James was saying to you?'

'Kind of. And I... need to sell the house.'

'The estate agents can handle that and I'm sure you'll work something out with James.'

'And there's Mitzi.'

'Of course you'll miss her but we'll take very good care of her. You don't need to worry about her. Now, come on, let's go and find Finlay. Nothing can be settled until we at least talk to him.'

Genevieve followed her mum but her mind was racing and her stomach roiling. Why had she thought this was a good option? How could she squeeze her way out of this without losing all credibility with everyone?

Chapter Twenty-Four

Finlay

Finlay rolled his shoulders and his neck, easing out the tension. He needed to be in fighting form, as the competition was starting in just over an hour. The competitors' tent was full of bulky men in wrestler vests, girls in Highland dance kilts and jackets, some people dressed for equestrian sports and various others in kilts or shooting gear. A hot musty smell filled the air, making it hard to breathe.

This wasn't exactly the way he'd have chosen to spend his last day with Genevieve, but that was because she hadn't even been on his radar at the start of the summer. Now she was... And not just on his radar. She was everything. And that was insane because she'd given him very strict instructions on how this was to go.

When he'd been engaged to Elise, he'd held back and had doubts. It had always felt a little too convenient and the outcome hadn't been wholly surprising – irritating and insulting, but frustratingly predictable. Genevieve had hit like a bolt from the blue, taking him off guard and rocking his world.

'Hey. You ok, mate?' Brann clapped Finlay's cheek in that funny way he had. Somehow he managed to match the tough warrior look with playful cheer and almost dad-like affection for his teammates. In fact, he was the father of the team, though he couldn't be that much older than Finlay.

'I'm good.'

'Aidan said you're off to Dubai tomorrow? That's quite a move.'

'Yup.' It was enough to be thinking about without Genevieve in the equation.

'I hadn't realised. I was going to ask you to be deputy leader for next year and run the warm-up sessions. You'd be great at that with your teaching background. But I guess you won't be able to.'

'Sorry, mate.' Pity too because it sounded right up his alley.

'Let's make this a games to remember then.'

'Yeah. I'm on it.'

Brann clapped his upper arms. 'Good lad. My daughter follows your girlfriend on Instagram.' He winked. 'I can see why you're distracted.'

Finlay's jaw stiffened. 'Your daughter? What age is she?' Surely he didn't have kids old enough to be on social media? What exactly had she seen on there?

That was a part of life with Genevieve he wouldn't miss.

'She's fifteen. And you're her P.E. teacher.'

'Oh god,' Finlay groaned. How many more of his pupils had seen his life prostituted on social media?

Brann laughed. 'Don't worry, mate. She thinks you're cool. Sounds like the kids will miss you now you've left.'

'If you say so. Sorry, I've not been a hundred per cent recently. I need to get my arse in gear.'

'I'm happy to kick it in the right direction,' Brann said with a smirk and gave him the thumbs up.

Finlay grinned back. 'Thanks,' he muttered. He needed to go for a walk and loosen up before the first round. Picking up his phone from his backpack, he checked his messages and spotted one from Genevieve asking her to come and meet her family. Was that really necessary? In a few short hours none of this would matter. But her pull was too strong. He wanted to see her.

People had left possessions lying everywhere, so he left his backpack too, but removed his wallet just in case. He didn't need that going missing the day before he left the country.

Outside, the air was muggy. A good crack of lightning was needed to freshen the air, though it could wait until later before it showed face. He didn't fancy the match in a rainstorm. One year, the weather had been so wet the competition had almost turned into a mud wrestling event. The ground had been so slippery they'd all fallen over. Not an experience he wanted to repeat. Plus, he wasn't sure he could afford the laundry bill for having his kilt cleaned again. It had been ridiculously expensive. He glanced down at it and ran his hand over the McBride tartan.

This would be mothballed in his mum's house for who knew how long. She thought she was putting it away for his wedding, perhaps hoping he'd be home in the summer next year to tie the knot. She'd probably even bought a hat, maybe a whole outfit.

'Oh god,' he groaned aloud. How many people would be let down by this farce?

Not far off, he spotted the tractor area and his eyes landed on Geoff Harrington. He was with a group of people Finlay didn't recognise but he guessed right away that one of them was Genevieve's sister. She had such a resemblance to her mum and Genevieve, though her hair was darker. She was sporting a very pronounced baby bump. A strong desire to see Genevieve like that surged through Finlay... But only if the baby was his.

As he got closer, he guessed the younger man next to Geoff was Rafe, Genevieve's brother. He had the family resemblance too and the same easy charm in his eyes that his dad had. He leaned over, talking to an older woman in a wheelchair. Where was Genevieve? It seemed odd approaching without her being there, but why not?

'Hi.' He sauntered up to them with a casual wave.

'Finlay,' Geoff said. 'Great to see you. Let me introduce you to everyone. This is my son, Rafe. My daughter, Cressida, and her partner, Tina, and this is my mother-in-law, Jeanette.'

'Nice to meet you all,' Finlay said.

Rafe shook his hand and the others gave waves of acknowledgement.

'About time too,' Jeanette said. 'I thought I wasn't going to see you in the flesh before you jetted off to the other side of the world.'

'Yeah. Sorry. It's been a crazy busy time.'

'Why Dubai?' Rafe asked.

'I've got a teaching contract out there. It's good money and a great experience.' He didn't add that most of the teachers he'd be working with would be about ten years younger than him, fresh out of college and ready for an adventure before they came back home to settle down. He had a knack for doing things all wrong.

'Sounds great,' Rafe said. 'I sometimes do business over there. Very interesting place.'

'I'm like Mitzi,' Jeanette said. 'And it's too hot for me, but Genevieve loves beaches, so I'm sure she'll enjoy it.' She smiled up at Finlay and he forced himself to smile back. Genevieve loved beaches. Her job was portable. Of course, there was Mitzi to consider, but was there a possibility they could make this move real? If Genevieve could part with Mitzi, they could maybe pull this off. Assuming she wanted to. Should he ask her? Maybe he could cut the contract to a year. Would they allow that? Or was he getting carried away in a fantasy even bigger than the one he was living in?

Am I so desperate to save one out of my three engagements?

'Here's Genevieve,' Geoff said.

Finlay took one look at her and knew something was up. Her expression was a poor attempt at that aloof face she put on to cover her true feelings. This time, he saw it for what it was. Her lips were too pinched, her cheeks too red and her eyes too bright.

'Hey,' he said.

Her eyes widened even more and she stumbled over her words before settling on, 'Hi.'

Hilary smiled broadly, almost a little falsely, and chivvied her daughter towards Finlay.

'Thank goodness you're here,' she said. 'Genevieve is desperate to talk to you.'

'Are you?' He glanced at her, trying to extract information from her telepathically – maybe his mum would manage, but it wasn't working for him.

'I... er...'

'Yes. She does. Go for a walk and talk.' Hilary almost pushed Genevieve into him. 'It's very important. She's desperate to go to Dubai. Let's not let any miscommunication get in the way.'

'What?' Finlay frowned but attempted to shrug off his confusion with a smile.

'It's fine,' Genevieve said with another poor attempt at a serene expression.

'No, I insist,' Hilary said. 'Go and have a chat.'

'Sure,' Finlay said. 'Though I don't have much time before the first round.'

'It can wait.' Genevieve flicked her hair over her shoulders. Maybe a month ago he'd have been fooled by her show of nonchalance, but not now.

'No, it can't,' he said. 'Let's go.' Painfully aware of everyone's eyes on him, he hooked his arm around her shoulder and led her away. 'What's wrong? What did your mum mean about miscommunication?'

'Oh god, Finlay.' Genevieve stopped and put her face in her hands.

He gave her a moment, then took her hands and parted them. 'I don't understand.'

'I tried to tell her I couldn't go to Dubai.'

'Why?'

'Because she was worried about us. She's been talking to Flora MacDonald and Flora thought you might have proposed to me to get revenge on Elise.'

'Interesting... I don't remember the exact events of that night but I'm pretty sure that wasn't the reason.'

'I know that and I told her. Then she said she thought it was obvious how much I liked you because I'd given up the house to go to Dubai with you...' She looked at him helplessly. 'Then I just kind of told her the story I was going to tell her on Monday. But she didn't believe me. She thinks I really want to go but all that's stopping me is... Uncertainty and this contract with Duchan Fayre.'

Finlay raked his hand through his hair. 'But how does she know about that? I thought you were keeping it quiet until I was gone.'

'I was, but James came over and was talking to us. Rafe told him I was going to Dubai, so now that contract is in jeopardy because he's gone off thinking I won't be around to do the photoshoots and events.'

'Wow... ok. And...' He needed to know for sure. 'Do you want to go to Dubai with me?'

'No,' she said, and it was very clear. So clear, it felt like she'd doused him in cold water. For someone who struggled to use that word at times, she'd used it now, good and proper.

'Well, you're going to have to suck it up then, because I'm going tomorrow night and I can't change that. I've signed a contract, booked flights. There's accommodation waiting and my job starts in less than a week.'

She looked away and shook her head. 'I know.'

'Listen.' He put his arms around her and tugged her close. 'This feeling is temporary. Just keep powering through. In a week or so it'll be fine.' Who was he trying to kid here? 'You'll be able to keep the contract with Duchan Fayre and you'll love it. It's what you always wanted.'

'Kind of.' She sighed or it might have been a little sob. 'Can't you just dump me? I'll give you the ring and I can go back and tell them it's over.'

'Why do I have to do the dumping? I don't want to look like the bad guy. This was your idea, so that neither of us would look bad.'

'I know. I've messed up.'

'We both did. I shouldn't have proposed in the first place. I mean, who does that?'

She let out a little laugh, and it lifted the ache in his heart for a moment.

'The proposal wouldn't have been so bad if I hadn't filmed the whole thing, so I think I'm still ahead in the messing up race.'

'Hey. We've both made a mess of this,' he said, holding her face in his palms. 'But you know what?'

'What?'

'It's been an enjoyable mess.' He leaned in and kissed her cheek. 'In fact, I've enjoyed this fake engagement a lot more than I enjoyed either of my real ones. And no matter what happens, I'll still care about you. That isn't fake.'

She wrapped her arms tight around his back, almost crushing him, but he didn't mind. The pressure helped relieve the aching tension in every part of him. 'I'm going to miss you.'

'Yeah.' Maybe she would, but not enough to make her want to come with him for real. 'I'll miss you too, but let's stick to the plan, ok?'

'Ok.'

'Listen, I'm sorry to rush off, but I need to go. The first round will be starting soon. Come and watch.'

'I will.'

'I luh… I'll see you later.' He had to go before he said or did something to get him even deeper in than he already was.

He ran back to the tent and found the team warming up. Brann said nothing as Finlay joined in. He couldn't say how grateful he was at not being drawn attention to. Aidan caught him as they made their way on to the field. 'You should have got a sick note,' he said. 'This is a lot for you to think about when you're leaving tomorrow.'

'Yeah. It would have been better if I'd dropped out this year.'

'Let's hope you can leave in a blaze of glory.'

He'd rather leave quietly and not draw any attention to himself, but that didn't seem likely. The team trooped onto the field to cheers and applause. Finlay didn't look towards the crowd. If Genevieve was there, he didn't need to see. She didn't want to come with him and that was that. He was going to Dubai alone. That had always been the plan, so why was he suddenly so cut up about it? Somewhere in a tiny corner of his mind, he'd believed she'd decide to come for real.

Reality was kicking in thick and fast now, and there was no stopping it.

After falling in line with his teammates, he lifted the rope. They took the slack, waiting for the whistle. The scuffle began. It was close and tough going. Eventually they got some momentum and on Brann's shouts they heaved. It was going their way. Finlay clung to the rope. When the whistle blew, he let go with a heavy exhale.

'That was a tough start,' he said.

'Not half,' Aidan agreed.

Finlay blew out a breath and wiped sweat from his forehead. Back in the tent, he grabbed a drink and snuck a look at his phone. A message from Hayley previewed on the screen. He opened it.

*HAYLEY: I just bumped into your grumpy friend in town *eye-roll emoji*. I asked him if he was still ok to take you to the airport tomorrow as I really don't mind doing it and let's face it you and G will get better chat from me, he's so dour. Anyway, he said he was doing it and that was that. I said 'be nice to Genevieve this is a big thing for her' and he gave me this snidey look and said 'she won't be there, will she? So I won't have to be nice'. Then he stormed off. What does he mean she won't be there?*

Finlay threw himself onto the ground next to his backpack with a groan. Oliver! Why had he opened his big mouth? As he stared at the phone, another message appeared.

OLIVER: think I might have put my foot in it with your sister. Are you still pretending to be engaged? I thought that stopped this weekend? Your sister cornered me in town and made some comment about Genevieve. I said she wasn't going with you tomorrow because I thought you'd told them all this weekend. Sorry if I've ruined it. You are telling them, aren't you? You're not keeping the charade going any longer, surely?

Christ, just what he needed. Hayley would hate the idea he'd confided the truth to Oliver and not her, and Oliver would go ballistic if he found out how deep Finlay had got in with Genevieve. He needed to reply quickly.

Hayley first. She'd pester him until he got back to her, even if she was at work, and Saturday was her busiest day.

FINLAY: Don't fret. Oliver probably just winding you up x

The next one to Oliver.

FINLAY: We're telling them tomorrow, but no worries.

No worries for Oliver anyway. Finlay's whole body was being eaten alive by worry mites, but there was nothing he could do except keep going forward. Feel the fear and do it anyway.

The team got to the tug-of-war final but fell in the last round to the Highland Haulers – again. Not exactly the blaze of glory Finlay had hoped for but they'd done their best. Brann high-fived everyone and told them all they were awesome and not to be down about it.

'I'm sorry,' Finlay said to him as he packed his bag. 'I don't think I was on my best form today.'

'Not your fault, mate. We're a team. We've got each other's backs. You hold your head high and enjoy your adventure. Seize the day while you're young and carefree because next thing you know, you'll have two kids hanging off your coattails and not a moment's peace for about eighteen years... make that ever.'

Chance would be a fine thing. 'Thanks.'

Finlay dodged the dinner with Genevieve's family. He was too exhausted and tomorrow was going to be gruelling enough. He thought she'd go, but she messaged, saying she wanted to spend the last night with him and after she'd taken her grandma home, she'd be there. She'd even put food on for him.

His house was empty but smelled delicious. Genevieve's slow cooker was about the only thing in the kitchen apart from some paper plates she'd also left. He lifted the lid and closed his eyes. Delicious. The few remaining items in the house, the bedsheets and his car were all going to his mum's the next day. She'd keep the house key and hand the spare to the estate agent so they could carry on with their business while he was away.

He sat on the balcony with a cold beer, looking out over the river. The sun dipped low, casting a warm golden glow over the rippling water. A slight breeze danced through the air, chasing away the mugginess from earlier. The distant chirrup of birds echoed in the trees. Everything looked more beautiful and home-ly than ever.

When would he next see this? Soon he'd be sitting alone in an apartment prepping schoolwork and enjoying peace – scratch that – being lonely.

The door clicked and Genevieve came in. Moments later, she dropped her bag on the table and took the seat beside him. He didn't look at her.

'The food smells good,' he said, when she didn't speak either. 'That was kind of you to do that.'

'You should take the ring back,' she said.

He turned to her. She was right behind him, holding it out, her face set.

'I don't want it. It's yours now.'

'But Finlay, I can't.'

'Please. If you don't want it, keep it safe somewhere. I don't have anywhere to put it now.'

'Ok.' She slipped it back on and looked at it.

Still not meeting her eye, he put his hand out and covered hers. 'We can still be friends, can't we?'

'Sure,' she said, her voice a little too jolly.

'Good.' He increased his grip. His mum was right. He would have felt much better about going tomorrow if he had someone to hold his hand. But he didn't. He'd reached the end of the road with their little game and he was going it alone. 'Let's eat.'

'Ok... The last supper.'

He nodded. Exactly that.

Chapter Twenty-Five

Genevieve

Genevieve moaned and dug her nails into Finlay's naked back. He held her tight, his toned weight pressing down on her. With ragged breaths, he lowered his head to her upturned face, bringing his lips to hers. His kiss was deep, passionate, and desperate. Genevieve returned it, chasing his tongue, needing to feel him everywhere. Her entire world depended on this. His deep thrusts drove her crazy, exactly the way she liked it, and she wanted to remember how good this felt.

When he kissed her and made love to her like this, it was so easy to believe he loved her as much as she wished he did – as much as she loved him. But sex didn't mean love and love wasn't enough. Not really. Not when love was just a game.

'Oh god, Genevieve,' he groaned, pushing her even higher. When her climax came, she clung to him so tightly she wasn't sure she'd ever let go. Her nails might have scarred him for life. Maybe she subconsciously wanted to leave her mark on him forever. She held him as they both lay spent and breathing fast.

Her heart was so full she could cry, but she held herself together. Just.

Later, as she curled in his arms, when she knew from his breathing he was asleep, she let the tears come. Silently, they trickled from her eyes onto his warm chest. The end had come.

The morning after was a long time coming, as Genevieve couldn't sleep a wink, but it still showed up too fast.

Finlay got up first, showered and dressed in almost silence. Genevieve took her turn and when she was fresh and dressed, she still didn't know what to say. He'd stripped the bed and the place looked dead.

What remained to be said?

Nothing.

She couldn't confess how she felt and send him off to Dubai feeling awful. He didn't need to know. If this was a fun game he was happy with, then so be it.

'Right,' he said in a businesslike tone. 'Everything's packed. I'm going to drive to mum's and unload everything. I guess this is goodbye.'

'I guess.' Her limbs felt heavy and unusually large, making her unsure what to do with them.

'We'll keep in touch.' He placed his hands on either side of her, clutching her upper arms. It steadied her for a moment. 'Yeah?'

'Of course.'

'And I look forward to the reels showing how you're getting over the breakup using the awesome girl power you have.'

She recognised the attempt to lighten the mood but smiling wasn't coming easy; her jaw had jammed. All she could do was stare into his eyes, the face she'd grown so used to and associated with so much fun and laughter. 'I'll do my best.'

'Good.' He dipped in and kissed her cheek. 'You keep being the amazing "Vieve".'

'I guess you won't miss being caught on film all the time.'

'Ha. That's true, though the risk kept me on my toes.'

The smile finally found its way to her lips, though it didn't filter into her heart. Like cool water was spreading through her veins, her insides chilled and she breathed slowly, welcoming back serene Genevieve. She was calm, cool and collected, and could handle this situation. The feelings she'd set free with Finlay over the past month would get locked up again.

'Well, good luck,' she said. 'You can let me know when you arrive. Hopefully the accommodation is good. If the facetime restrictions have been lifted, you can give me a call. Just don't do it from the beach or anywhere that'll make me jealous, especially if it's chucking it down here.'

His expression slipped momentarily and he looked almost taken aback at how well she was handling this. He blinked, then nodded. 'Noted,' he said. 'And you can let me know how the contract goes at Duchan Fayre.'

She drew in a long, slow breath and looked at him, then put her arms around his neck and hugged him. He put his hands on her back, but before he could pull her too close, she moved out of his hold and patted his arm. 'I'll go and let you get on your way. Have a safe flight.'

Without looking back, she darted out of the flat, down the stairs, and into her car. *Just drive and breathe.* She'd managed the first bit. The worst bit. Telling people they'd split up couldn't top this, could it? Tears would come. They were close, but she kept driving towards her house, swallowing back all the thoughts about Finlay, the missed opportunity at Duchan Fayre and everything else. She wanted to find the off-switch and give herself a break from her brain and her emotions.

Her house was cold and even the familiar ordered nature of the well-placed cushions wasn't enough to soothe her. Mitzi's basket lying empty by the sofa forced the tears out. If only she were here, Genevieve would sit and cuddle her, but of course she wasn't. She was at her mum and dad's house and Genevieve was supposed to be going there shortly to make an emotional goodbye. As it was, she'd be going there to tell them she wasn't going anywhere. What had seemed like a good plan all those weeks ago now had more holes than her Vieve range colander.

She stared at her face in the mirror, eyes red and blotchy, tears rolling down her cheeks. What a mess. She used the heel of her hand to push them away and the ring glinted on her finger. What should she do with it? She couldn't keep wearing it. Finlay had told her to look after it, but how could she? Everything about it reminded her of the fun times they'd shared. She laughed through the tears. How absurd it was that he had the ring with him at all that night. How was that even possible?

Fate?

That's what his mum would call it. Except something had gone wrong somewhere.

No point wasting time. This couldn't wait any longer, and Genevieve wanted Mitzi here. Nothing for it but to face the music. She got back in her car and drove. The journey to her parents was lost in a storm of thoughts and a tension headache.

When she arrived, her mum greeted her at the door. Her face was so struck with sadness, it was like looking in a mirror. She dabbed at tears as she welcomed Genevieve in.

'I didn't think this would hit me so hard,' she said. 'But you're my baby. I can't believe you're going so far away and for so long.'

Dad patted her mum's back. 'She'll be fine. It's a great experience.'

Genevieve could hardly breathe or bear to hear another word.

Cressida strolled into the room, nursing a mug of tea and smirking. 'Seriously, Mum. You're acting like she's two and she's going to be stolen from you for several years.'

'Wait until you have yours,' Hilary said. 'Then you'll know exactly how it feels.'

Cressida rolled her eyes at Genevieve in what should have been a sisterly moment of understanding about their mum, but Genevieve didn't react.

'I'm not going to Dubai,' she said and somehow her voice sounded normal, almost too normal and slightly robotic but at least it was working and not choked with emotion, despite the pain in her throat and head.

'What do you mean?' her father said. 'Why not?'

'Mitzi.'

'Oh come, come,' Geoff said, laying his hand on her shoulder. 'I quite understand. But you can come back at Christmas and during the summer. Three years isn't as long as it sounds. Also, wasn't there some talk of passports for dogs?'

'I've told you already, it's too hot there for her,' Genevieve said.

'Mitzi will be fine with us.' Her mum rubbed Genevieve's arm. 'She'll have a fab time with the boys and I'm looking forward to having her.'

'I'm not going,' Genevieve said.

Cressida frowned and gripped her cup. 'What's got into you?'

Genevieve sucked in her lips and looked up at the spotlights, willing her tears to stay back.

'I was never going to Dubai or engaged to Finlay.'

Holding her breath, she half expected a collective gasp, but silence prevailed. Slowly, she moved her gaze around the puzzled faces.

'You split up?' her mum said, almost in a whisper. 'Or... Wait? I don't understand. What happened?'

'We weren't really together. None of this was real. He was drunk when he proposed and didn't mean it. When you were all so happy, I didn't want to confess we'd just been fooling around and I didn't want all my followers thinking I was an idiot. Then when Flora wanted us to go to the retreat, I didn't want to back out in case Dad lost the deal and then we were stuck because if we split up straight after, Flora would think we'd faked it to get the deal and pull out. It all got so messy and now... I just can't pretend anymore.' She gave a little shrug.

Her father's expression was stern. 'I appreciate what you did to get me Flora's backing, but there's still the possibility she'll think we set the whole thing up.'

'I'm sorry.'

'Don't be,' he said, rather absently. 'The whole thing just seems very strange. None of it looked fake to me.'

'Or me,' her mother said. 'In fact, what you told me yesterday seems more like the truth. Are you sure this isn't something you've thought wasn't real, but actually it's what you want deep down?'

Genevieve froze at her mother's words. More truth was in there than she dared confess.

'Is it possible Finlay has similar feelings but neither of you have actually confessed it because you were too busy believing the other thought it was pretend?'

Was that the case? How could it be? 'I don't think so,' she said, though her brain was racked with uncertainty. 'We always knew he was going to Dubai. It was the perfect place to end this non-event. We hardly knew each other before this.'

'Love at first sight, perhaps?' Cressida said.

Genevieve remembered what Finlay had said to Elise not long ago. *'I realised I'd been attracted to Genevieve on some level for a long time and when she invited me to go to the party with her, it was clear she liked me too. Things were so easy between us, there didn't seem any reason to wait any longer.'*

Was there truth in those words?

'What's going on?' Rafe appeared at the door and leaned on the frame. The stance reminded Genevieve so vividly of the way Finlay propped himself in doorways that a fresh wave of tears washed through her. 'Why are you discussing love at first sight? I, for one, am not a fan or a believer.' His tone was light and jokey and he clearly hadn't noticed the grave faces.

'Shh,' Hilary said. 'Things are difficult.'

'Why?' He frowned and made his way into the room. 'I just came to say goodbye to Gen.'

'No need,' she said. 'I'm not going. I was never going. Please don't make me go through it all again.'

'It was all fake apparently,' Cressida said aside to Rafe. 'They got engaged by accident and carried it on to fool one of Dad's investors.'

'Fake?' Rafe pulled a face. 'No way. You don't expect me to believe that?'

'Believe it.' Genevieve said.

'Nothing is fake,' he said. 'Even fakes are real. They're just copies of the original. Sometimes good copies, sometimes so good they're only missing one or two elements that would make them as good as or better than the *real* thing. So forgive me for thinking that your engagement may have started off as fake but you can't tell me there weren't bits of it that were real.'

'I...' She wasn't sure what to say. Sometimes Rafe loved to rattle on and sound like the knowledgeable businessman he was, but he had a point. All that was missing in their 'fake' engagement was that she'd never confessed how deep her feelings were or discovered if Finlay felt the same. It was always meant to be fake, a mutually beneficial transaction like the arrangement she'd had with James. Both times she'd tricked herself into believing the feelings were real because that's what her lonely heart desired so hard. But this time, it felt so much worse.

'None of that matters,' she said, half to herself. 'Finlay is going to Dubai and no matter how you try to square it, Dad, or try to convince me three years isn't that long, it's too long in the life of my dog and I can't bear parting with her.'

'Then take her with you,' Rafe said. 'Some airlines these days will even let her in the cabin with you. I can get my company to arrange it for you so she wouldn't have to travel in the hold.'

Genevieve shook her head. 'No. I can't. She doesn't do well in the heat. It would be horrible for her. I waited a long time to get her; I can't just give her up.'

'It sounds like you don't really want to go to Dubai,' Cressida said.

'It's true, I don't want to live in another country. I like travelling and visiting new places but I don't want to live there.'

'But you do want to be with Finlay?' Her mum looked at her with wide eyes.

'Yes. Yes, I do.' She covered her face and the tears burst.

A group of arms surrounded her, offering comfort, but none of them were the ones she so desperately desired.

CHAPTER TWENTY-SIX

Finlay

'This is a bad joke, right?' Hayley stood on the doorstep of Lisa's house with her arms folded, looking more serious – and scary – than she ever had before.

'Nope. Not a joke,' Finlay said. 'The whole thing was fake.'

'Fake?' Lisa repeated, her expression flat.

'Yup. But don't go telling anyone else that. This is between me and the two of you. Genevieve doesn't want her followers to think she's the kind of person who would get drunkenly engaged to someone, so we're using this as the reason. And really, I don't want people thinking I'm like that either. One failed engagement is enough, two is getting silly and three is utterly ridiculous.'

His mum shook her head. 'But it wasn't fake.'

'I just told you it was.'

'You're wrong. It wasn't fake, it was fate.'

'What are you talking about?'

'Why else would you have had the ring with you? People don't go about carrying engagement rings in their pockets then suddenly find some random person to propose to. That wasn't a coincidence. It was meant to be. You and Genevieve are meant to be.'

Finlay cocked his head. This wasn't the first time his mum had given him the benefit of her belief in all things spiritual. Normally he let it wash over him but something struck him this time, an odd niggle, questioning him. *What if she's right?* But that was mad. He believed in small coincidences, sure, but this was too much. More likely his brain tricking him into hearing what he wanted to believe.

'I don't get it,' Hayley said. 'What made you ask her in the first place?'

'Prosecco.'

'Nonsense,' his mum said. 'It might have given you the courage and the freedom to open up but no way would you have done it if you hadn't felt something for her.'

'I'm not saying I don't like her. Of course I do. But we're not—'

'In love?' His mum narrowed her eyes. 'Because you did a very good impression of it.'

'And it's not like you weren't sleeping together,' Hayley muttered. 'No way were the two of you innocently cohabiting all those weeks and at that retreat.'

'That's got nothing to do with anything.'

'Yes, it does.' His mum shook her head and gave him a stern look like she used to do when he was eight and came to tell her he'd kicked his rugby ball into the neighbour's garden again. 'You're just too blind to see what's right in front of your nose.'

'It's not that simple.' He let out a low groan and ran his fingers through his hair. 'Even if I do like Genevieve.'

'Love Genevieve,' his mum supplied as though he'd made an obvious mistake.

'Assuming that,' he continued. 'That doesn't change any-thing. She doesn't want to move to Dubai.'

'How do you know that?'

'I asked her and she said no. It was very clear.'

'Pah,' his mum pulled a face. 'It seems like such a waste.'

'A waste of what?'

'A chance to be happy.'

Finlay shook his head and turned to where Oliver was in the car on the driveway, waiting. He tapped the steering wheel im-patiently and Finlay sighed. No time to debate.

'Listen, I'm sorry. I screwed up,' he said, 'Maybe some of what you said is right but I have to let go and accept this is it. Here stands Finlay McBride with three failed engagements to his name.' He held out his hands.

'Oh Finlay.' His mum sighed and pulled him into a hug. 'I don't know what to say. I'm going to miss you so much. Please take care.'

'I will.' His already bruised heart wasn't able to take much more. He pulled Hayley in to join the hug and she sniffed, not bothering to hide her tears. If he let it out, he'd have just as many, if not more, than her. 'I'll message you and let you know how things are going. I love you both.'

Hayley's gaze shifted to the car as Finlay pulled back. 'What have you told Mr grumpy face?' she asked.

'I told Oliver right at the start it wasn't real.'

'Nice,' she said. 'But not us.'

'It wasn't like that. You know how averse to anything romantic he is.'

Hayley rolled her eyes. 'Never met anyone as repressed as him.'

'Yeah, well,' Finlay said. 'Maybe he's got the right idea.'

After several more hugs, he made his way to the car. His mum and Hayley followed, still plying him with hugs and kisses through the open window as Oliver backed out of the driveway. He said nothing but Finlay got the impression Oliver thought the loving farewell OTT and pointless. Sometimes Finlay was frustrated by Oliver's cold indifference to people, though he understood why he was like that. He had a sad history. Then he remembered Genevieve and how she'd seemed cold like that at first. He knew Oliver much better though and was sure he wasn't hiding a soft centre, not a romantic one anyway. As a friend, he relaxed at times, but other than Finlay himself, he wasn't sure Oliver had anybody. His relationship with his family was strained and his hookups were... well, short and probably not even that sweet. Not that he talked much about that. Or anything deep. He was more of a receptacle for all Finlay's issues. Maybe Finlay should take a leaf out of Oliver's book. Close himself off and make himself immune.

'How do you do it?' he asked Oliver.

'Do what?'

'Stop yourself falling for people?'

Oliver drew his dark eyebrows together. 'Easy.'

'Not for me, it isn't.'

'Because you're more emotional than me.'

'I guess I'm doomed then.'

'You could probably get there with hard work and practise. Most things are achievable that way.'

Finlay smirked. 'Definitely doomed then. I've left it way too late for that.'

'Well, maybe in Dubai, it'll be easier to shut off. Did you tell your mum and sister the truth?'

'Yup.'

'And they didn't take it well?'

'They think it's fate and I'm throwing away a chance of happiness.'

Oliver huffed out a laugh. 'Fate? Right. No such thing. And don't worry about throwing away a chance of happiness. Happiness is a temporary and passing thing, like every other feeling. It's not like you won't experience happiness ever again. Just wait until you see your next wage sitting in your bank account. That'll bring a smile to your face.'

Finlay looked out the window as they left Glenbriar behind. Hayley had a point. Oliver was a right grump sometimes and such a cynic. Was he really shallow enough to value money over love? Or maybe that was genuinely his way of keeping content.

Bizarre thoughts whizzed into Finlay's head as they sped along the dual carriageway, passing buses and trucks, heading towards Perth – thoughts that involved Genevieve following him or messaging him, telling him to wait. But no messages from her came in. After negotiating the busy Perth roundabouts, they headed southwest to Glasgow Airport.

Even as he said farewell to Oliver over an hour later – minus any hugs or over emotional words – Finlay half expected to hear a shout and see Genevieve running towards him with a case, waving and saying she was coming with him. The fact she didn't have a ticket was neither here nor there. If this was fate, shouldn't there be a movie style moment?

He went through the busy check-in desk and waited in the lounge with a growing sense of nausea and unreality. This should feel exciting and new but with no one to share it with, he couldn't focus and time seemed to have slowed to almost a stop. Messaging friends who were excited for him didn't help and he tossed his head back and let out a silent groan.

The flight was delayed and he closed his eyes, hoping sleep would take him for a bit and when he opened his eyes, it would be time to board. No such luck. Sleep wasn't coming, even though he felt exhausted. Last night, he'd slept better than he expected.

Hot sex did that. He was relaxed and content and had dozed with Genevieve in his arms. Unlikely he'd be having nights like that again anytime soon. The way she'd clung to him with her nails was carnal. She'd owned him and he was hers... Except he wasn't.

He checked his phone for the three-hundredth time. What was she doing? How was she feeling? When they'd parted that morning she'd seemed ok-ish. Or had that been her summoning the serene face to cover how she really felt? He wasn't sure she'd want to hear from him but he could at least try.

FINLAY: At the airport. Flight delayed. How are you? How did your parents react? I told Mum and Hayley the truth. I couldn't help myself but I asked them not to say anything. Hope you're ok. x

That hardly covered it. He wanted her to be more than ok. His fingers hovered over the screen before he typed out another message to Hayley.

FINLAY: Hey, sorry about what I told you and Mum this morning. I know it must be a shock. Just to say in some ways both you and Mum were right. We did like each other and I still see her as a friend.

That was a nice little understatement.

If you have a chance to see Genevieve, can you check she's ok? It won't have been easy telling her parents about this and I know what she's like. She'll try to face it alone and pretend everything's ok, and maybe it is, but I'd feel better if I know she isn't on her own.

There. He sent it but it didn't ease the guilt worms eating away at his insides. A few moments later, Hayley replied.

HAYLEY: Of course I'll check in on her. No problemo. Has the flight not arrived yet? xx

Yes. Hayley was a kind, loyal friend and sister who'd never want anyone to suffer in silence. But that was exactly what he had to do.

FINLAY: Thanks, I appreciate it. Flight delayed but hopefully not much longer. x

He checked the board for the millionth time to see his flight still reading *boarding soon*. How much longer? He sent the text to Hayley and stared out the window, watching as a plane taxied to its take-off position. It settled into place, then with that rush of grace and speed belted down the runway before cruising into the air.

The speaker dinged into action, announcing his flight was boarding. With a heavy sigh, he lifted his bag and got to his feet. This was it. He was leaving the country and Genevieve wasn't coming with him.

Chapter Twenty-Seven

Genevieve

Genevieve's phone rang again. This was almost as bad as the morning the news of her engagement to Finlay had broken. Maybe worse. Ok, make that definitely worse. Why was Flora calling her? It couldn't come at a worse time. Viewers were coming to see the house and she didn't want to be bang in the middle of a dramatic call. She checked the time. Nearly five thirty. They'd be here any second.

Before Genevieve could hit the accept call button, her mind had already raced into speculation. One particular train of thought rising to the surface: had her dad told Flora this was a setup? Had she pulled the plug on her investment?

Do I really want to know?

But not knowing would be a hundred times worse.

'Hello.' She held up the phone.

'Genevieve, so glad to have caught you,' Flora said.

Genevieve waited. What could she say? Until Flora explained her reasons for calling, she didn't need to give her any more rope.

'I just wanted to check you were all right,' Flora said. 'Your father told me you broke up with Finlay.'

'Yes.'

'Dear, dear. I'm so terribly sorry to hear it. Of course I believed your father, but until I heard it from you, I wasn't sure what to make of it.'

Genevieve let out a sigh but couldn't do much else. No response seemed adequate. And she wasn't sure exactly what her father had told Flora.

'Your father is a very charming man,' Flora said. 'And surprisingly honourable for a businessperson. I've had business connections for a very long time and most people at the top have a fair few secrets or dealings in which they'd rather the whole story wasn't told.'

Genevieve's pulse drummed in her ear. Did that mean her dad had told Flora the truth? The hot, nauseous sensation she'd had in her stomach ever since Finlay left redoubled. The more people knew, the more stupid she felt. Her world was unravelling around her, and there was nothing she could do to stop it. 'Um, yes,' she said, thinking maybe Flora expected an answer.

'He seems to think you and Finlay were staging your engagement. He insisted it wasn't to gain my favour but he would understand if I wanted to withdraw my backing given the circumstances.'

'And are you going to?'

'No. And I still intend to fund the rugby club too.'

Genevieve silently willed her to carry on as she peered out the window for signs of the viewers.

'Perhaps you'd like to hear my reasons?'

'Yes. Of course I would.'

'Well, it's clear to me Geoff had no idea anything untoward was going on. And to be perfectly honest, I'm not sure I believe it. What was the point of staging a relationship if not to fool me? Was it to gain more followers or publicity?'

Genevieve winced. 'I... We were drunk when Finlay proposed, but when Dad told me about your offer, I didn't want to say no in case he lost your investment.'

'So it was just for my benefit.' Her voice was soft but had a steely note in it, like she was cross with herself for being duped.

'Partly, but my father had nothing to do with it. He didn't know what we were doing. And... Well, I actually liked Finlay a lot. It's just unfortunate...' That he didn't return the feelings she'd suppressed for years, but that was TMI for Flora. 'I can assure you he definitely didn't set out to con you.'

'I was pretty certain he wasn't as he didn't even know me when we originally spoke. I wonder though, if you liked him so much, could you go to Dubai with him?'

She was going to have trouble escaping this argument, even though she shouldn't have to justify not wanting to live abroad. It really wasn't for everyone. But the worst of it was Finlay had asked her. She'd taken it to be an aside, an offhand or rhetorical question. Her answer had rushed from her lips without any consideration because 'no' was the protective answer. Just like she'd blurted it out all those years ago when he'd offered her help with the rollerblading. This time her injuries were a lot more painful than sprained wrists and grazed knees. They cut right to her soul.

'Listen, I can't talk,' she said. 'I've got viewers coming around and that's them just pulled up.'

'Ok,' Flora said, not hiding her scepticism. Genevieve almost took a photograph of their car to prove it but why should she justify herself? 'But call me back when you have more time. I'd like to talk. I have another little proposition for you.'

Genevieve dreaded to think.

The little black car in the driveway reminded her of Hayley's car and she scooted away from the window before the viewers got out, so it didn't look like she was watching. Looking in the mirror, she smoothed herself down and tidied her hair. She was reminded irresistibly of that day back at Finlay's flat when she'd shown viewers around. Everything had been easy then, the chat, the banter... the growing sexual tension. She jumped as the doorbell rang, which was stupid as she was expecting it. Every little thing was getting to her at the moment.

Throwing open the door with a smile, she went to speak, but it wasn't viewers.

'Hayley.'

'Hi.' Hayley gave her a little wave. 'I had to come, sorry.' She pulled an apologetic face. 'You know I have to check you're ok.'

'Did Finlay send you?'

'He asked me to check you were ok but you were my friend first, so I would have come anyway.'

Genevieve glanced down the road. All around were houses, clustered together on the modern estate. They were neat and tidy but too close. It was part of the reason she wanted out. Even stepping into her small garden was like walking on stage. People would look her way whether they meant to or not and now more than ever the constant sense of being watched was overwhelming. Why did it feel like everyone knew her story and was out to judge?

'I can't really talk,' Genevieve said. 'I've got viewers coming.'

Hayley cocked her head in a manner that clearly said she wouldn't be got rid of that easily. Mitzi shuffled along the corridor, then, recognising Hayley, made a dash for the door and started hopping up and down at her ankles.

'She needs to go out,' Genevieve said, 'but I have to wait for these people. They're late.'

'How about I take her for a walk and I'll come back in half an hour? That'll give you time to see the viewers and we can chat after.'

How could she refuse? She got Mitzi ready and waved her off. Hayley had barely turned into the lane between two houses when the viewers pulled up, all apologetic that they'd got lost. It didn't take them long to look around and judging from their unimpressed tone, Genevieve didn't expect an offer from them anytime soon. Everything was 'too small' for them and they'd misread the specs and were expecting three bedrooms, not two. Genevieve wasn't sorry to show them out.

Hayley returned with Mitzi ten minutes later, rosy-cheeked and as smiley as ever. She pulled an almost commiserating face at Genevieve before heading straight for her and hugging her.

'Oh, Gen. I'm so sorry.'

'What for?'

'My brother.'

'Why are you sorry about him?'

Hayley stepped back and raised an eyebrow. 'Because of the way things have worked out. I love Finlay, don't get me wrong, but he's messed up this time.'

'We both messed up.'

Hayley took a seat and Genevieve followed, patting Mitzi's bed and indicating she should hop in.

'Finlay told us the truth.'

'I know,' Genevieve said. 'What can I say? We got drunk and the rest is history.'

'Except it isn't.'

'Meaning what?'

'I don't actually believe either of you are ready to give up on the other.'

Genevieve stroked her nails through her flyaway hair. 'Maybe on my side. I never told anyone, but I always liked him, even when we were young.'

'Mum said she thought that, but I never saw it.'

'I kept it well hidden.'

'Obviously.'

'But just because I feel like that doesn't mean Finlay does.'

'It's funny really, because Finlay's usually an open book. He's not scared of affection or showing his feelings, unlike that grouchy friend of his. But because he's been so unguarded about his feelings in the past, he's been hurt. What's silly this time is that it's the one time he has been guarded. He hasn't allowed himself to believe, which is annoying because this is the time someone feels the same way in return.'

'You don't know how he actually feels about me. Maybe he's not being guarded, he's just not serious. We don't know each other that well. Not really. We've only been together for a few weeks... If you can even call it being together because we both agreed to pretend. And we all know I'm the queen of pretending.'

'But not this time, and it doesn't matter how long you've been together. So what if you've known him for years, a week or hours? Sometimes I meet clients for the first time and feel like I've known them forever. We can talk about anything and everything is easy. Other times, I get clients I've had for years but never feel like I really know them or have much to talk about. It's not about time but about being comfortable in someone's energy. That takes as long as it takes. There's no ticking clock.'

None of this kind of talk was new to Genevieve, but she wasn't sure if she wanted to believe it or dismiss it as Hayley's love of all things spiritual.

'And you're still wearing the ring.' Hayley nodded at Genevieve's hand. 'That tells a story in itself.'

'I'm not sure what else to do with it. He told me to keep it safe.'

'That ring was our grandmothers. All of us, me, Finlay and our cousin, Aidan, got jewellery and keepsakes from her when she died. Some of it came with notes and that ring was for Finlay "to give to his one true love". He was going to give it to Elise but she hated old-fashioned jewellery, so he didn't. Then he had it restyled, which Aidan was angry about, but Finlay never actually gave it to Elise.'

'But that was just circumstance.'

'No, it wasn't. Finlay knew the importance of that ring. He took it to his engagement party, meaning to give it to her, but didn't do it. Something stopped him. I don't think he would have given it to anyone, not even when he was drunk, unless he genuinely believed his feelings to be true. Maybe alcohol tainted his judgement but I still think underneath there must have been a powerful emotion driving him. And I bet he was quite sober when he asked you to keep it.'

Genevieve ran her fingertip over the gem she'd got so used to on her hand. 'Yes, he was. But it changes nothing.'

'Doesn't it? I think it gives you a pretty good clue as to how he really feels. Now all you need to do is find out for sure.'

'It's not that easy at all. He's thousands of miles away.'

'Does that matter? You're selling this house anyway. Why not follow him?'

'Because I don't want to live in Dubai. I like living here. I can't bear to leave Mitzi and she really doesn't cope well with the heat here in summer, never mind in temperatures like that.'

'Oh dear.'

'I can't wreck this opportunity for Finlay either. Maybe guarding his heart was what he needed to do. He values his career and it wouldn't be fair for me to get in the way of that.'

'You're not getting in the way. Finlay made this move to get away from Elise and the talk surrounding that. If he'd got together with you before he signed his contract, I'm sure he wouldn't have gone through with it. It wasn't about career development as much as running away.'

Genevieve sank her head into her hand. 'That may all be true, but it doesn't change the situation. Let's not think about it anymore just now. It's making my head ache.' But it was nothing compared to the constant throb in her chest. How could she get out of this mess and get back to normal? Especially when normal wasn't a place she really wanted to be.

Her social media accounts had hundreds of new notifications and messages. She hadn't posted new content since the split and hadn't announced it. What could she say? After telling them all so emphatically she'd only ever get engaged to 'the one'. And she had… kind of. How could she suddenly go back to 'look at me,

I'm single again'? How the haters would hate. She really couldn't stand it.

A red number *99+* sat beside her notifications and she couldn't bring herself to read even a few of the comments. Good or bad, she didn't care. Maybe she should just delete it and be done with it.

Chapter Twenty-Eight

Finlay

Finlay loosened the collar of his shirt as he approached the school. The heat outside was intense but thank god everywhere he'd been had air conditioning, including his apartment. As lodgings went, his place was pretty good – clean, reasonably spacious and surrounded by people in similar positions as him. Well, as in they were teaching abroad, not that they'd just suffered their third failed engagement. He didn't expect to meet anyone else in that position – ever.

He approached the school building and allowed himself a grin. Photos hadn't done it justice. The pure white façade with domed mid-section looked almost like a temple and reminded him a little of the Harrington's eco house. But where it had been all glass and balconies, this was plain. Instead of the Harrington's cultivated rose gardens, palm trees grew around the front entrance and also lined the boundary.

He nipped up the front stairs and entered. The receptionist was already on her feet and seemed to be explaining something to another woman. They both gave Finlay a small smile. He wasn't sure why it should surprise him, but so far everyone he'd met had seemed so normal – probably a stupid thing to think, but for some reason when he'd imagined it, he'd thought people here would be different somehow. Perhaps with larger-than-life personalities like Flora, or snooty in some way.

'Hello,' the receptionist said, when the first woman moved away. Her accent was English and filled with cheer. 'I'm Leah.'

'Finlay,' he said.

'Ah yes. I have your I.D. card here.' She headed over to the desk. 'Finlay McBride.' She glanced at the photo on the card he'd emailed last month, then at him. 'Perfect. Now, you take that.' She handed it to him. 'There's a note here saying that the principal would like to talk to you before you start the development day. I'll take you through to meet him. He likes to personally welcome new staff.'

'Thanks.' Finlay slung the lanyard around his neck and followed Leah along the quiet corridors. Blissful cool air breezed over him.

She stopped at a door and knocked. When a reply came, she opened the door with a smile. 'I have Finlay McBride here.'

'Thank you.' The principal got to his feet and moved around the desk. 'Pleased to meet you. I'm Nicholas Fairley.'

Finlay shook his hand.

Leah left them and Nicholas Fairley indicated for Finlay to take a seat. Even though the principal was smiling, Finlay had an odd feeling that something wasn't right. This meeting itself was odd. While he liked the idea of being personally greeted by the principal, he didn't think it was common, especially on a development day when they were likely to meet anyway.

'I hope you don't mind me calling you in here before you've met anyone else,' Nicholas said. 'But I have a small matter I want to discuss with you first.'

'Ok.' Now his brain was racing. What small matter?

'I'm sure when you signed your contract, you made yourself aware of the stipulations regarding personal conduct, including the use of social media. As I expect you're aware, this school has some very conservative families who expect staff to behave accordingly.' He pulled a face. 'Almost expecting us to be saintly and completely above reproach, which is unreasonable in some cases, but there are times when...' Nicholas adjusted his tie and coughed into his hand.

Finlay's mouth had gone dry. He could sense what was coming without using any of his mum's psychic measures. Common sense told him someone had seen Genevieve's social media account and flagged it to the school.

'It's not possible to be squeaky all the time, I'm aware of that,' Nicholas went on. 'But it's been brought to my attention by a group of parents' – he seemed to steel himself as if these particular parents were a constant source of irritation – 'that you have appeared in some compromising ways this summer on social media. Almost as soon as I sent out the new staff list, I had a long message from one of them, detailing a very public proposal in which several bottles of wine were apparently visible.' He glanced up. 'Public drinking is, of course, a big no around these parts and viewed as criminal by these parents.' He kept his eyes on his screen as he read this out and his cheeks turned slightly pink.

'That's been twisted,' Finlay said, keenly aware it wasn't *that* far from the truth.

'Yes. I expect it has. I was hoping it would all have died down by the time you arrived and there would be no need to mention it, but I've had two more emails this morning.' Nicholas steepled his fingers and peered across the desk. 'I assume this fiancée of yours is here with you.' He looked back at the screen. 'Someone named Genevieve Harrington with social media accounts called The Vieve.'

What the hell? What lengths would some people go to in order to dish dirt? Did these people have nothing better to do?

'Genevieve and I aren't together anymore. We split up, so no, she isn't here.'

Nicholas frowned and leaned forward, resting his chin on his hand. 'You split up? Didn't this proposal only take place a few weeks ago?'

'Yes.' His insides squirmed. Did everything and everyone have to remind him of his stupidity?

'Oh dear.' Nicholas sighed. 'I hope the parents don't get wind of that.'

'Are you sacking me?' Finlay asked. How could he help it? Wouldn't it be just like his life to be sacked before he'd even started a job? Just like he'd been dumped three times before getting to the altar… though he couldn't really count the last one. That was the strangest part of all. The last one hurt more than both the others. For a fleeting second, the idea of being sacked appealed to him and he saw himself rushing back to Genevieve, telling her how he felt and begging her to make this real.

'No, you're not sacked,' Nicholas said. 'That would leave us with a real problem. I won't even call this a reprimand, just an informal chat, and a chance to put together an action plan for where we go next. To start with, please take care and ensure nothing else appears on social media. The parents play a powerful part in this school and I can only go so far to protect you.'

Finlay left the office some twenty-minutes later, his energy levels depleted. How much more could he take? Now he had to switch his focus to work and concentrate on learning about a new school, a different system, new colleagues and, all the while, panicking Genevieve might have inadvertently posted something else. He'd looked at her social media feeds more in the past few days than ever before. It was like a lifeline to her, but he couldn't very well pull out his phone and start checking now. Hopefully she'd be as quiet as she had been since they'd split. Nothing new had been posted. No announcements, cookery films or product endorsements. It was like she'd disappeared.

Finlay had to keep reminding himself it was only a week ago he'd got here. With the jetlag and getting used to a new place, it felt like a lot longer.

Even at lunch, he didn't want to appear rude and disappear into his phone, not when everyone else was chatting and getting to know the new staff.

When he finally checked later in the day as he walked towards his lodgings, nothing had changed. He would ask her to keep the news of their split quiet for now. Risking the stalker parents finding out anything else about his private life wasn't worth it.

Before he could message her, however, he noticed a chat head had popped up with Elise's picture in it.

With a sigh, he flipped it open and saw a long voice message. Pressing play, he held it to his ear.

'*Hi. I just want to say I cannot believe what you've done to Genevieve. I guessed right from the start you were only doing this to mess with me.*' He glanced around, hoping no one could hear this. Elise's message continued. '*I never thought you were like that and would use her in that way. It's cruel.*'

He hit the off switch and put his phone away without listening to the end. Seriously she had a nerve to say that to him. After the way she'd treated him. Talk about hypocritical, but his shoulders sagged. Cruel was a good word. Being so far from her felt cruel. This whole situation was cruel. He was here because of Elise when he actually wanted to be with Genevieve. That was twisted alright.

He let himself into his apartment building, took the lift, and headed inside. From the window, he had a good view of the city. The skyscrapers all squashed together reminded him of a game he'd played on his tablet as a teenager, where you had to build a city and the more money you earned, the bigger the buildings you could have. This place was like that, all money, business and noise. Unfamiliar. Hot, yes, but in other ways cold. He was alone and friendless and it wasn't a state he was used to. Would he grow accustomed to it over time? His mum was right. He was always better when he had someone to hold his hand and right now, the only person he wanted to do that was Genevieve.

Chapter Twenty-Nine

Genevieve

'It's such a shame there aren't any suitable properties,' Hilary said.

Genevieve nodded like she was still scrolling through estate agent websites, but she was actually looking at a message from Finlay.

'And I can't believe it was that couple you said were so dismissive that actually put in an offer.'

'I know, that was very strange.' She leaned on the breakfast bar where she was sitting, angling the phone away from her mum, so there was no chance she could see who was messaging. Staying at her own house was still ok. It wasn't officially sold yet and even if she accepted the offer, the couple presumably had to sell their house, then they would arrange a move in date. But she hated it being so empty. Not that it was much different from normal. The reason had everything to do with the man whose message picture was sitting on her screen and nothing to do with missing furniture or décor. Moving back with her parents meant she always had company, though it was a little awkward and the elephant in the room was getting bigger every day. Now he'd joined them electronically.

While her mum added some dishes to the washer, Genevieve opened the message.

FINLAY: Hey. How's it going? Hope you're ok. I think you'd like the shops and the bars around here, but it does feel a bit… different. I haven't really been anywhere much yet, other than school. It feels weird going on my own and I'm not quite chummy enough with my colleagues yet. Also, I've been warned by the principal to 'behave myself'. Some parents saw the engagement post. I notice you haven't posted that we split up. Can you please hold off doing that for the time being? The governors will have me strung up if they hear about that. God knows what the principal makes of it. His face when I said we weren't together anymore even though we only got engaged a few weeks ago… Well, you can imagine.

Anyhoo… I miss you

xx

She almost forgot what the rest of the message was about as her focus kept returning to the last bit. *He misses me.* Christ, she missed him too. So bloody much.

'Here's an idea,' Hilary said, taking a seat opposite. 'I know you said you wanted to sell your house anyway and it had nothing to do with…'

'Finlay. You can say his name. I won't break down about it.' Or she at least hoped she wouldn't.

'Finlay, yes. So he was also selling his apartment and didn't you say it was one of those lovely riverside ones?'

'Yes.'

'Why don't you buy that one? It's a much nicer location. It's a flat so I suppose it would all be on one level, but I guess about the same size as your house otherwise.'

Once upon a time, she'd joked about it with him, but how could she be there without him? She stopped herself blurting something out when actually it wasn't a bad idea. She had always loved those flats. The only thing putting her off was emotional baggage; the thought of being there alone, knowing what they'd done together there... how happy they'd been. But then maybe the opposite would happen. Maybe she'd feel safe there as she had been when he was with her.

'I'll think about it.'

What would he make of it? She typed a message in response to his.

GENEVIEVE: Sorry you got into trouble because of me. I'm going to look into a rebrand. I feel like I've outgrown prostituting my soul on social media but I like the cookery aspect of it. I phoned James at Duchan Fayre to discuss the contract and it's going ahead. I'm excited about it.

Or she was trying to be. James was a decent guy. He always had been and even when she told him about her split with Finlay, he'd been commiserative and didn't question why in her emails she'd acted like she was never going to Dubai. If he wondered in private, so be it. The thought of having her range in a place like Duchan Fayre was something she desperately wanted to share. James had talked of photoshoots, professional filming and live demos. He'd even mentioned commissioning a recipe book to sell with the products. If only she could be genuinely thrilled about it and not just serenely pleased.

I won't say anything online about our breakup, so hopefully you'll be fine. How is the job?

She paused again, trying to imagine where he might be and how it might look. He'd probably send a photo if she asked but she wasn't sure she wanted to make it so real. When it was just a vague fuzzy idea, it was somehow easier to handle.

My house is under offer. I haven't found anywhere yet. Mum thinks I should buy your flat. What do you think of that?

Miss you too

Xx

Her eyes pricked as she typed the last words. It didn't take long for him to reply.

FINLAY: I suggested that once before. Feels like I should give you mates rates... Or just give you the flat, full stop. Guess if you want to buy it, then you can, but doesn't it feel a bit bizarre?

X

It did and she couldn't deny it but it also had an almost circular feeling, like a perfect loop, keeping them both together while circumstances kept them apart.

Juicy red apples dripped from the trees as Genevieve walked Mitzi through the garden on her way to the woods. The roses were past their best, but still fragrant. That smell would always remind her of the proposal. She carried on walking. Finlay had been away for over a month now. Autumn was creeping in as September drew to a close, but it was still seasonably warm and the sky was bright after a few days of heavy rain. Genevieve had taken the plunge and put an offer in on Finlay's flat. Some other people had offered too and she hoped Finlay would be sensible and not sentimental and take the best offer. How would she feel though if someone outbid her? Would bitterness creep in if someone else got it? Finlay would know who made the offers and ultimately would have the decision. Perhaps she'd done nothing but put him in an awkward place... again. Her social media posts had almost lost him his job. How could she have forgiven herself if he'd been sacked?

She'd bitten the bullet and was in the process of rebranding The Vieve as cookery and homeware only. No more beauty products or relationships. James had been in touch again about the first photoshoot. Genevieve had also returned Flora's call to discover Flora also wanted a piece of The Vieve. She'd asked Genevieve to design dinnerware for the retreat, which would give even more exposure to her brand. How could she refuse?

Things were falling together in her career, but her love life was still dragging behind in a wagon with a missing wheel.

She opened a gate at the far end of the garden that led to the woods. Finlay used to come cycling here. She remembered him saying he'd seen her parents' house from up here, though never known who it belonged to. He'd be missing cycling unless he could hire a bike in Dubai. No doubt he'd put in some running or use the school gym. She couldn't imagine him not doing some sport or other. Maybe he'd set up his own tug-of-war team.

Her phone buzzed in her jacket pocket and she fished for it. The estate agent. She hastened to answer. Had her offer been accepted?

'Hello.'

'Hi, Genevieve,' Emelie Bright said in a tone that suited her name perfectly. 'I have an update regarding your offer for the riverside flat.'

'Yes?'

'I'm afraid it's not good news.'

Genevieve's heart sank. Of course Finlay had every right to choose whichever offer but she'd harboured a secret certainty that he'd pick her. 'My offer has been rejected.'

'I'm afraid so. There are circumstances surrounding the sale of this property but...' She hesitated and it sounded like she let out a sigh. 'Obviously it's all confidential and I can't talk about it to anyone but the seller. However... Can I speak off record for a second?'

'Go ahead.'

'Don't you and the seller have a relationship? I seem to re-call—'

'Oh, um, yes.' How could she forget Finlay had been with her when Emelie had done her initial valuation? This must look completely bizarre from her position. If they were actually a couple, then they could have done a private sale and cut out Emelie completely. 'Don't worry, I'll speak to Finlay about it.'

'Great,' Emelie said. 'That's the best plan and hopefully it'll work out better in the long run.'

Genevieve wasn't entirely sure what Emelie meant, but she didn't question it. The fewer people who knew about the state of her private life, the better. Well, that was that. The flat was going to someone else. Maybe someone who'd paid a lot more money. That was probably why Emelie thought it would work out better. She would think Genevieve would also benefit from that. The thought of messaging Finlay and asking him why he hadn't chosen her fluttered into her mind but she couldn't do it. Just like he hadn't chosen her as a life partner, he hadn't picked her for the flat either.

'Men,' she muttered. 'I don't know why I'm bothered. I should go back to being a happy single girl and be done with.' So what if she never managed the life with a husband and two point four kids? Did it matter? But no matter how hard she tried to bully her brain into believing she didn't care, it wasn't working.

She really did want that life and the only man she wanted for the job was Finlay.

CHAPTER THIRTY

Finlay

Autumn in Scotland was so gorgeous, even when it hadn't fully taken hold. The trees were changing; the air was breezy, slightly damp, and filled with scents of the harvest. By right, Finlay shouldn't be seeing it at all. He should be looking at bright blue skies, gleaming skyscrapers, palm trees and golden sand. Perhaps a quick scan through social media would show him his friends in some of his favourite haunts. Aidan's girlfriend Lilah was often posting pictures of the two of them on a walk somewhere or other with Luna their husky.

But seeing it in person was so much better, even if he couldn't completely chase away the guilt eating at his insides. Can't see an engagement through to a wedding – or a job in a foreign country either, it seemed. The rational part of his brain – which sounded very much like the man driving him north towards Glenbriar from Glasgow airport – was telling him he was an idiot to drop out.

'Oh god,' he groaned at the thought.

'What?' Oliver said. 'Are you ill?'

'No, but maybe I'm crazy.'

'I'd say there's no *maybe* about it.' Oliver took over exactly where the voice in Finlay's thoughts had left off.

'It just wasn't for me.'

'You were there a month. That's hardly enough time to decide.'

'I know, I know. I've beaten myself up enough about it. No need to add to that.'

'I don't get how you got out of your contract. Won't you be fined?'

Finlay gave a wry smirk. 'No. I had the option to leave before my probationary period ran out.'

'So you did.'

'Yup. Right from the start, a group of parents with too much time and more money than sense had run their own version of background checks on me, i.e. stalked me on social media. They knew all about me before I even arrived, thanks to Genevieve's films.'

'Oh jeez. I told you to stay away from her. Relationships are nothing but trouble.'

Finlay ignored that comment. Oliver was a one-track record sometimes.

'Anyway, I stupidly told the principal we'd split up and he was pretty shocked that we'd only been together a few weeks, then somehow that info got to the parents. God knows how because Genevieve didn't post anything.'

'He must have blabbed.'

'Yeah. I can't prove it, but I suspect he did. I think they were gunning for him about a bigger issue, and he used this to deflect them. Anyway, it wasn't a pleasant atmosphere, so I decided to jack it in. They think they've scored a point by getting rid of a teacher with no values but actually, it's because I have values that I'm coming home.'

'Oh yeah?'

'Yup. I value love above anything else.'

'Oh Christ.'

'Say what you want but it's true. I just need to find out if the woman I love loves me in return.'

Oliver shook his head with a barely concealed snort. 'And what about a job?'

Finlay shrugged. 'There are a couple of jobs going. One of them is the one I left at the end of term.'

'No one's applied for it?'

'Apparently not.'

'Would you want to go back to your old job?' Oliver glanced at him as they waited in a long line of cars waiting at a roundabout.

'Possibly. If they'd have me. I didn't hate it. What I hated was the shitstorm surrounding me and Elise.'

'Surely that's going to be even worse now.'

'Not if I can help it. I want to make things right with Genevieve.'

'And how are you going to do that?'

'By telling her how I feel and see if she wants to make the engagement real.'

'Oh jeez.' Oliver let out a low groan. 'That has disaster written all over it.'

'Possibly. But if it all goes pear-shaped, I know a very good divorce lawyer.'

'Jesus Christ.'

'No, you, but let's hope I don't have to call for intervention from either of you.'

The flat looked the same as ever when Finlay got back, but it was cold and completely empty. The for-sale sign was down as he'd instructed the estate agent to take it off the market as soon as he realised he'd be back. Oliver had offered him a bed for the night but he didn't take it. No one knew he was back and he told Oliver to keep it that way for now. The stories his mum and Hayley would want to know could wait. He had a job to do and it couldn't wait any longer. He had to see Genevieve now.

After dumping his stuff, he put on the only jacket he had, which wasn't very warm but it would do, and walked towards Genevieve's house. It was almost six o'clock. Daylight would hold for another hour, at least. Seeing everything familiar around him was like being cradled in a warm nest. This was where he belonged. The jetlag wasn't as bad coming this way and being out in the fresh air made him feel energised.

It was an easy walk to Genevieve's house in these shoes – not the heels she'd turned up in that first day. The irony wasn't lost on him. If she'd walked home that day from his flat, he wouldn't have had to give her a lift. She wouldn't have invited him to the party and they wouldn't be in this position. Maybe it was fate, after all. Fate or Elise's nonsense. She was the one who'd invited Genevieve in the first place for whatever bizarre reason. His mum would call it destiny. Maybe Elise was always the one who could unlock the gateway to Genevieve. He sniggered. Ok, that was stupid, but musing on it passed the time as he made his way through the town and up the hill. He skirted by the road that led to his mum's house and along the street where his aunt Tricia, Aidan's mum, lived. He gave her house a wave as he walked by. Wouldn't it be just the thing if she spied him and reported back to his mum or Hayley? But Tricia was usually occupied running the Crafty Bee Barn these days and if she was at home, she probably had her head down at a sewing machine making something.

The houses where Genevieve lived were bunched together on a newish development. Her house still had the for-sale sign by the fence with a giant yellow label *Under Offer* plastered across it. Her car wasn't there and the lights were off. Finlay didn't want to risk looking like a peeping Tom and press his nose up to the window to see if Mitzi was home alone. Casually he made his way to the front door and rang the bell. Silence. No barking or scuffling. They must both be out, but where?

She'd seemed so excited about the contract with Duchan Fayre. Could she be somewhere to do with that? Maybe having a business dinner with her old flame, James Charlton. Finlay didn't want to think about that. If she had, then maybe everything really had been pretend.

He shoved his hands in his pockets and walked back the way he came. How could he find out where she was? Would messaging and asking be a giveaway? He wanted to surprise her, but not just that. He had lots he wanted to say to her, but only to her face. Oliver would scoff or tell him the only thing she needed to hear was a gripe about posting his face all over social media. Thankfully he wasn't Oliver.

Ok, he could do this if he worded it properly.

FINLAY: Hey, how are you? I have something to tell you about the sale of my flat. You're probably wondering what happened. Are you at home?

He frowned at it. That sounded stupid. Why did she need to be at home for him to call her? Maybe he could say 'at home or somewhere you can talk'. Except he didn't want to actually call her. Not yet. He scratched the message and typed one to Hayley instead.

FINLAY: Hey. How are you? And how's Genevieve? Is she ok? Do you know if she's still living in her house or has she moved out? xx

It was possible she was out visiting someone but something about its vacant state felt final. Or was he just channelling his mum and all her spiritual stuff, making his imaginings seem real?

He walked briskly back down the street, past Tricia's house, and on to where a little green with a pond punctuated the houses. His phone pinged.

HAYLEY: I'm good. Think Genevieve is too. Haven't seen her for a day or two. She's moved out of her house and is back with her parents for now. Why do you want to know? Xx

FINLAY: Just curious. Xx

Genevieve was probably wondering why her bid on the flat had been turned down. She might even have discovered he'd taken the house off the market. Hopefully he could tell her soon. But the Harrington's house was a fair distance out of town. If he had his car or even his bike, he could do it, but they were both at his mum's house.

Nothing else for it. He'd have to go there. Either that or call Oliver and ask him for another lift. He didn't see that going well. It was only a short walk to his mum's house from here. He quickened his pace. When he reached the door, he rang the bell and held his breath.

His mum's eyes nearly popped out of their sockets as she pulled open the door. 'Good god, what are you doing here?' She clutched her chest, staring like she'd seen a ghost. 'Has there been an accident or something?'

'Hey, Mum.' He pulled her into his arms and melted into the loving hug only a mum could give. She was tiny compared to him but she still had the ability to make him feel like a little boy again, safe and protected, always loved. 'I'm fine. The job didn't work out. It's a long story but I can't hang about. I need my bike.'

'You're just back and you're going cycling?' She frowned up at him. 'With no explanation.'

'I need to cycle to Greenacres, you know, the Harringtons' house. I don't want to drive. It'll draw too much attention.'

'I see. Are you off to surprise a certain Miss Harrington?'

He nodded.

'Come to your senses, have you?'

'Allegedly.'

'And not before time. Make sure you tell her exactly how you feel.' She poked him in the chest. 'Then you can get back here and explain to me exactly what is going on.'

'I will. Just don't worry. Everything will be fine.'

She smiled. 'I know it will.'

He opened the garage, dusted off his helmet, and put it on. His bike was cold and he didn't want to waste time checking it too thoroughly but his mum insisted.

'It's been in here a month. It might have seized up or whatever bikes do. The last thing I want is for you to go off full of excitement only to have an accident on the way.'

'Ok, Mum.' He checked the brakes, tyres, pedals and had a quick scan over the bolts. 'It's all fine. I'll send you a quick message when I arrive, so you don't need to worry.'

She kissed him goodbye and he whizzed off, nipping through the woods and onto a track that led to the house. How often had he cycled up here and seen this house, never realising how significant a place it would be in his life? After a tough climb, he stopped at the edge where the house was visible. A small track led to a gate into the garden. The garden he'd proposed to Genevieve in a couple of months ago. Now he was back, he wanted to make that proposal permanent.

Dusk had arrived soft and velvety, not enough to obscure his view, but present. The lights in the eco mansion twinkled. Hopefully Genevieve was there. He just needed to lure her into the garden...

Chapter Thirty-One

Genevieve

Genevieve adjusted the blind in her dad's office. Weird wasn't the word for how she felt getting to use this place. It always seemed somewhere out of bounds or for people doing real business. Working on new cookware and homeware ideas for both Duchan Fayre and Flora at this time in the evening wasn't necessary but it was the nice side of choosing her own hours.

Writing a recipe book was a skill she was learning. It was fun pulling together all her favourites. She'd get to cook them again in the show kitchen at Duchan, where the finished results would be photographed for the book. Outside, the sky was darkening and even though this house was out in the sticks, she still preferred to have the blind shut.

Her phone vibrated with a message and she had a bizarre feeling it was Finlay, which she knew was silly as it was the same vibe sound for everyone. She lifted it and frowned when she saw his name.

'I knew it was you,' she murmured. Mitzi glanced up from the basket at her feet. 'Not you. It's Finlay.'

Mitzi's head raised fully like she recognised the name.

Genevieve opened the message. Maybe this was him finally explaining why he'd declined her offer on the flat. She flipped up the message.

FINLAY: hey. I wonder if you could do me an absolutely massive favour? Hayley told me you were back with your parents. If you're there now, would you be able to nip outside and take a photo of the fountain in the rose garden? I'd like to show it to someone. Hope you can help! Xx

She stared at it and shook her head. What the hell? Had he lost his mind? Or maybe he'd had too much prosecco again. Did she want to imagine him in a swanky bar in Dubai getting sloshed with glamorous colleagues? Probably not. And Dubai was four hours ahead. It must be going on eleven o'clock. And he was still out on a school night?

Laying the phone down, she returned to the screen. Nope. She wouldn't do it. Moments ticked by and she ignored her phone. It was completely black but still seemed to be jumping up and down, screaming at her.

Mitzi pulled herself out of her basket, lowered her front legs, and stretched.

'No way,' Genevieve muttered. 'You don't need a walk just now.' Honestly, why did it seem like Mitzi knew what was in that message and was trying to make Genevieve comply? Or maybe she genuinely needed out for a wee. 'Fine.' Genevieve got to her feet and went along the back corridor to the cupboard for her jacket. Her parents were in the living room watching TV and didn't mind if she came and went without saying anything. In fact, they probably didn't want her to disturb them as they were deep in the buildup for the first episode of the new series of *The Great British Bake Off*. Genevieve had considered watching it with them but she didn't like to disturb their together time too much.

She nipped out the French doors into the garden and Mitzi ran to a hedge. Perfect. If that was all she needed, they could go back in straight away. Genevieve had just turned to go in when Mitzi trotted off in the direction of the rose garden.

Seriously.

Raising her collar against the slightly chilly wind, Genevieve followed her. May as well take the damn photo, even though the light was fading and it might not come out very clearly. Ah, so what? He was lucky she was doing it at all. Mitzi skipped ahead like this was her first walk of the day. She sniffed around the rose hedges and bounded ahead as if she knew where she was going... Of course she knew her way around this garden but the way she was making a beeline towards the path to the fountain was highly suspicious. Sometimes Genevieve could swear that dog could talk or at least understand. But Genevieve hadn't even read the message aloud, so Mitzi must be a psychic.

Hurrying after her, Genevieve tried to catch the scent of the roses. It was still there, but nowhere near as strong as it had been in the height of the summer. Up ahead, Mitzi let out a little bark.

'Mitzi! Where are you?' Genevieve turned the corner into the clearing with the fountain and her heart stopped. She froze. A man was bending over, patting Mitzi. Who was out here and why? How could she get away? Before terror had a chance to set in, the man straightened up and his face became crystal clear, even in the fading light.

'Finlay.' Genevieve gaped at him, unable to form words that even touched on all the questions she had. 'What are you doing here?'

He stood still for a moment, just looking at her, then he moved slowly forward, closing the gap between them, but still out of reach.

'Why aren't you in Dubai? That message about the fountain.'

He lifted his left shoulder slightly. 'A ruse. I just wanted you to come out here so I could talk to you.'

'I don't get it.'

'I left. I realised there was something I needed to do.'

She raised her hand to her mouth and shook her head. 'What?'

She couldn't bear to move her hand from her lips. Her whole body was shaky and weak as she tried to process why he'd given up his job.

'I want to tell you something I wish I'd told you weeks ago, but it's taken me a trip halfway around the world to realise.'

'Realise what?'

'That I love you.'

'You do?' Her voice was as tremulous as her limbs.

He nodded. 'I think I did right from the start. It just seemed impossible. But the more I thought about it, the more I realised how much I missed you. Neither of my other failed engagements made me feel like that. When they ended, I was angry and humiliated but with you, I just felt sad and lonely. All I could think about was getting you back. That's why I wanted to meet you here. I want to ask you, for real, if we can be engaged, if you'll marry me, if we can spend the rest of our lives together.'

Tears had crept into her eyes and began to spill from the corner. 'You mean it? You really want that?'

'I do. I've never wanted anything else more. I can only hope you feel the same.'

'Yes. I do. I always liked you. But I taught myself not to and to look the other way.' She swallowed back her tears. 'Maybe it was stupid, but I made myself numb to other relationships, without really meaning to. When I met you again, I'd long given up hope of thinking you'd notice me. I thought we were just pretending and I didn't dare think it was real.'

He took two steps forward and wrapped his strong arms around her. She was instantly hit by his warmth and she closed her eyes, sinking into an embrace that felt like home, kindness, and love.

'It might have taken me longer to see you for who you really are, but once I did, I couldn't look anywhere else and I never will again. You're all I want.' He pulled back a little and glanced at his feet. 'Well, you too, Mitzi. We're a whole package. And maybe one day we can add to that with little baby Harrington-McBrides.'

Hot tears pricked the corners of her eyes again but she wiped them away and smiled. 'It sounds perfect.'

'That's why I took the flat off the market. I needed somewhere to stay. Sorry I didn't tell you. My head's been all over the place trying to get a flight back. I realised there was so much I wanted to say to you but not over the phone or in a message.'

'Emelie didn't tell me it was off the market. She just said my offer hadn't been accepted.'

'Did she? Oh. I suppose she wasn't allowed to say. Well, I accept your offer. You are now the official co-owner of the flat.'

'Don't I need to pay some kind of deposit?'

'I accept payment in kind. After all, I know you to be a guru in many things. I'm sure we can come to some arrangement. Keep your money. We might need it in the future for a down payment on somewhere bigger.'

She ran her hand over his cheek, savouring the feel of his neatly trimmed beard against her palm. 'Good thinking. Shall we go in and surprise my parents with the news?'

'Assuming you haven't been secretly filming this and broadcasting it all around the world.'

'No.' She laughed. 'I've rebranded my accounts and I'm working on the contracts with Duchan Fayre and Flora.'

'Wow, that's brilliant. I'm so proud of you.'

He raised an eyebrow. 'I think my mum was right. This was all fate. Everything we did happened for a reason.'

She smiled. 'I love you so much, Finlay.'

'And I love you too, beautiful Genevieve.' He kissed her on the forehead. 'You're my everything.'

'Can we not wait too long to get married?' she said. 'I don't want an engagement that lasts years.'

'Sounds perfect. Six months then? Is that enough time for wedding prep?'

'Should be... Though we'll need to check venues before we set a date.'

'I think we should do it here... Where it all began.'

'That's not a bad idea. Oh, and can I choose Hayley as a bridesmaid?'

'I'm sure you can, though it's not up to me. You better ask her.'

'I will, but will you be choosing Oliver as a best man?'

'Hmm. I'd like to, though I know he hates weddings, so maybe I shouldn't.'

'He also hates Hayley and she doesn't like him either.'

Finlay frowned. 'Does that matter? They don't have to marry each other. They just have to get through one dance and smile for the photographs.'

Genevieve could see Hayley taking the role a lot more seriously than that, but time would tell and it definitely wasn't something they had to worry about right now.

This was a moment to forget everything else. She took Finlay's hand and they strolled along the dusky path through the roses.

'I definitely want a bouquet of roses,' Genevieve said.

'Very fitting, though I'm not sure we should serve prosecco.'

'Why not? Without it, we might not have got this far.'

'True. Let's make a monument to it, a prosecco fountain in tribute to the drink that brought us together.'

Genevieve laughed and squeezed his hand. 'Maybe we should thank Elise for bringing me to you that afternoon.'

'Yeah, who'd have thought after everything she did to me this year it would be her actions that brought about the proposal?'

'Bizarre really, but I'm not complaining.'

'Whatever happened, our stars aligned that night.'

'They really did...' Genevieve looked up to where one or two stars were twinkling. 'Do you believe it was always written up there?'

He stopped to look at her, gently took her face in his hands and kissed her on the lips. 'I believe in roses and prosecco. I believe in you, I believe in us and I believe in love.'

'I believe in it too. For a long time, I gave up on it, but I believe in it now. With you.'

Together they stood among the roses, gazing at each other for a long time, until Mitzi broke the moment with a little bark.

'Let's head in and get warm.' Genevieve took Finlay's hand and Mitzi led the way through the garden towards the house. Everything was perfect at last.

The End

MORE BOOKS BY MARGARET AMATT

Scottish Island Escapes

1. A Winter Haven

2. A Spring Retreat

3. A Summer Sanctuary

4. An Autumn Hideaway

5. A Christmas Bluff

6. A Flight of Fancy

7. A Hidden Gem

8. A Striking Result

9. A Perfect Discovery

10. A Festive Surprise

The Glenbriar Series

1. Stolen Kisses at the Loch View Hotel

2. Just Friends at Thistle Lodge

3. Pitching up at Heather Glen

4. Two's Company at the Forest Light Show

5. Highland Fling on the Whisky Trail

6. Snowdown at the Old Schoolhouse

7. Starting Over at the Crafty Bee Barn

8. A Surprise Proposal in the Rose Garden

9. Cutting it Neat for the Wedding

10. A Classy Affair in the Country

11. Mix Up under the Mistletoe

12. A Fresh Start on the Bridle Path

13. Last First Kiss at the Village Church

14. Fight or Flirt on the Scenic Route

15. Love Match on the Road Home

16. Christmas Wishes at the Station Bookshop

17. Faking the Grade at Glenbriar High

18. Summer Nights at Hillview Farm

19. Love Song at the Music Festival

20. Holly Dates at the Christmas Cottage

Love on the Edge – Barra Series

1. The Castle in the Bay

2. The Lighthouse by the Sea

3. The Gateway on the Sands

About the Author

Margaret Amatt

Margaret has told and written stories for as long as she can remember. During her formative years, she spent time on long walks inventing characters and stories to pass the time.

Writing books is Margaret's passion and when she's not doing that, she's often found eating chocolate, walking and taking photographs in the hills around Highland Perthshire. Those long walks still frequently bring inspiration!

It's Margaret's pleasure to bring you the **Scottish Island Escapes** series, **The Glenbriar Series** and the **Love on the Edge – Barra** series. Each series features interconnected stories for those who enjoy inhabiting Margaret's world but each and every book can be read as a standalone if you'd rather dip in and out.

You can find more information about Margaret on her website or by signing up for her newsletter

www.margaretamatt.com

ACKNOWLEDGEMENTS

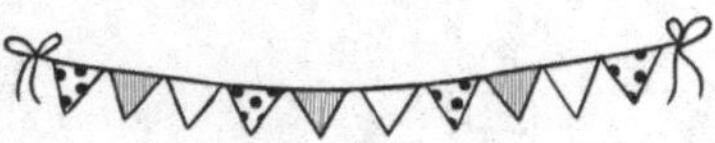

Thanks goes to my adorable husband for supporting my dreams and putting up with my writing talk 24/7. Also to my son, whose interest in my writing always makes me smile. It's precious to know I've passed the bug to him – he's currently writing his own fantasy novel and instruction books on how to build Lego!

Throughout the writing process, I have gleaned help from many sources and met some fabulous people. I'd like to give a special mention to Stéphanie Ronckier, my beta reader extraordinaire. Stéphanie's continued support with my writing is invaluable and I love the fact that I need someone French to correct my grammar! Stéphanie, you rock. To my lovely friend, Lyn Williamson, thank you for your continued support and encouragement with all my projects. And to my fellow authors, Evie Alexander and Lyndsey Gallagher – you girls are the best! I love it that you always have my back and are there to help when I need you.

Also, a thanks to the editors at Leannan Press for their work on this novel.

Of course a huge thank you goes to the readers who continue to support me in so many ways. I appreciate each and every one of you and hope that I can keep bringing you more books to enjoy! Big love.

Margaret XX

www.ingramcontent.com/pod-product-compliance
Lightning Source LLC
Chambersburg PA
CBHW011218190726
48287CB00008B/2668